I0663650

The Casino Mystery

*An
Inspector Reynolds
of Scotland Yard
Mystery*

By Elaine Hamilton

Originally published in 1936

The Casino Mystery

© 2015 Resurrected Press
www.ResurrectedPress.com

Published by Resurrected Press

This classic book was handcrafted by Resurrected Press. Resurrected Press is dedicated to bringing high quality classic books back to the readers who enjoy them. These are not scanned versions of the originals, but, rather, quality checked and edited books meant to be enjoyed!

Please visit ResurrectedPress.com to view our entire catalogue!

ISBN 13: 978-1-937022-91-4

Printed in the United States of America

Resurrected Press Books in A. E. Fielding's *The Chief Inspector Pointer Mystery* Series

RESURRECTED PRESS CLASSIC
<u>MYSTERY CATALOGUE</u>

Journeys into Mystery
Travel and Mystery in a More Elegant Time

The Edwardian Detectives
Literary Sleuths of the Edwardian Era

Gems of Mystery
Lost Jewels from a More Elegant Age

Anne Austin
One Drop of Blood
The Black Pigeon
Murder at Bridge

E. C. Bentley
Trent's Last Case: The Woman in Black

Ernest Bramah
Max Carrados Resurrected:
The Detective Stories of Max Carrados

Agatha Christie
The Secret Adversary
The Mysterious Affair at Styles

Octavus Roy Cohen
Midnight

Freeman Wills Croft
The Ponson Case
The Pit Prop Syndicate

J. S. Fletcher
The Herapath Property
The Rayner-Slade Amalgamation
The Chestermarke Instinct
The Paradise Mystery
Dead Men's Money
The Middle of Things
Ravensdene Court
Scarhaven Keep
The Orange-Yellow Diamond
The Middle Temple Murder
The Tallyrand Maxim
The Borough Treasurer
In the Mayor's Parlour
The Saftey Pin

R. Austin Freeman
The Mystery of 31 New Inn from the Dr. Thorndyke Series
John Thorndyke's Cases from the Dr. Thorndyke Series
The Red Thumb Mark from The Dr. Thorndyke Series
The Eye of Osiris from The Dr. Thorndyke Series
A Silent Witness from the Dr. John Thorndyke Series
The Cat's Eye from the Dr. John Thorndyke Series
Helen Vardon's Confession: A Dr. John Thorndyke Story
As a Thief in the Night: A Dr. John Thorndyke Story
Mr. Pottermack's Oversight: A Dr. John Thorndyke Story
Dr. Thorndyke Intervenes: A Dr. John Thorndyke Story
The Singing Bone: The Adventures of Dr. Thorndyke
The Stoneware Monkey: A Dr. John Thorndyke Story
The Great Portrait Mystery, and Other Stories: A Collection of Dr. John Thorndyke and Other Stories
The Penrose Mystery: A Dr. John Thorndyke Story

The Uttermost Farthing: A Savant's Vendetta

Arthur Griffiths
The Passenger From Calais
The Rome Express

Fergus Hume
The Mystery of a Hansom Cab
The Green Mummy
The Silent House
The Secret Passage

Edgar Jepson
The Loudwater Mystery

A. E. W. Mason
At the Villa Rose

A. A. Milne
The Red House Mystery

Baroness Emma Orczy
The Old Man in the Corner

Edgar Allan Poe
The Detective Stories of Edgar Allan Poe

Arthur J. Rees
The Hampstead Mystery
The Shrieking Pit
The Hand In The Dark
The Moon Rock
The Mystery of the Downs

Mary Roberts Rinehart
Sight Unseen and The Confession

Dorothy L. Sayers

Whose Body?

Sir William Magnay
The Hunt Ball Mystery

Mabel and Paul Thorne
The Sheridan Road Mystery

Louis Tracy
The Strange Case of Mortimer Fenley
The Albert Gate Mystery
The Bartlett Mystery
The Postmaster's Daughter
The House of Peril
The Sandling Case: What Would You Have Done?

Charles Edmonds Walk
The Paternoster Ruby

John R. Watson
The Mystery of the Downs
The Hampstead Mystery

Edgar Wallace
The Daffodil Mystery
The Crimson Circle

Carolyn Wells
Vicky Van
The Man Who Fell Through the Earth
In the Onyx Lobby
Raspberry Jam
The Clue
The Room with the Tassels
The Vanishing of Betty Varian
The Mystery Girl
The White Alley
The Curved Blades

FOREWORD

The Casino Mystery published in 1936, is the eighth of a series of mysteries featuring Inspector Reynolds of Scotland Yards' C.I.D. that appeared through the 1930's. Little information is available about the author, Elaine Hamilton beyond the list of books she wrote.

The Westminster Mystery, the first book in the series, was written in the style that has become known as "Hum Drum" not because the books are lacking in excitement, but because they try to portray the reality of a police investigation. This style arose in the 1930's as a reaction against the more flamboyant style of detective fiction as epitomized by Agatha Christie's Hercule Poirot or Dorothy Sayers' Lord Peter Wimsey. In place of the eccentricities of these amateur detectives, this style revolves around rather somber police detectives who achieve their results by hard work, dogged attention to details and common sense.

By the time Hamilton penned *The Casino Mystery*, the series had evolved somewhat, becoming more melodramatic in nature, probably as a result of what the publisher thought would be popular. The story has been spiced up by the introduction of Mimi, a French woman with somewhat tenuous ties to the French *Surete,* and Inspector Reynolds and his wife don't make an appearance until quite late in the book. Romance has been added to the mix as well, not for Inspector Reynolds, who is happily married, but in the person of Jill Caryll, a young woman who finds herself posing as the niece of a wealthy American who may not be as American as he seems.

The story finds a set of ill-matched guests staying at the Villa Lorne, a large house in Monaco, rented by Lady Daventry. In addition to her nephew Tony and Glen Armitage, a friend, the guests include Mr. and Mrs. Lucas, a British stockbroker and his wife, an Austrian

Baroness, a Dutchman and his son, and lastly, John Caryll, a wealthy American and his "niece." None of them seems to particularly care for the others, and none seems particularly happy to be there. There are, of course, hints of past events tying some of them together, but these remain concealed, at least at the beginning.

Lady Daventry, concerned about several jewel thefts that have occurred at the villa, has hired Mimi to act as her secretary, though her real purpose is to catch the thief. Mimi, who had appeared in several previous books in the series, including *Peril at Midnight*, finds the focus of her investigation changing when Mrs. Lucas dies under suspicious circumstances at the Casino. Mimi plays a much larger role in this book than in her previous appearances, leaving Inspector Reynolds the duty of tying up the loose ends.

While perhaps not as realistic as the works of some other mystery writers of the time, Hamilton tells her stories with a certain panache that is both witty and entertaining. There is plenty of action and suspense in *The Casino Mystery*, and more than a hint of romance.

Elaine Hamilton is today a nearly forgotten author, but during the 1930's at least nine of her novels were published though they are hard to find today. It is with pleasure that Resurrected Press offers this new edition of *The Casino Mystery*.

About the Author

Not much is known about Elaine Hamilton other than she wrote a series of mysteries in the 1930's featuring Inspector Reynolds of Scotland Yard. *The Westminster Mystery* published in 1930 was the first of these. Other titles in the series include *Murder in the Fog* (1931), *The Green Death* (1932), *The Chelsea Mystery* (1932), *The Silent Bell* (1933), *Peril at Midnight* (1934),

Tragedy in the Dark (1935), *The Casino Mystery* (1936) and *Murder Before Tuesday* (1937).

Greg Fowlkes
Editor-In-Chief
Resurrected Press
www.ResurrectedPress.

TABLE OF CONTENTS

I. A Shattered Dream

Monday afternoon.

"THERE'S your beloved Monte Carlo at last. Does it come up to expectation?" John Caryll demanded.

The girl swung round from the rail of the steamer and smiled up into the speaker's face. Then she turned again to the panorama that stretched before her across the blue bay of the Mediterranean.

"It's different: incredibly beautiful and a little unreal," she answered.

Caryll—middle-aged, clean-shaven, with keen eyes showing behind horn-rimmed spectacles—gave a short laugh.

"It's real enough, Jill. Some folks would tell you that it's even materialistic."

"Then I don't want to meet them. To me, it's a cross between an enchanting fairy-tale and the toy towns that children make with cardboard."

"Keep your fancies as long as you can, my girl. They'll fade quickly enough." He pointed to a headland. "Every fairy-tale should have a prince. There's his castle on that rock; and from the edge of it people who no longer share your illusions occasionally hurl themselves to a watery grave. Still, I admit the coast is a pretty sight from here. Particularly so at night when the harbour and town resemble a lighted Christmas tree. That white building facing the sea is the Casino. I wonder what you'll make of it."

"I'm going to love it all, only," the girl sighed. "I can't help being sorry this wonderful cruise is over. There must be a limit to happiness I've a frightened feeling about landing and meeting strangers."

"Nonsense. Nobody's going to frighten you." Caryll put his hand under her chin and tilted her head up for his inspection. He saw large wistful grey eyes, dark hair blowing softly in the breeze, an oval face and complexion only lightly tanned by the sea voyage. Her mouth was too frank and sensitive for concealment of her moods, the man thought, although its beauty was undeniable. "Nobody *can* frighten you—unless you let them. Understood?"

She nodded, a little uneasily.

"I'm not quite the philanthropic genial person you imagine, Jill," he went on abruptly. "but even I am sorry to be obliged to rouse you from your dreams of what you term my generosity. Up to now it has amused me to bask in the role of benefactor—to receive your undoubted gratitude, to watch your delight in the luxury of travel. Now you must know the truth. I've fought hard for what I possess, and usually when I give I exact value in return. This is where you being to pay your bill."

Jill's expression was unchanged as she regarded him.

"Of course I will," she promised "Please tell me what I can do. You don't know how much I long to be of some practical use to you."

Caryll smiled grimly.

"Oh yes, I do. I've studied you pretty closely these past three months You're neither greedy nor selfish as so many of your generation are; you're full of generous impulses, singularly sweet-tempered and far too trustful in human nature."

"People have never let me down," she objected.

"Perhaps on the principle that traffic rarely injures a blind man. On the other hand, the blind man never sees what has knocked him down when an accident does happen. How much money had you, Jill, when that employment bureau sent you along to my London hotel to fill the post of temporary secretary?"

"About eight shillings. Oh, how I prayed that you would engage me!" she said "I often wonder why you did.

You must have had many applicants far more skilled than I."

"Hundreds," he replied bluntly. "Here's where you begin to wake up, Jill. I chose you because you were on your beam ends, an orphan and with no living relatives."

"You had to choose me for something, hadn't you?" she asked, unperturbed.

"After a month of close watching, I decided that you would suit my purpose. With all the acting that I was capable of, I made you my offer. Any average girl would have suspected that there was a snag in it. You accepted blindly and unhesitatingly."

"You forget I did hesitate about changing my name."

"For a while, yes. Then you swallowed all my 'lonely-old-man-longing-for-someone-to-bear-his-name' stuff without a murmur." The man threw up his head. "Bah! How I hated pulling that trick. Jill, didn't it occur to you that I could have asked you to marry me if my story had been true? Men of fifty-odd often marry girls of twenty-two, you know."

"Yes, but clever, wealthy men of that age needn't marry penniless and not-very-efficient secretaries," she protested. "They have the world to choose from."

"Have it your own way. At any rate, I've no thought of marriage, and on that point only my intentions are strictly honorable. I persuaded you to change your name to Caryll legally, and for the sake of appearances adopted you as my niece." He gave a harsh laugh. "A sweet domestic picture of a benevolent bachelor uncle trotting round with his devoted young relative to cheer his declining years. As such, we went to America and came back here."

The girl flushed.

"You must have thought me a fool and an egoist to accept the situation so readily."

"Neither. You acted as I intended. Now comes the jolt: unless you back out and go to England."

"I'll stay and earn what I've already cost you," Her tone was decided and the grey eyes held a look of hurt pride, "What do you want me to do?"

"Go on with the devoted niece stuff. If anyone asks, say that you're my heiress. Don't forget that bit, thought it's not true."

"How long is this masquerade to last?" she asked. "I'm not that convincing a liar."

"You'll have to be, until I'm through," Caryll told her sternly. "It won't be difficult."

"Have you met this Lady Daventry with whom we are to stay?

"No." The man pulled a letter from his pocket. "You'd better read what she says."

Jill read the business-like communication.

Villa Lorne,

Monte Carlo, February 1st.

Dear Mr. Caryll,

The sum you mention is quite adequate for a stay of three months. I shall be pleased to receive you and your niece here at my villa, act as her chaperon and give her every social advantage in my tower. When the Riviera season ends we shall go to my London house, and the same conditions will continue.

I note that you will land at Monte Carlo on February 15th and suggest that we meet at the Hotel Napoli, near the Casino. I will give a cocktail party there, on that date and expect you both, about six-thirty. You will thus be able to meet the other guests who are staying with me. An interview at the hotel will be more impersonal than at my villa.

Should you wish to withdraw from your arrangement after our interview, you will of course be at liberty to do so.

Yours truly,

Eve Daventry.

"So I'm to be launched into society in this commercial fashion!" Jill commented.

The niece of a Californian millionaire might not get there otherwise. Lady Daventry does this social business rather, well, I believe." John Caryll laid his hand on the girl's shoulder. "Whatever she's like, remember you and I are under no obligation to her.

She'll be paid for all she does, so keep your chin up."

"Thank you." Jill hesitated. "I can't see what you will gain by this plan."

"You don't need to," he retorted. "Come along. There's the tender waiting. I'll see about our luggage. We're due at the hotel in an hour."

Jill caught his hand.

"In spite of what you've told me, I'm very grateful," she said.

II. Introducing Mimi

Monday Afternoon.

☐

GLEN ARMITAGE flung open the heavy glass door of the Hotel Napoli and dashed out impatiently. Before he could check his speed he collided with a girl who was about to enter and caused her to lose her balance.

She gazed with indignation at the young man who had made this stormy exit. His lean sunburnt face and greenish eyes showed no penitence.

"Do you often make the departure like that?"she demanded severely.

"Not often," was his reply. "Sorry I bowled you over. You're so small that I didn't see you. Is all well or do I call an ambulance?"

"I am unbroken, thank you," the French girl observed with dignity, and with the impersonal bow of royalty swept past him into the hotel.

Armitage's lips pursed to a whistle of amazement as he looked after her. Then he hurried towards an older man who was approaching at a leisurely pace

"Thank, goodness you've turned up, Lucas," he exclaimed. "The mob are clamouring for their drinks."

"I'll quiet them," Lucas promised. "Hasn't Lady Daventry come?"

Armitage nodded.

"Some time ago. We had a peach of a row; then she went to make a trunk call to Paris and I came out to look for you and cool off."

Lucas's calm face broke into a smile.

"You appeared to be having another peach of a row at the front door," he commented. "Who was the little girl in black, Armitage?

"Hanged if I know: a young Balkan princess or Hollywood star, judging by her cool poise. She withered me with a glance when I barged into her."

Lucas, a retired London stockbroker, looked at his watch.

"The liner was in some time ago," he observed. "Lady Daventry is expecting a Mr. John Caryll and his niece. This cocktail-party is to welcome them."

The younger man assumed a sardonic expression.

"We can make a rough guess as to what they'll be like! He'll be a canned meat king with a huge cigar, diamond studs and millionaire stamped all over him; niece will wear big spectacles and proclaim nasally how much better Amurrica is than France."

"Possibly they won't be as bad as that. Caryll is certainly very wealthy." Lucas paused. "It would be tactful for Lady Daventry's sake if you treated the newcomers amiably, Armitage. They might be staying at her villa."

"I get you. I've no love for social climbers but I won't queer our hostess's chances by bad behaviour, if that's what you mean."

"Stout lad. Let's get in and I'll M.C. the proceedings."

Inside the hotel lounge Lucas left the younger man and, going towards a crowd of well-dressed men and women, sorted them out and guided them to little tables.

Glen Armitage eyed the throng with a frown for a while; then he too looked for a chair. The only vacant seat was at a table occupied by a small, dark-eyed girl in black.

Fresh from a sharp quarrel with a tall blue, eyed girl in white, Armitage had no immediate interest in blondes or brunettes. Indeed he resented the fact that he would have to put up with one of the latter variety being *vis-à-vis* if he wanted to sit down.

It added nothing to his joy to discover that this particular brunette was the one who had suffered by his hasty exit from the front door.

With his hand on the back of the chair, he studied her as she sat reading a letter. She wore no jewellery, and her clear pale skin was void of make-up, save for a touch of colour on the lips. Her piquant delicately-featured face was thrown into relief by the black hair and straight thick fringe cut in the fashion of a Florentine page. In figure she was petite and her slender hands were exquisite. She looked so young that his description of her to Lucas seemed now to be inaccurate. It was more likely that she was some consequential chit of a French schoolgirl, parked here by her mother for a while.

The "chit" suddenly raised grave dark eyes and regarded him disconcertingly, aware of the frown on his face.

"You wish to sit, yes?" she inquired.

"It's the only place vacant." Armitage's answer, revealed ill-humour.

"Then why not take it? I shall not disturb you and I shall not permit you to disturb me."

Distinctly nonplussed by her for the second time within a quarter of an hour, the man sat down and, lighting a cigarette, fidgeted restlessly. He felt bored and irritable.

Why on earth had he been fool enough to promise Lady Daventry that he'd come? He knew only too well his fellow-guests who were staying at her villa, and he had no wish to meet any of the others. If he'd wanted a drink he could have bought himself one; a plain drink, not cocktails, which he detested.

He kicked the table, savagely, knocking the ashtray on to the girl's lap.

At his gruff apology she put away her letter and looked at him with the expression of a sorely-tried mother about to deal with a tiresome child.

"You are out of the temper," she remarked. "The English rarely exhibit emotions so."

Armitage stared at her in surprise.

"How did you know I was cross?"

She flicked her finger negligently.

"It was so obvious as to be dull. The cause might be more amusing, but I think even that is easy to guess."

"Indeed." The man was piqued to interest now. And might I ask what you imagine made me angry?"

"A quarrel with a lady," surmised the French girl.

"You happen to be quite right, but what made you think so?"

"You explode from the hotel, knock me over and are too angry with all women to make the correct regrets to one. Also you are annoyed to find that you had to share this table with me. I think the quarrel is not yet finished because you are still so upset."

Armitage's mouth twisted bitterly.

"We certainly didn't do the 'kiss and be friends' act," he admitted. "I say, you're terribly clever for a kid of your age. What are you called?"

For a second the girl hesitated.

"My name is Mimi," she told him. Adding seriously, "But I am quite old."

"Really! You bear your age remarkably well. I thought you were about sixteen."

Mimi was not flattered.

"I am nearly twenty-four," she said in an aloof manner.

"Astounding." Armitage looked round for a waiter. "Let's drink to your advanced years."

The French girl shook her head.

"*Merci, m'sieur*; I do not allow strangers to pay for me."

"We're not strangers; we're healthy old enemies. Besides, nobody need pay. Lady Daventry is giving a cocktail-party here to-day."

"I am not a guest," the girl objected. "And in any case I do not care to drink the cocktails with an angry man whose name I do not know."

"That's easily rectified. I'm Glen Armitage, quite old— I was twenty-nine last June—a bachelor, and on a visit to the hostess of this party. I've very little money, lots of ambition, and still more temper. Does that introduce us sufficiently?

Mimi bowed.

"Almost it is enough for a police dossier." She gave him a speculative glance. "So you are staying at the Villa Lorne."

"Yes. Do you know Lady Daventry?"

The girl took out her cigarette-case.

"*Non*," she replied. "But one has heard of her. She makes much entertaining, I believe."

"Fills her house with a pack of stuffy people, if that's what you mean. Rich and dull classifies 'em, excepting me. I'm poor and odd. Social functions, clothes, food and gambling: that's all they live for. I love gambling, but not for their reason."

"You like it for adventure, yes?"

Armitage eyed her shrewdly.

"Perhaps. You know you'd have been burnt for a witch not so long ago. I wish you were staying at the Villa Lorne. It would brighten up life considerably."

"Has not life been bright enough here this season with the recent jewel robberies in hotels and villas?" Mimi demanded.

"That cheered things up a bit," agreed the man, "but the novelty's worn off now."

Why?"inquired the girl. "The thief has not yet been caught. Also there was a murder, I believe."

A shadow darkened Armitage's face.

"A couple of murders. Unnecessary and unsporting ones, too."

"You have uneven ideas, monsieur. Can murder ever be sporting or necessary?"

"Possibly; at times," he asserted. "These were neither. In both cases the victims were servants who were killed while loyally defending their employers' interests. That spoilt the jewel robberies for my taste."

"*Toujours le sport!*" murmured the girl.

"Yes, the thief certainly had a delicious sense of humour." Armitage looked up as a debonair young man paused beside him, cocktail in hand. "Hallo, Daventry, can't you find anybody to play with?"

The newcomer gave an impudent grin and deftly tilted the contents of his glass on to the gown of a squat-figured woman who was passing.

"Things are looking up now, thanks," he observed with a significant glance at the French girl. "I'd like to be introduced, please."

Armitage's face bore its most cynical expression as he complied with the request.

"Mademoiselle Mimi, this is Tony Daventry, stepson of my hostess. Don't blame me if you don't like him."

Mimi bowed and looked into Armitage's eyes as he rose.

"Monsieur Daventry seems to have the delicious sense of humour also," she observed "But perhaps not so delicious a sense of sport."

Tony Daventry slid into the seat which Armitage had vacated and glanced impishly at the amber satin gown adorned with the latest cocktail.

"That's Mrs. Lucas," he confided. "I detest her. She nags her husband who's quite a good egg; and she's crazy for a gigolo called Guido. He's with her now."

"Pardon if I seem stupid, but surely it is the good egg who will suffer if you spoil his wife's gown, is it not?" Mimi inquired blandly.

"I hadn't thought of that," Tony admitted.

"You don't do much thinking, anyhow, do you?" Armitage said to him with a hard look.

"Perhaps not. You think enough for both of us, Armitage, so that levels things up. Beware of him, mademoiselle. He's a mysterious bloke; hears all and says nothing—or nothing that matters."

There was a touch of malicious antagonism in his tone, almost a daring challenge in his swift upward glance at Armitage.

The latter seemed unmoved by the attack.

"We can't all be frank and impulsive, Daventry," he replied. "You supply the high lights; I, the more sombre shades."

The younger man chuckled.

"Good word, sombre!" he commented. "What about the row you were having half an hour ago with Eve? That seemed nearer black than sombre, my lad. By the way, I don't see her doing a spot of work with her guests. Is she sobbing her heart out in seclusion?"

Armitage's expression stiffened.

"I can't imagine Lady Daventry doing that in any circumstances," he retorted. "She had to telephone to Paris. There she comes now."

A tall, slim woman advanced slowly from the back of the lounge, pausing with a word here and there to greet her guests. She wore no hat, and her severely-cut afternoon gown of soft white silk made the elaborate toilettes of the other women seem garish by contrast. Mimi watched her with interest. Eve Daventry was of the type known as arrogant and polished. Her blue eyes alone seemed alive in her cold rather-bored face with its finely-cut features. A beautiful sophisticated woman, who had known many phases of life and allowed none of them to scar her chiselled perfection.

Her pale gold hair, gleaming in smooth broad waves, was swept back, revealing her ears which held large pearl studs. Even the fashionable curls at the back seemed to obey the classic role demanded of them, for the contour of that proudly-carried head was unspoilt. She might have been twenty-eight in years, and a hundred in experience.

Graceful and assured, Lady Daventry approached until she was close to the table occupied by Mimi and the two men.

"Like to meet my step-mamma?"questioned Tony, taking a drink from the tray of a passing waiter. "I'll get her to ask you up to the villa. A pretty kid such as you are would be easy for me to fall in love with."

Mimi rose.

"I think your introduction might bring me a poor advantage, monsieur," she said dryly.

Then with complete composure she walked towards the radiant figure in white.

"You wished to see me, madame," she said in French. "I am Mimi."

III. The House of Hate

Monday Afternoon.

LADY DAVENTRY'S eyes swept swiftly over the girl who stood before her with a dignity that equalled her own. From the chic little hat, tailored black silk suit, to slim ankles and well-shod feet, Mimi was good to look at.

"Here are my references, madame."

The Englishwoman scanned the letters that Mimi gave her and handed them back.

"They are entirely satisfactory," she said, and smiled. "You are not very tall, are you?"

"I have exactly sixty-one inches of your English measure," Mimi proudly told her.

Lady Daventry turned to Tony and Glen Armitage.

"How much is that complicated sum?" she asked them.

"Five feet one," replied Glen.

"If you will permit me to say so, madame," Mimi interposed, "I am very strong and"—her dark eyes met the Englishwoman's sapphire eyes in an odd glance—" I know my work."

Lady Daventry nodded.

"Can you come to me at once, mademoiselle—or may I say Mimi?"

"Mimi, please. I am at your service now."

A faint sigh of relief came from the Englishwoman.

"Good." She again addressed the two men. "Mimi is my new companion secretary," she explained. "I like someone to speak French to, and she will be able to translate for my guests and see to my foreign correspondence. She knows German and Italian as well as English."

"I trust better," Armitage wilfully misinterpreted, "or your reputation for clarity may suffer."

There seemed some secret meaning behind his words intended for Eve Daventry. Mimi stepped into the breach.

"English I have only learnt recently, and although I speak it with a fluency and many idioms, yet I make many faults and write it even worse," she stated, "Particularly so when I have talked much with irritable strangers who love quarrels."

Lady Daventry's lips twitched.

"I fancy that you boys have met your match," she observed. "I should be glad if, after this party, one of you will take Mimi up to the villa and show her round. Dinner is at eight, and we're going to the Casino later." She laid her hand on the girl's arm.

"You will take my orders daily for the staff, Mimi. Rule them with a rod of iron, particularly the housekeeper. I'll back you up."

"Is your potted-meat millionaire going to fail you, Eve?" came in Armitage's cynical voice.

"Even in civil war there are times of truce" she replied in low tones. "I can't bear any more hostilities to-day, Glen."

"Our war was of a very uncivil variety," he reminded her. "Still, you shall have your way. Consider the white flag to be flying—for the time being. What is your ladyship's pleasure?

"Thank you. Ah! at last, the Americans," Eve exclaimed as the hotel door opened and John Caryll and his niece appeared. "The girl is lovely. Please take her round and introduce her to people. Take Mimi, too: she must meet the guests. I've got to have a talk with Mr. Caryll."

"Do you include baths?" Armitage inquired. "Sorry, Eve, but why are you such a fool when—"

His sentence died away as Lady Daventry went forward to meet the newcomers. Armitage turned to the French girl.

"Well, what do you make of your new employer?" he demanded. "The emotionless aristocrat type probably does not appeal to your Gallic temperament."

"She is brave and has determination, monsieur, and I think is not at all cold," Mimi replied slowly. "Perhaps she has suffered and is too proud for the world to know it."

"Queer child," Armitage remarked. "Come along and meet this Yankee and his niece."

"She looks lonely and scared," Mimi observed.

"Who wouldn't be scared, brought straight into this bear garden after a placid sea voyage?" he demanded.

But it was not fear of a social function that clouded Jill Caryll's face as she stood there, replying automatically to Lady Daventry's questions. Her mind was on that strange interview she had just had on the boat when her "uncle" had deliberately shattered her illusions about him.

The two men whom her hostess presented did nothing to change her mood. Tony Daventry she visualized as charming and irresponsible; Glen Armitage as clever and bitter.

Her wistful grey eyes, however, grew a shade less troubled at Mimi's warm greeting. At once there seemed a wave of understanding between the two girls.

Already John Caryll, her pseudo uncle, was transformed from the personality she had woven round him into a different being as he strolled off with his hostess.

It was as though a chill finger had been laid on Jill's heart as she watched them. What dread reason was in John Caryll's brain? Was she merely a cat's-paw in his grim schemes? She started as a man's voice broke in on her thoughts.

"Like one that on a lonesome road
Doth walk in fear and dread,
And having once turned round walks on

And turns no more his head."

It was Glen Armitage who had spoken softly at her elbow.

"Sorry," he murmured. "I've an incurable habit of talking to myself."

Mimi gave him a warning glance as she saw Jill Caryll's uneasy expression.

"Take no attention of Monsieur Armitage," she said comfortingly. "He is a mysterious bloke."

The colloquialism sounded so quaint coming from the little Parisian that Jill smiled.

"The description is rather alarming," she said. "Are you also mysterious, Mr. Daventry?"

"Lord, no," Tony said decidedly. "I'm not clever enough for that pose. All my goods are in the shop window. Anybody can see through me. Fond of a lark and a practical joke. You know the style."

Armitage's eyes narrowed.

"Yes, I'm sure Miss Caryll will recognize that formula, Tony, but why bore her with a personal analysis? She'll find out our faults in time."

The strained, far-away look in Jill's face urged the French girl to loosen the tension in the conversation.

"Would you like tea?" she asked with a touch of inspiration.

"Very much, if one can obtain it." There was relief in Jill's voice.

The 'five o'clock' is very usual now in France," Mimi assured her as Armitage went off to order it. "It will be quiet at this table."

"This is all rather strange and bewildering," Jill said apologetically. "I suppose it is because I'm new here and these people all are friends of one another."

"I also am quite new," Mimi consoled her. "Since only half an hour I am Lady Daventry's secretary. You must not be bewildered by those people." Mimi waved her hand towards the crowd. "They are neither clever nor amusing, and very few are friends. They smile with their lips and hate with their minds, I think. But," she added gently, "I am your friend, mademoiselle; my name is Mimi."

Jill caught the French girl's hand impulsively. "Thank you, and mine is Jill."

Tony Daventry overheard the last phrase.

"My friends call me Tony," he remarked pointedly.

"I'll remember, should we reach that stage in our acquaintance," was Jill's retort.

Presently Armitage returned carrying a tray of tea.

"Put it down here, waiter," Tony ordered facetiously. "You needn't stay. We can get along without you nicely." There was a malicious glint in his eyes.

"Thank you, sir," returned Armitage. "What about settling up?

"Oh, of course, my man." Tony made a gesture towards his pocket. "How much?"

"Forty-two pounds," came from Armitage evenly.

Tony muttered something under his breath.

"Miss Caryll is longing for her tea," interposed Mimi tactfully. "Please help me to pour it out, Mr. Armitage."

Once more the tension between the young men was eased, and they chatted pleasantly to Jill and the French girl.

Behind them at a table sat the squat figure of the woman whose dress Tony Daventry had stained. She was arguing violently now with her companion, a sleek, dark-haired Italian with "gigolo" stamped all over him.

"Nonsense. Of course you did it, Guido. Nobody else has been near me," her voice shrilled. "It's terribly clumsy of you. My new gown, too, and after all I've done for you!"

The Italian raised his hands despairingly.

"I assure you, madame, I did not drop my wine on your robe," he protested.

Mimi rose suddenly and went towards the pair.

"Pardon, madame," she said, "but I observed the stain on your beautiful gown when you entered the hotel. You stood near me for a moment."

Gratitude was in Guido's eyes, and the woman showed no resentment at this unexpected defence of her dancing partner.

"That's very nice of you," she said. "Are you one of Lady Daventry's party?"

Mimi explained. "You are Mrs. Lucas, I think," she added.

"Yes. Where's my husband?" There was a sharp edge to the question.

"With Mr. John Caryll and Lady Daventry, madame."

Mrs. Lucas compressed her lips to an ugly line. "Of course she'd be there! So the Carylls have arrived, eh? What are they like?"

"Jill Caryll is with me at the next table," Mimi warned quickly.

Unabashed, the woman twisted round and favoured Jill with a prolonged stare.

"Not the smart gilded lily type," she commented.

"Miss Caryll is too lovely to require gilt," Mimi said.

Mrs. Lucas promptly transferred her attention to the French girl.

"It's a long time since I heard one pretty girl pay compliments to another," she remarked. "You're as loyal as you're honest, apparently. Lady Daventry is lucky to have you for a guardian angel. I wish you were mine."

There was a bitter inflexion in her voice, Mimi noticed.

"I shall be happy to do anything I can for you, madame."

Shortly afterwards John Caryll appeared with his hostess and Mr. Lucas; all three seemingly in the best of spirits.

"Well, my dear," Caryll greeted his niece, "having a good time?" His tone was jovial, but there was firmness in his eyes as he looked at Jill, as if counselling her to make the correct answer.

"Yes, thank you, uncle," she replied with bright obedience.

"Good child. Lady Daventry's offered to take you under her wing and show you how the wheels go round on the Riviera. That's almost a joke, eh?"

His bluff hearty manner was totally unlike that of the John Caryll whom Jill had known.

"After dinner to-night we're going to be very gay," he went on. "Opera for those who like it; the Casino for those who don't. I'm inclined for a gamble. Would you like a flutter with some of your old uncle's money, my dear?"

Jill assented, again responding to what she felt was his wish.

"I'm sure that you two travellers would like to go to the villa and get your things unpacked," their hostess suggested. "I can't leave for a while, but my stepson will drive you there."

"May I also go, madame?"inquired Mimi. "Perhaps I could assist Miss Caryll."

Jill gave her a grateful glance, and was thankful to hear Lady Daventry agree to the plan.

"In that case, I'll take Mimi and her luggage in my car," Armitage offered.

"Well," he said to the French girl as they drove away from the hotel, "are you going to like your new job and us?"

"A new job is always interesting. And," Mimi's lips crinkled, "I like some of you."

"I wonder if I'm included in the number. Let me see: you've met Lady Daventry and charming stepson. Mr. and Mrs. Lucas and her dear Guido. By the way, you saved him from a spot of bother, and I fancy his heart is yours if you want it."

"I do not," Mimi stated emphatically.

"And you know me and the Carylls," Armitage continued.

"You are wrong, monsieur. I only know Miss Caryll. You and Mr. Caryll are both mysterious blokes."

Armitage cocked an eyebrow.

"You've been pretty quick in noticing that there are two of him!" He steered through some large iron gates and curving along a wide drive, stopped the car. "Here's your new home."

Mimi looked round. She saw a beautiful white stone villa standing in still more beautiful grounds.

"The Villa Lorne," she said. "Who gave it that name?"

Armitage shook his head.

"I don't know, but he should have called it the 'Villa Forlorn.' Its three previous tenants have all met with sudden death; suicide or accident, I believe. Lady Daventry only rents it furnished, so let's hope she'll escape that fate." He paused and looked at his companion. "You've already noticed that those of its occupants whom you've met don't exactly love each other, haven't you?"

"Yes," Mimi sighed. "It is a pity; the villa is so lovely."

Armitage gave a harsh laugh.

"Lovely? Do you know what I call it? The house of hate."

IV. THE PEARL NECKLACE

Monday evening.

IN a small sitting-room at the Villa at nearly ten o'clock that evening, Mimi unfolded a letter. She had received it at the Hotel Napoli that afternoon but had only had time then to scan it hurriedly.

The letter was from England and bore an address in Highgate. She read it with a smile.

Dear Minx,

Here is the reference you ask for. It speaks perhaps a trifle highly of your virtues, and not at all of your phenomenal faculty for poking your nose into danger and other people's business.

Yes, I can arrange matters so that you can come to England in Lady Daventry's employment, if you and she still wish later on. Why you want to do so is beyond me!

What in the name of fortune are you doing in Monte Carlo as a secretary? As you say, "your spoken English is of a fluency," but Heaven help the individual who has to solve the mystery of English as you write it.

All this probably reads a little harshly. In reality I send you as always my best wishes, and a warning to keep out of mischief, which I'm sure you will disregard.

My wife sends her love to you and begs you to call about four o'clock at the Hotel Napoli at Monte Carlo,

*on Wednesday next. A friend of hers will be at the hotel
and will expect a message at the reception bureau from
you. Telephone a message if you're busy, giving your
name.*

*Things are fairly quiet here at the moment. My last
effort had for me a successful ending, although it was
unpleasant for—shall we say?—my opponent.*

Every good wish,

Thos. Reynolds.

For a girl who had just received a communication
from an old friend, Mimi's next action was curious.
Lighting a match, she burnt the missive.

She had barely finished when there was a light tap on
her door. It was Jill Caryll, in a very becoming chiffon
frock of a delicate shade of green.

"You didn't come down to dinner, Mimi," she said. "I
was so disappointed."

"No. I was busy and dined here. This is Lady
Daventry's study where I am to work."

Jill walked round the room, glancing at the various
articles in a preoccupied manner.

"Come to the Casino with me to-night," she pleaded,
after her survey had ended. "Please do."

"But perhaps I shall be needed here, and not at all by
your party."

"Lady Daventry and—" Jill hesitated perceptibly, "my
uncle want you to come; and I, most of all."

"*Bon.* Give me ten minutes to make my toilette," Mimi
agreed.

"Who else is going, Jill?" she asked when they were
upstairs in Mimi's bedroom.

"Tony Daventry, Glen Armitage, Mr. and Mrs. Lucas
and a funny Dutchman and his son," Jill told her. "I hear

they're diamond merchants from Rotterdam. There's also an Austrian baroness: I didn't catch her name."

"Anyone else?" Mimi inquired as she slipped an exquisite black lace frock over her head.

"No. Glen Armitage says they're dull nobodies." Jill flushed. "I forgot that's what uncle and I are, of course."

"Mr. Caryll *certainement* is not; nor you either."

"One would not expect Lady Daventry to have this type of friend," Jill went on. "She's so beautiful and fascinating. Mimi, I don't believe she likes any of them, except perhaps her stepson and Mr. Lucas. All through dinner the conversation reminded me of the calm before a storm. That broke afterwards."

She bit her lip. "Perhaps I ought not to talk in this fashion."

"You can say anything you wish," Mimi assured her. "It helps one to speak openly at times. Won't you smoke while I make my face a little?

Jill lighted a cigarette absently.

"Why are they all under the same roof if they dislike one another?" she asked in a puzzled tone. "Lady Daventry surely is wealthy enough not to be obliged to have them. I mean," she added awkwardly, "there is no other girl of my age to need a chaperon as—" She broke off in confusion.

The French girl filled in the blank.

"There might be many reasons for their presence," she remarked in loyalty to her employer, and then allowed her curiosity a little latitude. "You say the storm broke after dinner. Who made the thunder?"

"Nearly all of them; in different places. Lady Daventry and Armitage were quarrelling in the hall; Mr. and Mrs. Lucas in the library, about the gigolo. Tony Daventry annoyed the Baroness and she slapped his face—they were in the garden. Even the old Hollander was not very amiable to Lady Daventry. Nobody seemed to be peaceful. That's why I came up to you."

"I'm ready," Mimi announced, throwing an embroidered Chinese scarf around her.

"Oh, I forgot," Jill said. "Mrs. Lucas wants you to go to her room before we leave for the Casino."

Mimi ran along the corridor and knocked at the door.

"You've been a long time" Mrs. Lucas said peevishly. "Will you ring up my hairdresser at Nice early to-morrow morning and make an appointment for me? I sleep very late."

"I will not forget, madame," Mimi promised as she took the address. "Is there anything else I can do for you?"

The woman fastened the clap of a magnificent necklace of pearls round her throat and frowned at her reflection in the long mirror. Neither jewels nor exquisite clothes could do much for Bella Lucas's heavy discontented face and clumsy figure. Jewels! She was wearing far too many, she thought. Even this French girl, who was only a secretary, looked more distinguished in her black frock devoid of colour or adornment than she herself did.

With impatient movements Mrs. Lucas drew off some rings and two ruby and diamond bracelets.

"These don't go well with my pearls," she explained. "Open that wardrobe trunk and lock them in the jewel-case which you'll find on the bottom tray. Here's the key."

Mimi unlocked the trunk and jewel-case while the woman was selecting a wrap.

"Push them in anywhere," Mrs. Lucas called across the room. "There isn't much space. I've a lot of jewellery, as you see. I need a larger case."

The French girl caught her breath as she raised the lid. Not much space! For, a moment she hesitated. Then she placed the trinkets inside and turning the key, handed it to its owner.

"Does your maid look after your jewellery, madame?" she inquired as they went downstairs.

"Never," declared Mrs. Lucas. "She is ill now, but no one opens that case except myself; or my husband on rare occasions." She laughed. "I see. You think I would let any stranger touch it because I trusted you. Lady Daventry told me about you, Mimi. Besides, I admired you this afternoon when I was scolding poor Guido."

She patted Mimi's shoulder.

"Forgive me for snapping at you," she went on. "My head is bad to-night. The doctor was terribly stern yesterday; said my blood pressure was far too high and I must not rush about so much or—" She .waved her hand expressively. "But if I'm quiet, I start thinking of my enemies; a regular hymn of hate."

The echo of those words rang in Mimi's brain for long afterwards.

Outside the Casino Lady Daventry spoke to the French girl.

"You won't be allowed in as you're an employee," she said vexedly, remembering the rules of the establishment. "I'm so sorry."

"Don't worry, madame. I am acquainted with one of the officials. He will admit me," Mimi reassured her. "I will join you very soon, Jill," she added, with a smile at her new friend.

The luxurious Atrium—that famous vestibule leading to the gambling rooms on one side and the opera house on the other—was glowing with light and filled by eager spectators as Lady Daventry and her party entered.

Every eye was turned towards the theatre doors through which a throng of beautifully dressed women, accompanied by their more soberly clad escorts, drifted slowly.

"What is happening?" Jill asked as she gazed wonderingly at the brilliant scene.

"The first act of the opera is over," Eve Daventry told her. "I thought you might be interested if you'd never been here before."

"Interested!" exclaimed John Caryll beside her. "Why, I guess my niece and I are a pair of perfect rubber-necks. Some show, isn't it, Jill?"

The girl nodded. Why was he speaking with a strong American accent now, and using expressions which she had never heard him employ before?

"It's amazing, uncle," she said a little shakily.

For a few moments Eve Daventry stood there with her guests, pointing out to them the various well-known people as they appeared, and occasionally being greeted by acquaintances.

Her own fair loveliness was not eclipsed by any woman there that night. A graceful trailing gown of pale blue brocade enhanced the sapphire of her eyes, and formed a background for the diamonds that sparkled at her neck and slender wrists.

"Our hostess is a very distinguished-looking woman, isn't she?" Armitage murmured to John Caryll.

"She certainly is not easily forgotten," was Caryll's reply, uttered in a tone that roused Armitage's surprise.

"Here is Mimi," Jill said hastily as the French. girl came towards them.

Lady Daventry glanced at her guests.

"If you've seen enough of the fashion parade, shall we go in and watch the gambling?" she inquired casually.

"Always the perfect hostess!" Armitage remarked to her cynically, as they led the way into the rooms. "Better watch your step, Eve, with Mr. Caryll. He's not a bluff fool as he hopes you think he is."

A trace of uneasiness flickered in Eve Daventry's eyes, but her voice was cool and undisturbed as usual.

"You like making mysteries where none exist, don't you, Glen? The American is genial by nature. He is perhaps assuming heartiness, to disguise the fact that he is strange and a trifle out of his element."

"Your judgment of, human nature would be amazing if it were correct," Armitage retorted. "What d'you make of his accent?"

"A bit pronounced, but I've not met many Californians before "

"Well, he gave a pretty good imitation of an ordinary English accent a few minutes ago, I noticed. That's all, Eve. You have been warned!" Armitage slipped to the rear of the party and joined Jill and Mimi, who had paused near the first roulette table.

"Is your first visit here as big a thrill as you anticipated?" he asked, looking at the English girl.

Jill's brow puckered perplexedly.

"It's quite different," she confessed, "but then, most realizations are, aren't they? I thought there would be a tense dramatic atmosphere, and the players either elated or distressed."

"And instead, it's as hushed and subdued as a cathedral," he remarked, "with the gamblers stolidly doing sums in their notebooks or apathetically pushing a small stake on at slow intervals."

Mimi touched his arm.

"See," she exclaimed, "there is one who is not doing sums!"

At the opposite end of the table at which they were standing was Lady Daventry with a group of her guests. Conspicuous amongst them was the commanding figure of John Caryll, as with a nonchalant gesture he flung a packet of notes on to the table.

"*Rien ne va plus*," called the croupier in a voice void of interest.

Jill watched the ball with fascinated eyes as it rolled and hesitated before finally tumbling into one of the numbered sockets.

"*Treite-deux; rouge, pair et passe*," chanted the monotonous voice at the wheel, while another croupier picked up the packet of notes and counted them.

"Has he lost?" Jill asked breathlessly.

"*Ma foi, non*," Mimi replied. "He has won ten thousand francs!"

"How much is that?"

"Roughly about one hundred and twenty pounds" Armitage replied. "Ah, wise man, he's only going to risk five thousand this time."

In silence they waited until the wheel had been spun and the result announced.

Once more Caryll was successful; and once more he played on red.

"He's won again," Jill exclaimed eagerly. "Oh; all the party except Lady Daventry are following him this time."

"Not with the same stakes, though," Armitage remarked. "There they go, like sheep. Mr. and Mrs. Lucas, the two Hollanders and the Baroness she's probably borrowed her stake. Hello, Mrs. Lucas is plunging heavily. She'll bring your uncle bad luck, Jill. I'm going to join them and watch the fun." Armitage strolled off and left Mimi and Jill standing together.

By this time a small crowd had gathered round the distinguished-looking group whose play obviously belonged to the Sporting Club, and not to these tables where the average stakes were low.

Mr. Caryll frowned as he saw the attention they had attracted, and that the party were imitating his play.

Leaning down, a second or two before the ball fell, he changed his stake to the colour black.

"*Vingt-neuf; noir, impair et passe,*" called the croipier.

John Caryll's luck held good—on black.

Mrs. Lucas raised her hand to her lips to hide her vexation as she saw her notes raked away, thrusting aside her wrap as if she needed air.

The next moment a shrill cry broke from her.

"My pearls! They've gone!" she exclaimed in piercing tones.

V. Tragedy in the Casino

Monday Night.

A SHOCK of surprise at that unusual sound paralysed the players.

Several things seemed to happen at once. The chef at the table clapped his hands. Two men in blue and gold livery appeared as if by magic at his side and received whispered instructions. Another official in black arrived swiftly and began to talk in a calming undertone to the victim.

"Be assured, madame; a thorough search shall be made," he said soothingly. "Your necklace will surely be found. You are certain that you were wearing it when you entered the Casino?"

The suggestion infuriated the agitated woman; her face reddened with indignation.

"Of course I was wearing it," she asserted. "All my friends saw it."

"Then it will be found. Perhaps madame will repose herself a little." The official waved his hand towards a large leather settee against the wall in a secluded corner.

"It's no use making a scene, Bella," Mr. Lucas urged. "Go and sit down while the men are searching."

His wife pressed a hand to her head and allowed him to lead her across the room.

Several people surged nearer Mrs. Lucas as she sat talking excitedly of her loss. Someone brought water and a fan; someone else brandy. A smelling-bottle was passed to her.

The guests from the Villa Lorne stood round or seated themselves beside the distracted woman, endeavouring to console her.

Lady Daventry drew the wrap from Mrs. Lucas's shoulders, and opening the fan, waved it gently to and fro.

"Why don't they send for the police?" demanded Mrs. Lucas feverishly. "I've been robbed and nobody's doing anything about it. My necklace was worth thousands." She drew the stopper from the scent-bottle and inhaled its pungent perfume deeply. "My head!" she moaned.

Swaying forward, she collapsed into her husband's arms.

"She's fainted. Stand back." It was Glen Armitage who spoke.

In a moment he seemed to dominate the situation. Flinging Mrs. Lucas's wrap around her loosely, he helped her husband to support the sagging form.

Before they had time to lay her on the settee, the Casino officials began to work with characteristic swiftness. It was a matter of only a couple of minutes from the time Mrs. Lucas collapsed before her inanimate figure had been transported through a door into a private room. Her husband and Eve Daventry followed.

It was perhaps five minutes after that when a doctor arrived on the scene and found Lady Daventry trying to pour brandy into the woman's mouth.

Moving her aside a little brusquely, he bent over the still form and after an examination stood up. "I regret to say that the lady is dead."

Mr. Lucas stepped forward.

"She is my wife. A few minutes ago in the Casino she missed her pearls and was very agitated. My name is Lucas," he explained in a curt jerky manner that gave evidence of the shock he had suffered.

The doctor bowed gravely.

"My sympathy, monsieur," he said, exchanging a significant glance with one of the Casino officials. "Your wife has possibly been ill recently?"

"She has been attended by a doctor here for high blood pressure and sleeplessness, but I had no idea—" Mr. Lucas broke off.

"No, no, of course not," murmured the medical man.

"Mr. and Mrs. Lucas have been staying with me at the Villa Lorne for some time," Eve Daventry told him.

Again the doctor bowed.

"I have heard of the Lady Daventry," he observed, with a hint of admiration in his eyes for the gracious English beauty who was dealing with this crisis so calmly. Walking over to the Casino officials, he held a whispered conversation with them.

"Monsieur Lucas," he said after it was concluded, "you can rest assured that we will arrange this melancholy business as delicately as possible for you. I, myself, will see your wife's doctor and explain about the sudden heart attack. I suggest—" He dealt briefly with the necessary details of removing the body."

Mr. Lucas showed signs of distress.

"You will not take her to the Villa Lorne?"

The doctor seemed pained to give his reasons for not agreeing to that suggestion.

"Custom of the country—funeral in forty-eight hours—unnecessary to disturb the ménage of the Lady Daventry." Another bow in that lady's direction. "Everything to be done with the utmost consideration for the bereaved husband."

In the Casino, meanwhile, the disturbance caused by the loss of the necklace had been subdued by the unobtrusive methods of the staff, trained to preserve a placid atmosphere at all costs.

Two stout valets in blue uniform, known as "blue boys" were continuing a perfunctory search near the spot where Mrs. Lucas had first proclaimed her loss.

One or two of the more curious onlookers had tried to discuss the situation with the black-clad chefs. Their questions were rebuffed blandly.

Back on the settee, vacated so tragically by Mrs. Lucas, sat five members of Lady Daventry's household: John Caryll, Tony Daventry, Mimi, Jill Caryll and Glen Armitage.

There was no trace of excitement in their faces as they sat there, as yet unaware that Mrs. Lucas was dead. It was as if by common consent they had agreed not to make any further scene. Yet, they were all keyed up, waiting for news from that inner room to which the unconscious woman had been so deftly conveyed.

Mechanically their eyes strayed to the "blue boys," still occupied with their task.

Beside her, Jill felt the French girl's hand grope along the back of the seat.

Have you lost—" she began, and stopped abruptly as Mimi gave her a sharp pinch.

John Caryll rose.

"Come for a turn round the room, Daventry?" he invited. "Not much use staying here. There might be something amusing on at the *trente-et-quarante* table. I'd rather like to try my hand at that. They say the odds are slightly better for the player than at roulette."

Tony Daventry seemed reluctant.

"My stepmother might need me," he said hesitatingly.

Armitage leaned forward.

"I can't think why," he observed. "She never has before; and anyway, Lucas is with her."

Tony made no reply. Standing up, his cigarette case fell open on to the settee, and the contents rolled to the back of the seat.

"Can't afford to waste these. They're English cigarettes," he said with a laugh as he searched the couch to find them.

Armitage watched him with an amused glint in his eyes.

"Retrieved the lot?" he inquired.

Tony made no reply. He snapped his case, and placing it in his pocket, sauntered away with John Caryll.

"Queer little episode that," Armitage remarked to the two girls.

"Not very hygienic, perhaps," Jill said.

"And not very fruitful, certainly," added Mimi cryptically.

Glen Armitage gave her a keen glance.

"Like that, eh, Mimi?"

She nodded.

"Like that, monsieur," she replied.

"And now, what?" he demanded with a grin. Jill turned from the man to the French girl. "You two seem to have a secret code," she laughed.

"I'll stroll over to that table and watch the game for a while. Maybe I'll even be bold enough to play. It's so enticing."

"You're a sweet child," Glen told her. "Most people would have said that Mimi and I were insufferably rude." He thrust some counters into her hands. "Play with these. It will save you from changing your money and you may make my fortune. The novice always wins."

"Only at games of chance, I think," Jill replied in a subdued voice. She added anxiously, "Mrs. Lucas is not ill, I hope. They've been gone a long time if it is only a faint."

"She's probably recovered from that and is wailing about her lost necklace to a fresh audience in the room where they took her," Glen said. "Run along, Jill. Put a counter on a dozen; you get two to one if you win."

He turned to Mimi when they were alone. "And now, what?" he asked again.

She opened her bag and showed him something that was inside it.

Armitage whistled softly.

"My hat, you're a smart kid. Better try to get to the poor lady, though I doubt if you'll manage it. Casino officials are hard nuts to crack, and they won't admit you."

"Will you make the two to one bet?" Mimi asked demurely. "In francs, of course."

"By all means; but you'll lose your money," he warned.

"Come and see me crack the nuts," invited the girl. Armitage followed her as she approached a man who was evidently a head official.

Drawing a card from her bag, she gave it to him and stated her request in clear authoritative tones.

"*Immediatement*, mademoiselle," he assented, and led the way across the vast room. Over her shoulder Mimi drooped an eyelid at Glen Armitage.

"Behold the cracking of the nut," she said under her breath. "It has cost you two francs."

The official paused and gave a preliminary knock at a door in a narrow corridor.

"I will announce you, mademoiselle," he said impressively.

Mimi shook her forefinger in a negative and imperative gesture.

"No. You will say, please, it is Monsieur Armitage and Lady Daventry's secretary."

The official obeyed her wish, closing the door behind them as they entered the room.

In a split second the significance of the grim tragedy was apparent to Armitage and Mimi as they observed that still form covered by the evening wrap.

"Poor Madame Lucas," breathed the French girl. "If only I had found the pearls sooner!"

Mr. Lucas swung round as he caught her last sentence

"You have found them!" he gasped. "Where?"

Mimi's dark eyes rested for a moment on Eve Daventry's startled face before she replied steadily:

"Under the settee. They must have caught in the lining of madame's wrap and rolled on the floor beneath the seat when we took her there to repose herself."

"I'll take the necklace," Lucas said, extending his hand.

Mimi gave it to him and, going towards the couch, bent over the lifeless figure. She looked up as one of the officials and the French doctor drew near and regarded her with a frown.

Their expressions changed as she murmured something to them.

"But all has been arranged to the satisfaction of poor madame's husband," the doctor said, giving her the details. "It would be a great and unnecessary inconvenience for Lady Daventry otherwise."

Mimi debated the point inwardly.

"Very well," she agreed, and rejoined the others.

"If only I had given her the brandy more quickly!" Lady Daventry was saying in remorseful accents. "My failure possibly cost Bella her life!"

Mimi touched her arm.

"You must not distress yourself, madame," she said in a quiet voice. "It is not that you failed, but that someone perhaps succeeded."

VI. A Midnight Discovery

Monday Midnight.

JILL sat on the edge of Mimi's bed in the Villa Lorne at a little past midnight.

"Forgive me for coming up here at this hour, but I'm afraid to be alone," she explained "My first night here, and this ghastly tragedy of Mrs. Lucas's death happens! Don't you think it's a bad omen?"

"Of what?" Mimi inquired.

Jill shivered

"I'm not quite sure. Maybe I ought not to have come to Monte Carlo." There was a distressed shadow in her grey eyes "If I had not been such a blind fool, lost in dreams of an impossible fairyland, I should have had more strength of character and—" She paused abruptly and added, "I don't know what I'm talking about."

The French girl studied her. Jill was certainly not talking about Mrs. Lucas with whom she had not exchanged a dozen words and whose sudden death could surely not have affected her so strongly. Neither did Jill appear to be of a fanciful or morbid type. Yet she was obviously suffering from some secret nervous strain that appeared to be connected with her visit to this villa.

Mimi's thoughts drifted to Jill's uncle. Could he be the cause of the anxiety? She recalled the picture of John Caryll's strong face, his decisive, masterful speech and eminently sane brain. It seemed unlikely that a man of such personality would need to claim the resources of his sweet, mild-mannered niece to aid him in any scheme he might be contemplating.

Caryll was the kind of man who would scorn assistance and prefer to fight his battles alone.

Could it be the atmosphere of the Villa Lorne that was subconsciously disturbing Jill? The house of hate, as Glen Armitage had called it.

Midnight was not the perfect time to investigate that theory, Mimi decided.

"Jill, tell me who was standing nearest to Mrs. Lucas at the roulette table when she missed her pearls," she said in an endeavour to change the subject. "I was behind a tall man and could not see clearly. You remember, Lady Daventry and her party were at one end of the table and you and Armitage and I were at the other watching your uncle's lucky play."

Jill wrinkled her brow.

"I remember perfectly," she said after a moment. "The Villa Lorne party were grouped in three rows. Tony Daventry and the young Hollander were in front, Mrs. Lucas was immediately behind Tony with Lady Daventry on one side and the Austrian Baroness on the other. Mr. Lucas, uncle and the older Hollander stood behind the three ladies."

"Tony was in *front* of Mrs. Lucas!" Mimi said questioningly. "You are sure?"

"*Quite*," Jill replied. "Then Glen Armitage left us, slipped into the group and stood at the back of Mrs. Lucas; I could see his head just above hers."

"And a moment *after* Glen Armitage arrived there, she screamed that her pearls were gone."

"Yes, I'm sure Glen was there before she called out," Jill replied. "Oh, you don't think that he took them, do you?"

Mimi gave a little laugh.

"One may never know who played the funny trick, but it is perhaps unimportant. Poor madame is dead and her pearls are found—too late to comfort her, alas. I forgot you didn't know that."

Jill's eyes widened as Mimi related the discovery of the necklace, giving the same version that she had given Mr. Lucas previously.

"Mimi, you pinched my arm when we were on the settee in the Casino to prevent me asking if you'd lost anything."

"It was not the moment for questions." Mimi's face was serious.

There was silence for a moment Then Jill said in a low tone: "You found the necklace thrust in the cavity at the back of the seat and not on the floor."

Mimi sighed wearily.

"It is found, so what does it matter? Leave the explanation as I made it, *chérie*."

"Anyone sitting there might have concealed it," pursued Jill. "Lady Daventry, Tony, or Armitage."

"Or you or me," Mimi reminded her. "It is better forgotten. To continue might cause unpleasantness."

"But poor Mrs. Lucas's death was caused by the shock of her loss," Jill persisted.

Mimi shook her head.

"Perhaps; and perhaps not. One may never know. Please, we will not talk of this any more, Jill. You see, it is finished."

Jill caught Mimi's arm.

"It is *not* finished," she said earnestly. "There are queer things happening in this house even tonight. Let us be frank with each other. If you won't be my friend, I can't bear to stay here I'm —I'm frightened. Don't please treat me as a child."

"Calm yourself, Jill," Mimi urged "We shall be—as you wish—frank friends. I will tell you what I can, and you shall tell me what you wish. And no more. You understand? We both have some secrets that for different reasons we may not share, is it not? The others, we will make the pool of, yes?"

"Yes," Jill agreed with relief.

"*Entendu. Alors,* why do you say that the affair of the necklace is not finished when you know that Mr. Lucas has the pearls?"

"To-night," Jill bent nearer to the French girl and lowered her voice, "I felt uneasy and thought I would like to come up and talk to you. The house was almost uncannily silent as I crept along the corridor on the. floor below. And then suddenly I heard a man and woman quarrelling—"

"Who were I they?"

"I don't know. The man might have been Mr. Lucas, Tony or Armitage, or even the Hollanders. The woman, might have been Lady Daventry or the Baroness."

"What were they saying?"

"I only caught a few words and then I hurried on to your room," Jill explained. "It meant nothing until you told me that the pearls were found. They were quarrelling about the necklace being false, and there was something about Mrs. Lucas's empty jewel-case."

The empty jewel-case! Mimi's thoughts flashed back to the incident in Mrs. Lucas's bedroom at ten o'clock that evening when she was locking away the trinkets. "Push them in anywhere. There isn't much space. I've a lot of jewellery, as you see," Mrs. Lucas had said. And the jewel-case had been empty when Mimi had opened it! At the time she had been a little startled, but later had dismissed the subject, concluding that Mrs. Lucas had momentarily forgotten she had placed her jewels elsewhere.

Now a new light was beating fiercely upon that incident through the fragment of conversation which Jill had overheard. Could it mean that the necklace was false?

"In which room were they?" she asked. Jill shuddered.

"That is what is so horrible. They were in Mrs. Lucas's bedroom! I had to pass her door to get to the staircase. It sounded so uncanny to hear voices in there, when she—" Her words trembled to silence.

The French girl looked at her with sternness.

"Listen, Jill. This is terribly important. I love your sweet nature, but I despise softness in character and too much of weak sentiment. Death, voices in Mrs. Lucas's room—"—she flicked her fingers disdainfully—"that is nothing to bring fear to your heart. It is the ugliness in life, and what those voices said, that makes me afraid."

Jill accepted the rebuke.

"You're quite right, Mimi; I'll try to have more courage. All my previous friends were as foolishly spineless as I was. I've never met a girl like you before."

"I'm no great shakings," Mimi assured her, producing one of her inaccurate English colloquialisms with pride. "Things occurred years ago to teach me to fight and not to cry." She got out of bed and hurriedly pulled on a black dressing-gown, as severely tailored as a coat. "Stay here until I come back," she urged. "I'm going to make the snoopings."

Moving lightly down the thickly-carpeted stairs, she paused outside a room on the first floor. Only one dim light showed in the long corridor, leaving the passages which branched to the side rooms in darkness.

It was to one of these passages that Mimi went, and standing motionless, listened intently. The silence was so profound that the ticking of the hall clock was distinct to her ears. Yet Mimi felt it was the silence of tense watching, and not of peaceful slumber. Almost she visualized that behind those closed doors stood the occupants waiting with bated breath for something to happen.

Along the corridor a door opened stealthily. Peeping from her shadowed retreat, Mimi saw the figure of a woman in a purple and gold negligee advance towards the head of the staircase. It was the Austrian to whom Mimi had scarcely spoken, but whose acquaintance she determined to improve very soon. A man's voice came from the head of the stairs.

"Hello, Baroness, can't you sleep either?" he asked.

"Oh, it's you, Mr. Caryll," she exclaimed softly. "I was going down to get a book and perhaps a drink."

"That's what I'm after," the man declared. "Let's forage together."

Although they had spoken in low tones, every word was quite audible to the listening girl.

She crept along the landing as Caryll and the Baroness descended to the hall, and looking down, saw them enter the dining-room.

"I presume you can't sleep either and came down to get a book or a drink," murmured an ironical voice behind her. "Guests always do that in novels of the thriller class."

Mimi swung round swiftly. Before her stood Glen Armitage, regarding her with his usual expression of cynical amusement. He was still in evening clothes, and hands in pockets, seemed in no way disconcerted by this nocturnal encounter.

"I always sleep well and I require neither drink nor a book, otherwise your guessings are correct," she retorted. "Probably you and I have the same reason for being here, monsieur."

"To listen-in," he replied coolly. "What made you think there was anything interesting going on?"

"There were voices in Mrs. Lucas's bedroom."

Armitage nodded.

"Yes, I heard 'em. I was in there," he remarked nonchalantly. "Standing behind those thick stuffy curtains became rather boring."

Mimi gave him an impish glance.

"I trust monsieur was rewarded for his pains."

"Oh, quite, thanks. We detectives get tiresome at times. You didn't know I was connected with Scotland Yard, did you?"

"No, monsieur, and I do not know it now," she replied flatly.

"Don't you?" Armitage's eyebrows cocked to a quaint angle. "Maybe you're right. I thought I could get away with that one. Well, what do we do next?"

"Will you tell me who was in Mrs. Lucas's bedroom?" she inquired.

"I shouldn't think so. Why should I give away all my hardly-won secrets?

"Because I know what was said in there," she stated boldly, "so naturally I want to know who said it."

"I'll bet you do!" Armitage exclaimed. "Bit of a shock for you, wasn't it?

"It was rather," she owned, fully aware that Jill might only have heard a small portion of that conversation but hoping to draw Armitage into admissions. "Tell me, do you think it is true or was the man pushing the bluff? Remember I showed you the pearls in the Casino."

"So you did; that's worth something in return, I suppose you think. I'll be generous. Lucas was in his wife's bedroom."

"Lucas!" Mimi exclaimed in surprise.

"Why not? He's the only person who has a right to be there. You seem to doubt my statement."

"I thought you Englishmen played fair," Mimi reproached him. "Mr. Lucas was sleeping very loudly when I stopped outside his door a quarter of an hour ago. I could hear his heavy slow breathing, and the conversation took place only a few minutes before."

"H'm. That's awkward. I'll have to think of a better answer than that." Armitage suddenly became grave. "I was wrong to jest about Lucas. It's correct that he entered his wife's room over an hour ago, but he was alone. The poor chap seemed very worried. It was pretty foul to be hidden there behind the curtains, spying on him. He only stayed a few minutes and then went out of the room, and to bed, I suppose."

"Does he know that his wife's jewel-case is empty except only for a few trinkets?" Mimi demanded.

"How can I tell?" Armitage's tone was irritable, his mind on another subject. "I say, Mimi, this is a rotten house for Jill to come to."

"Jill shall be safe, monsieur. I will take care of her."

"Thanks. I believe you will. Her uncle's American accent is too good to be true somehow." The man seemed to be nonplussed. "That was a slippery bit of work with the fake necklace."

"So it was a fake—the one I found?"Mimi asked

"Of course; put there for you or some other fool to find while the thief got away with the real goods. One thing is certain: the pearls taken from Mrs. Lucas's neck were genuine."

Mimi raised her eyebrows.

"You seem very sure of that, monsieur," she said. "Who were the two people who said that the one I found was false?"

The sound of soft footsteps came from the hall below.

"Clear out quick," warned Armitage. "Caryll and that Austrian Jezebel are coming."

The French girl caught his arm as he was opening his door.

"Tell me, please," she pleaded, "who were the man and woman in Mrs. Lucas's room to-night? You promised."

"Oh yes, of course." He slipped inside his room and putting his head out whispered mysteriously: "Dr. Jekyll and Mrs. Hyde. Now scram!" he added, and closed the door.

VII. A Confession of Guilt

Monday Midnight.

MIMI sped up to her room, angry with Armitage for the trick he had played her, and still more angry with herself for giving precious information away and receiving nothing in return. In the future he should learn that she too could play his game with skill.

Jill regarded with astonishment the French girl's dark eyes, blazing with indignation, the stormy mutinous mouth from which poured a flow of incoherent English.

"If you tell someone something and they promise and tell you nothing, what is it?" Mimi demanded of her bewildered friend.

"I don't know. Is it a conundrum?"Jill inquired.

"I am in a fury with the rage," Mimi continued. "Ah, my sweet Jill, I disturb you with my bad temper, but that man," she shook her fist, "I could—"

Jill grasped the small hand and smiled whimsically.

"You couldn't do much damage with that tiny thing," she observed.

"*Peut-être non*, but with my brain, yes. That I could make such a foolishness as to trust him!" Mimi groaned. "He is bad, isn't he?"

"Very bad," agreed Jill calmly. "Who is he and what has he done?"

The anger in Mimi's face changed to a comical grin.

"How this is *drôle*! Only a little half-hour ago and I was telling you to be calm, and now, behold me!"—she lighted a cigarette—" l am *tout-a-fait* normal again, except my English, and she is—how you say?—all wore out, bust."

"Then give it a rest and speak your own language," suggested Jill. "I went to a French convent school."

A sigh of relief broke from her companion.

"That will be perfect," Mimi went on in her mother tongue. "In future I can explode easily because I know so many more words in French to say when I am angry. But—"—she waved her forefinger to and fro in her characteristic gesture—"—I tell no more secrets, even to you. To-night I have learnt my lesson. You are not vexed with me, Jill?" she inquired anxiously.

"Not a bit. I'm sure you have some wise reason, though I would like to know whether it was Glen Armitage or Tony Daventry who annoyed you."

Mimi evaded reply.

"You like them?" she asked.

"Ye-es. They're totally unlike each other, yet both so sure of themselves in different ways. Tony, because he knows he is charming and can get away with his impudence; Armitage, because he realizes he is clever and unusual."

Mimi nodded, her lips pursed.

"So sure of themselves that I would like to bang their heads together until they crack," she declared.

"And which of them upset you?" Jill asked again." Mimi yawned and stretched her arms.

"I forget whether it was Dr. Jekyll or Mrs. Hyde," she said with a reminiscent smile. "Now scram, Jill, and go to bed."

*   *   *   *   *

Mimi was already dressed when a maid brought coffee and rolls at eight o'clock. On the breakfast-tray was a message from her employer.

Hope you slept well. Please come to my room at nine o'clock for the day's orders.

Eve Daventry.

Smoking a cigarette after her light meal was finished, Mimi churned over in her mind the strange and tragic events of last night. There were three questions to which she badly wanted answers.

A. Where were the real pearls?
B. Who had taken them?
C. When was the exchange made?

Her ears caught the sound of stealthy footsteps in the corridor. They paused outside her room, and she saw the handle move quietly.

Flinging the door open, she confronted a sallow, hatchet-faced woman of about fifty-six, clad in a severe black dress.

"So you're not down yet," the woman said in a belligerent manner. "Very much the fine lady for a secretary's job, aren't you?"

"Good morning, Mrs. Warren," Mimi remarked with pointed politeness. "I believe you are the housekeeper."

"I am and have been for twenty-odd years," Mrs. Warren stated bluntly. "Her ladyship told me she'd engaged you. You'd better know at once that I'm taking no orders from a French bit who's little more than a child."

If the woman thought that she had intimidated the newcomer, she was instantly enlightened.

"Your mistress, of course, knows of your decision?" Mimi's tone was disarmingly mild.

Mrs. Warren glared at her with beady hostile eyes, but avoided a direct answer.

"There's too many foreigners and enough trouble in this house already," she mumbled "Her ladyship's my mistress, not you. I only obey her instructions."

"Those are the only ones I shall ever give you," Mimi said clearly. "If ever I usurp her rights you may complain to her. Until then, you will please address me as courteously as I address you. You understand, Mrs. Warren?"

There was a reasoned authority in her words that the housekeeper was forced to recognize.

"Yes I s'pose you want me to call you 'Mamzel.'"

"Since your French accent is so bad, I prefer you to say 'Miss Mimi,'" was the girl's cold reply. "You will find that it is not wise to make an enemy of me, Mrs. Warren. As you say, there is trouble enough here already, and your mistress has many worries. I am here to help her, and as you have been with the family so long, I am sure that is your wish also."

"I've slaved for the Daventry family." The woman's face wore an artful expression and her voice held a whining note now. She was defeated into outward submission and knew her only chance lay in currying favour with this surprising girl who undoubtedly would hold the household reins in future. "Mr. Tony was only a baby when I entered his father's service: Sir Neale Daventry, that was. His first wife died when her baby was born," she added with apparent sentiment.

Mimi was fully alive to the woman's cunning, but decided to use it to her own advantage by learning a little about the family.

"You must remember when Sir Neale married the present Lady Daventry?" she inquired casually.

"They were married abroad. I don't know where. He was a retired barrister—a King's Counsel I think it's called—and went on a trip round the world about six years ago. When he came back he brought his new wife with him. Nobody ever expected it, him being a widower for so long. A hard kind of man was Sir Neale. She was a slip of a girl, about two- or three-and-twenty."

Mimi made a swift mental calculation.

"Mr. Tony must have been nineteen then," she mentioned. "How did he like the idea of having a young stepmother? Many young men would have resented it."

A queer fleeting look chased across the woman's face.

"It worked better than I—anyone thought," she admitted. "Mr. Tony was for ever getting into scrapes and he and his father were always quarrelling before that. But from the very first her ladyship took Mr. Tony's part, and him and her was like brother and sister."

"They appear to be excellent friends now," Mimi observed. "He stays with her often?"

The woman scowled.

"Where else can he go?" she demanded. "An only child, and his father making that will! Every-body knows about it or I wouldn't gossip to you. Mr. Tony only gets a hundred a year; and except for a few legacies, her ladyship was left everything else. And her only married three years when Sir Neale died! I must say though she's very good to Mr. Tony."

"Can't he earn his living?" inquired the girl.

"He's tried several things.'" Mrs. Warren reverted to the will again. "Sir Neale wasn't a millionaire, but nearly two thousand a year isn't poverty, and that's about what Lady Daventry's got; for life, too."

"Mr. Tony must have annoyed his father very much."

"Sir Neale was the unforgiving sort, and never had any patience with his son. The master was a lawyer to his dying day, so to speak, for all he had retired."

Remembering the incident of the cocktail which Tony had poured on to Mrs. Lucas's dress, Mimi felt she could understand the antagonism that existed between his legal-minded parent and the boy's wild irresponsible nature.

Her sympathy and admiration were drawn to Lady Daventry, who apparently had trodden a difficult path with grace and tact.

She glanced at her watch and rising, dismissed the woman.

"Thank you, Mrs. Warren," she said. "It is interesting to know something of the family with whom one works. I must go to her ladyship now. Later I will see you in your room and give you the day's orders."

Mrs. Warren detected the firmness in Mimi's last sentence and realized that for all her chatty revelations to this new member of the household, she was no whit nearer her goal of independence than when she had made this call. It eased her mind considerably, however, to give a wholly fictitious account of the interview to the butler.

"So that haughty French piece knows I won't be under her thumb, Mr. Oswell," she ended.

"She didn't seem haughty to me," the butler remarked. "Very capable and ladylike, I call her, and she'll be no end of a help with her French. I'm fed up with translating and telephoning that lingo for the guests."

Meanwhile Mimi went to keep her appointment with her new employer. She was about to knock on the door when she heard the sound of voices from within. The first sentence made her resolve to pause and listen.

"Did anyone hear you quarrelling with Bella Lucas?" It was Glen Armitage who put the question.

"I don't think so," Eve Daventry replied. "They were all having rows of their own elsewhere. Does it matter much?

"It might, if there's an inquest or whatever they have down here, and some busybody mentions that you and Bella had a violent scene just before she went to the Casino last night. What caused the row, Eve?"

"Strangely enough it was not the usual reason of jealousy on her part. This time she made an unpleasant threat. I managed to pacify her, but she said the subject was shelved and not finished. And now she's dead," Eve ended in a spiritless tone.

"And now she's dead," Glen echoed significantly

"Eve, don't you realize that you'll be in a ghastly mess if that quarrel comes out?"

"Shall I? That won't be new. I've been in a more or less ghastly mess for years, Glen. Oh, why did you crop up in my life again? You're not helping me. Sometimes I think you hate me by the way you act."

"I neither hate nor love you," the man asserted coldly, "but at times I'm extremely angry with you. You're as proud as Lucifer and more foolish than an ostrich, Eve. What induced you to get entangled with this bunch?"

"Bella Lucas primarily; fear of her, I mean. And Tony secondly and indirectly, for reasons which you won't understand."

"Crazy about your precious stepson, aren't you?" Glen sneered.

"I consider his father was unjust to him," Eve declared. "Tony and I suffer something in common— injustice, though I hope and pray he'll never know it."

"Are you sure he doesn't know?"

"Absolutely certain. Tony's very transparent and his manner to me has never changed. I can't forget how decent and sporting he was about his father's will. 'I'd rather you had his money than anybody, if I can't have it,' he said."

"You haven't let him suffer much financially," Glen retorted.

"I've given willingly. Listen to me, Glen. You've had your knife in Tony for a long while. You'd have me think that he is worse than a practical joker. I know, better."

"Splendid!" Glen's tone was sarcastic. "Three pieces of jewellery have been missed within the past two months at various intervals by guests in this villa. Guests who were making short visits and were rich parvenus, very much under the spell of your social position. Two of them pretended they'd lost it outside the villa, because they didn't want to offend dear Lady Daventry! The third made a very unladylike fuss and suggested calling in the police, and lo! the trinket was mysteriously found. Am I right?"

"Yes, and Tony could not possibly have taken the things," Eve replied.

"Oh, he had his alibis in order, I grant."

"They certainly were well tested by you," Eve reminded him. "You forget though, four things were missed, Glen."

"You mean Bella Lucas's necklace."

"Yes. And Tony didn't take that either," she replied. "He was in front of her and me when she missed it. I should have seen him if he'd touched it."

Glen Armitage gave a short laugh.

"No, he didn't take that, for a very good reason."

"Why?"

"Because I took it when I stood behind Bella at the Casino," he said calmly. "And that, my dear, is all you're going to know."

"Are you mad?" Eve asked in startled tones.

"Perhaps. If so, it's quite a pleasant condition and one that affords me no end of fun. A new kind of hide and seek: find the real necklace. I wonder who'll win. By the way, I shouldn't be surprised if your astute little Mimi does. You had another of your brain-waves when you got her here, didn't you? She fancies herself as a pocket Sherlock Holmes, I think."

"That reminds me. She'll be here any minute," Eve said quickly. "You'd better go, Glen, though I'm sure Mimi is honourable."

"I'm sure she is," the man emphasized mockingly. "I'll stay and have a squint at her."

Outside the room the French girl retreated with light steps. Then walking firmly, she tapped at the door and was bidden to enter.

"Good morning, madame," she said, and, turning, acknowledged Armitage formally.

"So we meet again, shadow," he remarked cynically.

"Found Dr. Jekyll and Mrs. Hyde yet?"

"Not yet, monsieur," Mimi replied with the hint of a smile.

Armitage rose and walked to the door.

"Cheer up. You will in time," he said. "I wonder how much you heard of my conversation with Lady Daventry!"

VIII. THE SEARCH

Tuesday Morning.

EVE DAVENTRY glanced at the intelligent piquant face of the girl when they were alone.

"Well, Mimi, you've come to a strange household. A pearl necklace is stolen and a guest dies suddenly before you've been here twenty-four hours! You know that the necklace you found is a clever imitation?"

Mimi made a gesture of assent.

"Would it make you happy if the real one were recovered, madame?"

The older woman seemed startled by the question.

"Oh, of course," she replied hastily. And then: "You have no idea where it is?"

"None, madame." There was blankness in the girl's tone. She produced a notebook and stood waiting.

Eve's slim fingers toyed restlessly with her cigarette while she detailed a list of things for Mimi to attend to.

"You'll find my cheque-book and things in one of these drawers. This desk is yours, as much as mine now. Has the housekeeper crossed your path yet? She's a perfect dragon! I hope you won't be afraid of her."

"Mrs. Warren called on me in my room this morning," Mimi mentioned. "I am not at all afraid of her."

"She's a loyal soul in her queer fierce way, and really devoted to my interests. Old servants are sometimes a bit trying: she's inclined to rule me, and poor Tony is still a naughty child to her. I hope she won't master you."

"She tried and failed." A flash of amusement was in Mimi's eyes. "It is strange that Mrs. Warren dislikes your stepson."

"Yes," Eve agreed, "particularly as she was here when he was a tiny infant. Yet she constantly reports his faults to me. However, I'm glad you've conquered her. Oswell, the butler, won't be any trouble to you. By the way, would you mind answering all the telephone calls to-day?

"Certainly, madame, but my English is far from perfect, and it gets worse when I talk it much," Mimi warned.

"That doesn't matter. You have tact and discretion and we shall have dozens of people ringing up or calling here to-day because of Mrs. Lucas's death. I'm seeing no one until after the funeral. Oswell will keep visitors away, if you'll deal with the telephone. I'm afraid it will mean a long day on duty for you. Give no information to anyone on the wire, please, or to guests in the house either."

"You have my promise," the girl assured her.

"Thank you. Mimi, you are here—for my sake, are you not?" There was a strange note in Eve's voice.

"For no one else, madame. I like Jill Caryll very much, but she is not my mistress." Mimi paused and looked straight into the tragic sapphire eyes before her. "I am entirely at your service. Are there any letters for me to write?" she inquired, deliberately lessening the tension.

Eve drew forward a diary that lay on her desk.

"Decline all my engagements for a couple of days, please," she said. "You can do it by telephone in some cases. 'Owing to the death of Mrs. Robert Lucas'; you'll know what to say. I must meet Mr. Lucas presently and see to the arrangements. We must wait, of course, until the doctors give the certificate. He has gone to see them. If you've any spare time, make yourself amiable to the guests. Tony will introduce you to those you haven't met."

"Am I to use the hall telephone, madame?"

"It's in too public a position. Use this one." Eve indicated the instrument on her desk. "I shan't be in here much to-day. I've told Oswell to switch all inquiries through to you. There's your first call," she said as the bell rang.

Mimi lifted the receiver and heard a man's voice ask for Lady Daventry.

"It is Mr. Lucas, madame," she said. "He has seen the doctors."

"Take the message," Eve ordered sharply, and waited in strained silence.

"Both the Casino doctor and Mrs. Lucas's own medical man agree that she died from a heart attack following unusual agitation," Mimi reported. "The funeral is to take place to-morrow. Mr. Lucas will meet you in half an hour in the lounge of the Hotel de Paris."

Eve nodded and went into her bedroom to dress, her face bearing no sign of the relief Mimi was sure she had experienced.

The French girl gave her employer's orders to various members of the staff and returned to Lady Daventry's study. She was about to enter when she heard an unusual sound from within. Someone was opening and closing the drawers of the desk. She went into the room.

Lying back in an armchair, with a cigar in his mouth, was John Caryll, apparently engrossed in a newspaper.

"Hello, Miss Mimi," he said with a genial smile. "I looked in to see how Lady Daventry was after last night's distressing scene."

"Madame is well and has already gone out," Mimi answered with polite reserve. Sitting down at the desk she began to write a note. She could feel John Caryll's eyes watching her as she bent over her task.

"You seem one hundred per cent efficient, as we say in the States," he observed.

"Monsieur is too kind." Her tone was distant.

"You've been mighty nice to my niece," Caryll continued with a strong American accent. "I must buy me an automobile and take you two girls for a run one day. The scenery looks pretty good in these parts from what I could see from our boat as we came along the coast."

"It resembles California perhaps?" Mimi's words had a questioning note and she was conscious that the man shot a keen look at her before he replied:

"I guess we've all kinds of scenery in my quarter of the globe. You've been there?"

Mimi escaped an answer by knocking some papers off the desk.

"Ah, *merci*, monsieur," she murmured as Caryll helped to pick them up. "Your niece is one hundred per cent English, yes?"

Caryll grinned.

"You bet she is. I dug the poor kid out in London a while ago. Her old uncle's giving her the time of her life. Jill's on velvet now. She's a lucky girl, eh!"

"She deserves to be, monsieur. You too are lucky. Jill's affection is worth having; she is so sincere."

"Quick to find that out, aren't you?" Caryll demanded shrewdly.

"One cannot find that out. One feels it."

"Well, I'll quit hindering you and buzz off," Caryll remarked.

Directly he had gone, Mimi opened the drawers of the desk which Lady Daventry had told her to use. They contained chiefly letters, menus and invitations.

The top right-hand drawer was devoted to account books and bills. Mimi had noticed her employer carelessly thrust a cheque-book inside it, a moment before she went to dress.

The cheque book was not on the top of the papers now. Mimi discovered it under some crumpled bills. Smoothing the papers, she felt something hard beneath them.

Second later she drew out a triple necklace of pearls with a diamond clasp!

Almost breathlessly she tested the pearls with her teeth. There was no doubt. This was the genuine thing. And it was in Lady Daventry's desk!

Here indeed was a dilemma! Had Caryll placed it there, or had he merely discovered its presence?

Calling the Hotel de Paris she asked if Lady Daventry was in the lounge.

"Milady Daventry left a few moments ago with a gentleman," she was told.

What was she to do now? Only one point seemed clear. While the pearls were there, for her employer's sake, she must not leave this room.

There was a second door which led into Lady Daventry's bedroom. In there Mimi found Felice, a serious, middle-aged Frenchwoman who was the personal maid, mending some garments.

"Who went into madame's study after she went out?" Mimi asked.

"I cannot say, mademoiselle, but the door into the corridor was opened and closed several times. I have been in here all the morning."

Mimi bit her lip in despair.

"Try to think of some little thing, Felice," she urged. "It might be important. Did anyone cough or speak? Mr. Caryll was there, I know."

"I heard a woman cough half an hour ago but thought it was you," Felice explained. "And I'm sure I heard Mr. Tony's quick step in the corridor, but I don't know if he went into the study."

Mimi left the maid, feeling extremely anxious. In desperation she rang for the butler and asked him if he could find out who had entered the study during her absence.

"I've mislaid an important letter," she said as an excuse.

"Don't worry too much on your first day, miss," Oswell said consolingly. "I'll ask the maids and let you know."

Presently he informed her that a maid cleaning the corridor had seen the Dutch gentleman and his son go in and come out almost at once. Also the Baroness and Mr. Tony Daventry, each only for a minute or so.

"Mr. Tony's a rare hand for a joke, miss. Maybe he took the letter. I'm sure her ladyship won't mind. She's very indulgent about his tricks."

There was a solid kindliness in Oswell that made Mimi long to tell him the real trouble.

"Nearly all the guests drop in here in the morning to see her ladyship about something or other," he went on. "And of course, after poor Mrs. Lucas's death, I expect they wanted to hear the doctors' report. As her ladyship was not here, they naturally didn't stay. Mr. Armitage was the only one who saw her; he was here before nine. Excuse me, Miss," he said hurriedly, "that's the front-door bell. Very impatient some folks are," he added, as a second peremptory peal rang out.

Mimi never knew what induced her to go to the head of the stairs, and, keeping out of sight, try to ascertain what the imperative callers wanted.

There were three men. Two were of a class she at once recognized as police officials in private cloths. The third man was speaking in French.

Oswell apparently was having a little difficulty in understanding him.

"I must see her ladyship's written orders first," he said at last with reluctance. The spokesman of the trio gave the butler a letter. "I represent the Casino," he said. "You will appreciate that as the deceased lady claims the pearls were lost there, we must protect ourselves by searching this house. We understand that the necklace found in the Casino was an imitation. Lady Daventry agreed to the search when we explained the matter to her this morning."

Oswell read the letter from his mistress authorizing him to admit the bearers and go round the rooms with them

"It seems most irregular to me," he said, "but if her ladyship permits this business, I've no power to stop you. Come in."

Mimi saw the men enter the hall and wait until Oswell had closed the front door.

"Who's in the house at the moment?" one of the men asked him.

"Her ladyship and all the guests have gone out. Only her secretary and the servants are here," the butler replied icily. "The secretary is a young French lady and is very busy with correspondence."

"We'll go there first then," was the decisive answer that Mimi heard before she tiptoed back to the room.

Their heavy feet tramped firmly up the stairs behind Oswell who, a second or two later, flung open the door and ushered in two of the men, while the third presumably kept guard in the hall below.

They cast a cursory glance at the slip of a girl in her simple black frock who faced them with wondering eyes.

"Sit over there," one of them ordered, indicating a wooden chair in a corner of the room. Mimi retreated obediently, and sat with her hands folded in her lap, watching the men perform their task.

One by one the drawers of the desk were inspected: thoroughly, but with no result.

"Finished?" demanded the butler, with disgust plainly depicted on his stolid countenance.

"There is nothing here," the men agreed. "I think we will now inspect the main bedrooms and reception-rooms."

"Better make a thorough job of it and turn out the servants' quarters, too," Oswell suggested. He brightened as an idea occurred to him whereby he could wipe off one old score with his enemy, Mrs. Warren; "There's the housekeeper's sitting-room, you haven't seen that yet," he added, and conducted the trio along the corridor.

He came back much later and announced that the search-party had gone.

"Don't disturb yourself, miss," he said kindly. "I knew the necklace couldn't be in the house. If you ask me, it's the work of that clever crook who's done so many jobs this season in various villas in Monte Carlo. I'll send you up a nice luncheon and you try to forget this nasty business. I could see you were upset by the way you never took your eyes off those men while they were in here turning out her ladyship's things. You never turned your back on them once."

That was the last thing Mimi could have done, she reflected to herself with a chuckle. For in that fraction of time while the men were mounting the stairs' to this room, she had hurriedly threaded the necklace through the back of her leather belt! And had she ceased to face the searchers for one moment, they would have noticed the long ropes of pearls hanging from her waist, only too visible against that plain black frock.

IX. Visitors for Mimi

Tuesday afternoon.

DIRECTLY a maid had cleared away her luncheon, Mimi made a short excursion to her own room.

She returned to her duties considerably lighter in mind. To the best of her ingenuity the necklace was securely hidden. There she determined it should remain until she could discuss the matter with Lady Daventry. Shortly afterwards Tony appeared, his gay impudent face unusually perturbed.

"I say, Mimi, do you know why my stepmother hasn't turned up for luncheon? Old Lucas never came for his nosebag either. Did she tell you where she was going?"

No," the girl replied noncommittally, and volunteered no information concerning Lady Daventry's movements.

"Felice says that the police have ransacked the house. She had to unlock my stepmother's jewel-case, he continued. "The Baroness's personal maid had to turn everything out. The balloon will go up when she hears that! Oswell ought not to have let them in."

"Lady Daventry gave her permission," Mimi informed him, "so the butler had no alternative, had he?"

"I s'pose not. He's a dark horse is our Oswell. Never mentioned the raid to any of us."

Mimi was sure that Tony would soon rectify the omission.

"Seen Glen Armitage?" he asked.

"I have been here all day," Mimi fenced, strong in her determination to disclose nothing to this inquisitive young man. "There have been many telephone calls and much correspondence."

Tony's eye caught a pile of letters on the desk.

"I'll seal and post these," he said.

Mimi laid her hand on them.

"Lady Daventry, must first inspect my replies," she said firmly.

"My hat, you had the Gipsy's Warning rammed into you when you were an infant, didn't you? So long, cautious one."

A moment or two later, an extremely large man, of about sixty years of age, burst noisily into the study after a preliminary knock. He was followed by a younger, thinner and quieter edition of himself, plus a rimless monocle. Evidently these were the Hollanders, whom Mimi had as yet only seen in the distance at the Casino.

The elder man's jovial face beamed amiably as he introduced himself and his offspring.

"We are the Van Godchens, fader and zon," he announced in a deep booming tone that would not have disgraced a ship's foghorn. "And you are the very leedle new segretary of Lady Daventry that we zee?"

In comparison with Van Godchen's towering bulk, Mimi felt that there was indeed very little of her to see, but such as there was, she agreed, was the secretary.

"And now Lady Daventry we would zee, my zon and I, on a leedle matter of business. She is here come, yez?" There was keenness in the Hollander's eyes that belied the geniality of his countenance.

"She has not yet arrived," Mimi replied.

Van Godchen turned to his son and exchanged a few swift words with him in Dutch. The language was sufficiently like German for Mimi to gather that he doubted her word. The knowledge did not endear him to her.

"My lady perhaps wishes to sleep," he insinuated, directing his glance towards the door leading to the bedroom.

Mimi flung it open.

"Felice," she called, "has madame come?"

"No, mademoiselle," the maid replied.

"You are satisfied, messieurs?" Mimi demanded. Van Godchen grunted.

"We are annoyed, my zon and I, about the men who zearched the house for the necklaze," he explained. "We are not griminals."

Mimi knew that a common grievance can often melt anger.

"I too was annoyed at first, monsieur," she confided, with an enchanting smile. "But after all, when one has nothing to conceal, what does it matter?

Van Godchen solemnly churned over the point and looked at his son questioningly.

"She is right, father," the latter answered.

"You are wize in that leedle head, Miss Mimi," boomed the elder man. "My zon and I will bid you good day."

Mimi wished he had left it at that, instead of extending a hand the size of a small ham that gripped her slender fingers in a vice. She got off lightly with "zon," who contented himself with a click of the heels and a formal bow.

The telephone bell rang and she picked up the receiver to hear again the oft-repeated request for particulars concerning the late Mrs. Lucas.

"The doctors certify that death was caused by a sudden heart attack," she replied automatically.

Over the wire she heard a man's low chuckle.

"More and more like a gramophone record," he declared. "This is the third time to-day you've graciously given me that information."

"If it amuses you, please ring often, Monsieur Armitage," flashed back her answer.

"It doesn't amuse me particularly, but at least it lets me know where you are," was the man's retort.

"Why do you want to know where I am?" she demanded sharply.

"Well, in the study, I feel you're safe. Whereas, out of it, who knows what risk you're running! Forgive me if I should seem inquisitive, but are you practising for an act in a circus?"

"No." Mimi's heart was thumping with alarm. How much had Armitage seen?

"I'm immensely relieved. When I saw you perched on that table, leaning dangerously out of your bedroom window a while ago, I was really anxious for your physical safety. It seems I need only worry now about your mind."

"Why worry about me at all?" she tried to say lightly.

"Just my kind old heart," Armitage replied. "You're a big girl now and too old for birds'-nesting in the gutter of a roof."

"Someone is coming," Mimi said desperately, and ended the conversation.

She set her teeth in a strong effort to recover her normal control. Was the atmosphere of this villa affecting her so much that Armitage's taunting words could disturb her? It was incredible that she, who had been in tough spots in some of the worst quarters of Whitechapel, Montmartre and Marseilles could be unnerved by a series of minor if odd incidents connected with a number of strange people. The sudden death of Mrs. Lucas was certainly tragic, but it was medically proved to be natural. To think otherwise now would-be sheer morbid stupidity. And yet—

Her fingers drummed restlessly on the desk. Why had she been in any doubt concerning that fatality? There had been a faint suspicion in her mind last night about something. She tried in vain to recall what had given rise to it.

Suddenly she rushed up to her room as a far more alarming idea came to her. Bolting the door, she dragged the table to the open window and climbed on to it. She leaned out and, clutching the top of the casement with one hand, groped with the other in the gutter of the roof, among the collection of leaves and dust. The packet was there safely!

But she dare not let it remain lest Glen Armitage should retrieve it during her absence from the room. Where now could she hide it? Her thoughts darted to the only person in the house upon whom suspicion could not possibly turn: Jill Caryll, who had been at the opposite end of the roulette table when the necklace had disappeared.

Jill was fortunately not in her bedroom. Mimi opened her friend's wardrobe, and taking out a large black fox fur, ripped a few stitches of the satin lining and deftly slid the necklace inside. Stretched out at full length upon the padding of cotton wool, it was scarcely discernible. In any case, she could easily warn Jill.

Distinctly comforted by this maneuver, she hurried back to the study only a moment before the telephone bell rang again.

"You still there, shadow?" Armitage's mocking voice inquired.

"I am still here, monsieur," she replied sweetly.

"Your voice sounds as if you were happy. Now I wonder if that's because you know I'm watching over you tenderly, or because you've been up to some fresh mischief."

"I wonder?' she echoed, and hung up the receiver with a pleased sensation of having at last scored a point over Glen Armitage.

She was puzzling her head over a long column of figures when loud voices outside the door disturbed her.

"They searched every room?" shrieked a woman. "Mine?"

"That's what I said, my dear," replied Tony Daventry with a laugh. "As you were out, your maid obligingly unlocked your cases."

"Preposterous! An outrage!" exclaimed the woman. And then, in nervous haste; "What did they find?"she demanded.

"Nothing," Tony told her, and ran downstairs.

The door of the study was opened and a tall, woman of commanding presence entered swiftly. She was perhaps forty-five years of age. A bright green hat, composed of birds' plumage, was perched on a mass of red curls, and her clever, attractive face, although no longer youthful, hinted that she had a strong if fiery personality. The fiery part predominated at the moment.

"Is Lady Daventry here?" she demanded with a wave of her hand.

Mimi was reminded vaguely of someone who resembled this dramatic-looking person. There was a theatrical aura surrounding her vivid make-up, bizarre attire, and imperious gestures. In such garb and manner might an actress have made a stage entry.

An actress! That was it. This woman of whom she had only caught a glimpse last night must be Baroness Pertzoff. But, unless Mimi was very mistaken, she was also Hester Taranova, a Viennese actress whose name was famous in every European capital, and whose work was considered comparable with that of the great Bernhardt.

Was this fact known in the house, Mimi wondered. If not, what was such a woman doing here? For the present it was a useful card to have up the sleeve.

It would also be wise to remember that if Hester Taranova or Pertzoff could hold a vast audience enthralled by her acting, she could likewise employ those same arts to trick the inhabitants of this household. Had she become Baroness Pertzoff by marriage, or had she assumed the name for some purpose of her own?

Meanwhile, presumably the lady would not think it worth her while to waste her histrionic ability upon an insignificant girl-secretary, so her present mood might be genuine, and therefore interesting to study.

With polite reserve Mimi replied that Lady Daventry was out.

"This house search, she knew of it?" demanded the Austrian woman impatiently.

"The butler received her written permission, madame."

The Baroness wrung her hands, whether in anger or despair Mimi could not tell.

"Ah, it was mad," she muttered. "You are certain they found nothing?"

"Quite sure, madame," Mimi assured her with perfect truth.

For a while the woman stared absently across the room, as if trying to decide on a course of action. Then, raising her hand with that same imperious gesture, she pointed to the door.

"Leave me," she ordered. "I wish to telephone."

Mimi stood her ground.

"Will you not use the other instrument in the hall, madame? Lady Daventry told me to remain here on duty to-day."

Once more came that gesture of dismissal. "My call is urgent and private. Go."

With a faint shrug, Mimi went into the adjoining bedroom, leaving the door ajar.

"Shut it at once," called out the Austrian.

Felice was not in the bedroom and Mimi had no scruples in attempting to listen to what was being said over the wire.

The Baroness was speaking in German; fragments of two sentences were all that Mimi could understand, and to whom they were spoken she had no clue.

"What am I to do now that—No, no. I won't let you touch him. He is not—"

The receiver was replaced with a clash, and for long moments there was dead silence.

It was broken by almost an anti-climax as the study door was opened and a girl's voice rang out.

"Mimi, I had no idea where you were hiding all day," exclaimed Jill's voice. "Oh, I beg your pardon, Baroness; the butler told me Lady Daventry's secretary was here. Shall I go?"

"No. I have finished," the Baroness replied in her deep resonant tones. "You may return, Mimi," she called.

Jill's face was alight with excitement. But Mimi's attention was centred on the Austrian woman, who, gathering up her handbag and gloves, swept from the room without a word, her brilliant eyes blinded with tears beneath the heavy mascara'd lashes.

X. A GREEN SCENT BOTTLE

Tuesday afternoon.

NEITHER girl spoke for a few moments. It was as though a cyclone had passed through the room, leaving them breathless and shorn of thought.

"That's the Baroness Pertzoff," Jill said at last "She's extraordinary. I don't know whether I like or dislike her, or am merely afraid of her. One feels she could pull down empires, or build them up, if she wished."

"She might be quite an ordinary person inside assuming this pose to attract attention," Mimi replied, not believing what she said, "Where have you been today, Jill?"

Jill lay back in an armchair and lighted a cigarette.

"This morning Tony Daventry took me to Nice in his car. The Hollanders came too. Old Van Godchen has a terrific voice. He bellowed so loudly as we drove along the Promenade des Anglais that people stared as if he were shouting through a megaphone. Have you met him?"

Mimi nodded.

"Also his 'zon,' she remarked. "And then what did you do?"

"We saw uncle as we were driving back, by Monaco harbour. I went off with him and had sandwiches in an American bar. After that he took me to the Casino. Tony and the Van Godchens came back here to lunch, I believe. Mimi, I won nearly three hundred francs." Jill's voice rose in excited semitones. "Do come out to tea. I'm dying to spend some of my winnings."

Mimi shook her head.

"I can't leave until Lady Daventry comes." Her friend looked disappointed.

"You've had a terribly dull day. Nothing but telephone calls and letters to answer."

The French girl repressed a smile: the day had not been quite so void of incident as Jill imagined.

"Talking in English for so long was the worst part," she remarked—she and Jill were now speaking French. "You seem happier and less worried than you were last night."

"I am. One of my worries was about uncle and Lady Daventry. I fancied he didn't like her or—" Jill stopped abruptly.

"And now you think he does," prompted Mimi.

"He talks about her; said that he feared Mrs. Lucas's death and the loss of the necklace must have been a great shock," Jill explained. "Nice of him to be so thoughtful, wasn't it?"

"Very. Did Mr. Caryll also play at the Casino?" Mimi asked.

"I expect so. He wandered off and I was too engrossed in the game to notice. He joined me about twenty minutes ago and we walked here together. If you won't come out, can we have tea here? It's a quarter past four."

Mimi rang the bell and received a surprising answer in the shape of the housekeeper, apparently ready to do battle again.

"The maids aren't here to wait on you," Mrs. Warren said tartly. "What d'you want?"

Ignoring both the woman and the question, Mimi pressed the bell again.

This time the butler answered the summons.

"Will you bring tea for Miss Caryll and myself, please, Oswell?" Mimi requested.

"Certainly, miss," replied the butler, favouring the housekeeper with a stony glare.

"You may go, Mrs. Warren," Mimi said calmly. "If I want you at any time I will send for you."

Oswell stood aside for the housekeeper to pass him before he addressed the French girl.

"Excuse me, miss, but if I may venture a compliment, you handled that old bag of acid drops perfectly. If ever she annoys you, send for me."

"Thank you, Oswell," Mimi replied.

Over tea the two girls chattered, occasionally being interrupted by the telephone.

As the bell jangled again, Jill darted to the instrument.

"Let me reply," she said. "I know the formula!"

She smiled over her shoulder at Mimi as she repeated the phrase she had heard the French girl use.

"Oh, it's you, Mr. Armitage," she exclaimed. "Jill Caryll speaking—Yes, Mimi is here—No, I don't think she's missed you particularly—Uncle's having tea in the lounge downstairs, I think—A good walker—I don't understand." Jill's face was perplexed.

Mimi took the receiver from her friend's hand and replaced it on the stand sharply.

"Don't let that man annoy you with his ridiculous questions, Jill."

"What on earth does he mean? He says, uncle is a good walker, and—"—Jill's voice dropped to a troubled note—"I think he had a queer meaning behind his words." She rose and strolled aimlessly around the room, glancing at the various photos and trinkets. "Glen Armitage is difficult to—Oh, there's Lady Daventry's pretty bottle. She says the Casino is so overheated that she always carries it in her bag," indicated a small article on a table near the door, half hidden by a bowl of carnations.

It was a green cut-glass scent bottle, which had certainly not been on that table when the luncheon tray had rested there, Mimi reflected.

"So it is," she commented, and recognized as being the facsimile of that which Mrs. Lucas had used a few moments before she died.

That, Mimi suddenly knew, was what had eluded her memory: who had given that bottle to the dead woman? And who had taken it from her and brought it to Lady

Daventry's study? First the necklace placed in the drawer of the desk, and now the scent bottle! Was someone trying to incriminate Lady Daventry?

Mimi's thoughts raced backward to those few minutes after luncheon when she had taken the pearls from the roof gutter and concealed them inside Jill's fur. Who had entered this room in her absence?

And then she remembered the agitated visit of Baroness Pertzoff. Had the Austrian placed the bottle there? Or even Tony Daventry?"

Probably its contents were aromatic vinegar and she was merely imagining the terrible possibility that had occurred to her last night in the Casino. Who could wish to kill Mrs. Lucas? Besides, the doctors had found nothing to warrant any suspicion of foul play.

This house was undoubtedly getting on her nerves, she decided, and pivoted her mind to another subject that was indeed of pressing importance.

"Jill, please ask no questions," she begged urgently. "Go and fetch your fox fur and throw it round your shoulders. Don't take it off until I say so, and don't touch the lining. Go quickly, chérie."

Her friend hurried out, promising to come back at once.

Mimi was staring at the scent bottle when Felice came to her from the bedroom.

"Milady has returned and is lying down," she whispered. "Her head is very bad and she has taken aspirin. *Ma foi*, she looks so white and ill."

"No one shall disturb her," Mimi promised.

The maid caught sight of the green scent bottle.

"Why, there it is!" she exclaimed. "I couldn't find it this morning. I'll take it now in case milady needs it."

"Leave it," Mimi said breathlessly. "It needs refilling. Did madame have it in her bag last night when she went to the Casino?"

Felice looked dubious. "I cannot be sure, but it is most probable. Unless, as you say, the perfume had gone and she thought it would be useless. Shall I give any message to madame if she asks?"

"Say all is well and I will remain here until she feels better," Mimi told the maid.

"Truly the devoted secretary?" remarked Glen Armitage 's mocking voice from the door. "So her ladyship has at last returned, has she?"

"If you heard what Felice said, Monsieur Armitage, I need not say it again when I have already repeated so much to you to-day and wasted my air."

"Ha! Devoted secretary's English is slipping a peg or two, I observe." Glen sank into an armchair near the table. "Just what I wanted," he exclaimed, picking up the green bottle. "I too have wasted my air to-day, and in consequence have a headache."

"No not—" Mimi cried as he twisted the glass stopper round before lifting it out. "Don't touch it, please."

The man's eyebrows lifted.

"Devoted secretary has a fit of the jumps, eh? I wonder why!" His fingers still twisted the stopper round as he spoke. "You'd make a marvellous house-dog; especially if you were kept on a chain. But really you go too far when you want to prevent me from having a sniff of your employer's salts. I'm sure she wouldn't object."

Mimi gazed in horrified fascination as he pulled the stopper out and raised the bottle to his nose.

"Here's to you, shadow," he remarked, and inhaled deeply.

With her heart pounding she stood as if her limbs had turned to stone. He slowly replaced the stopper and, grasping the, bottle, leaned back and closed his eyes.

Still and quiet he lay, no breath, so far as she could detect rising and falling in his chest.

Wrenching herself from the grip of terror that held her rooted to the spot, she moved forward fearfully. Was his face already more pallid?

"*Mon Dieu!*" she cried desperately. "Why didn't I stop him?"

Rushing to the door, she called a maid who was in the corridor.

"Bring me brandy at once, please," she ordered breathlessly; and turned back to see Glen Armitage regarding her out of one open eye.

"You might tell her to bring two," he suggested coolly. "I'm too big to be content with a sip out of your glass, shadow."

The French girl's eyes flamed with anger.

"I hate you for your cruelty," she exclaimed, and was still angrier to find herself in tears. "Never, never do I forgive you for tormenting me with this wicked trick."

Glen Armitage sat up and looked at her curiously.

"When you have finished your most excellent imitation of the Baroness Pertzoff in a first-class temper," he drawled, "will you please explain what this is all about?"

"Explain? I?" Mimi stared at him dumbfounded.

"That is what I said. I sat down, said I had a headache and wanted to use Lady Daventry's smelling salts. For some profound reason you tried to prevent me from doing so. Having been out of the nursery for some years, I didn't obey you, but sniffed at the bottle. Then, as most people do when they're tired and have a bad head, I leaned back and closed my eyes. And behold! a marvellous scene a la Pertzoff."

Mimi pressed her hand to her head in bewilderment.

Of all the plausible arguments, this was the most convincing. There not a flaw in it, and it left her exposed mercilessly to this man's ridicule.

"It was the bottle that Mrs. Lucas used last night," she faltered.

"Who said so?" Glen Armitage's tone was languid, but his eyes had narrowed to alert slits.

"Jill Caryll recognized it as belonging to Lady Daventry."

The man glanced over her head to the door.

"There she is," he remarked. "We'll ask her. Ah, and there's my brandy too," he added as the butler brought a decanter and glasses. "Oswell, you've saved my life again. Pour one for Mademoiselle Mimi too. She's been overdoing things to-day, I fancy."

XI. A Woman's Foes

Tuesday afternoon.

"JILL, you sweet angel, come and tell me what you know about this pretty thing," Glen Armitage continued after the butler had left them. He balanced the smelling bottle on the palm of his hand.

"Isn't it the bottle that Lady Daventry always carries? Also," Jill added nervously, "it's the one—"

"That Mrs. Lucas used in the Casino," the man finished for her.

"Yes."

"Are you sure?" he demanded.

"Not quite." Jill's voice had a flattened note.

"Of course you're not," Glen said definitely.

"There must be thousands of bottles of this kind. Whether Mrs. Lucas used this particular one or no, what does it matter? She died a natural if sudden death. Surely you're not morbid enough to be scared of a thing touched by her at the last, are you?"

Again, Mimi reflected inwardly, his specious reasoning had succeeded, for the troubled look was erased from Jill's face as she replied.

"No. It, was stupid of me, Let's talk of more cheerful subjects. I've been gambling this afternoon and won quite a lot."

"Keep it, my child," advised Glen. "Who was your guardian angel?"

"My uncle was about the Casino somewhere; he likes playing alone, he says."

"H'm," grunted the man. "He got on very well with a crowd around him last night. If I'd known you were there alone I'd have joined you. As it was,"—he cast an odd look at Mimi—"I was in most of the afternoon and thoroughly bored by the book I read."

Mimi frowned.

"You telephoned to me this afternoon."

"More than once, shadow," he agreed. "I used the hall instrument; there's a special switch so that one can speak through to this room; I ought to have told you where I was. You'd have felt happier if you'd known I was on the premises, wouldn't you?"

"Your thoughtfulness for me is undeserved, monsieur."

Glen waved his hand negligently.

"I'm built that way," he mentioned. "My heart runs away with my head, as the palmists say."

The door from the bedroom was opened and Eve Daventry came towards the trio.

"Hello, children; has Glen been teasing you?" she questioned. Turning slightly, she caught sight of the green bottle of smelling salts in Glen's fingers. Her nostrils dilated and she drew her delicate satin wrap with its heavy sable collar around her as though the air had grown chill.

"Oh, here's your scent bottle, Eve," Glen said in a casual tone. "You might be glad of it if you've a headache." He raised the stopper and sniffed vigorously. "It doesn't seem very strong."

His eyes held hers as he spoke, Mimi observed.

"No," Eve replied, gazing at Glen as if she were hypnotized and awaiting his orders. "No, it must be refilled," she added with the slow care of a child repeating a lesson of which it is not very sure.

Glen Armitage blinked quickly; it might have been an unconscious contraction, it might also have been a signal that Eve Daventry had answered as he wished, Mimi decided.

"Catch!" he said, and tossed the bottle to her.

Eve's fingers were perhaps a fraction too late, or perhaps they trembled, for the bottle crashed on the shiny parquet and splintered to a thousand fragments.

"It seems to be rather bent!" Glen remarked as Mimi swept the particles of glass out of range. "Sorry, Eve. I'll buy you another to-morrow to match your eyes." He studied her white face critically. "Why didn't you stay in your room and rest? You look—"

"Never mind how I look," she broke in. "I can't sleep during the day, and I wanted to speak to Mimi. Had a good time, Jill?" she asked, smiling at the English girl. "I'm afraid you'll think me a terribly poor hostess."

"I've had a glorious day, Lady Daventry, but I'm afraid yours has been very tiring." Jill's face showed kindly concern. "Can I do anything for you?"

"You might muzzle Glen," Eve replied. "That indeed would be a help. You've probably discovered that he can be extremely—" She paused, searching for a word.

"Persistent, tiresome, inquisitive," suggested Glen obligingly. "Where's Lucas?" he demanded. Jill caught him by the sleeve.

"Come along, or I shall put you out in the kennel," she told him. "Lady Daventry's had enough of us for a while."

"Can I wear your fur if I'm good?" he whined, dragging back with assumed reluctance.

"No," said Jill firmly. She pushed Glen outside the door and looked at the French girl inquiringly. Mimi answered that unspoken question.

"I'll take your fur up to your room presently, Jill, if you like," she offered.

"Thanks, so much."

Mimi laid the fur across her lap as she sat down facing her, employer.

"Well, what has happened?" There was a world of weariness in Eve Daventry's beautiful eyes. "Tell me the worst."

"There is nothing to worry you, I think, madame," Mimi said reassuringly. "Dozens of telephone inquiries: I answered them as you wished. See, here are the names, excepting for one or two who did not give them."

Eve scanned the list with that swift intelligence which belied her usual manner of listless ease. She flicked the paper away.

"Nothing here of importance. What else? Don't hide anything. Who called here?"

Mimi spread her hands eloquently.

"All the world, I think." She ticked the names off on her fingers. "First this morning, Mr. John Caryll: only to inquire for you, he said. Later, but not in this order, came Felice, Oswell, Mrs. Warren, Mr. Tony, the two Hollanders, Mr. Armitage, Jill and the Baroness."

"You were here when these people came?" There was strain behind Eve's quick words.

"Mr. Caryll had been here alone a few minutes when I returned from seeing the housekeeper this morning."

"He did not seem angry or annoyed?"

Mimi shook her head.

"*Au contraire*, he was charming and invited me to go for a drive with his niece. A maid told me that before I came into the study the Van Godchens, Baroness Pertzoff and Mr. Tony ran in for a moment."

"They usually do to wish me good morning. You didn't see them?"

"Not then, madame. I saw them all after luncheon. The Baroness requested me to go out while she made a private telephone call. I did so." Mimi waited to see the effect of that statement, but Eve was staring blindly, at the window as if she had not heard.

"Get it over, child," she said impatiently. "It's no use trying to spare me. The detectives, what did they find?"

The French girl's fingers, toying with the fur, snapped a cotton in the lining.

"Nothing, madame," she said smoothly, while her hands tugged unseen beneath the fur. "Bah! those men they were sheep; I said there was nothing to worry you, even as yesterday I said that I was strong and knew my work. *Voilà*," and she laid the glistening rows of pearls across Eve Daventry's knees.

No word of surprise came from Eve's lips as she gazed at those gleaming treasures. Almost unbelievingly she touched them with a tentative finger as though they were a dream.

"They are real, madame; have no fear." In low gentle tones Mimi related her discovery of the necklace in the drawer and the subsequent hiding-places in which she had concealed them. "Mr. Lucas will be glad they are found," she added.

"Mr. Lucas! Oh yes, of course," Eve said hastily. She laid her long slim hand on Mimi's arm. "You've been very comforting, child, aside from this." Her fingers touched the necklace again. "You won't desert me, will you?"

"No. While I can be of use to you I will gladly stay."

Eve shivered, and pressed the bell.

"I think I'd rather these were not in my possession."

"There's a large safe in the butler's pantry for the house silver." She raised her head as Oswell entered. "This is the lost necklace, Oswell. Lock it up, please, and give no one the key," she requested.

The butler took the pearls with a murmured, "Yes, my lady," and withdrew.

"You trust Oswell," Mimi commented.

"He is at least human. He might rob me in household goods, but not to do me a personal injury."

"Forgive me if I ask a question," said Mimi. "Do you know who placed those pearls in your drawer today?"

Eve shook her head wearily.

"No. Neither do I know who sent an anonymous message to the police stating that the pearls were in this house. That's why I was forced to permit the search. Someone seems to be scheming to get me into a trap. I can't talk about the past, but at least I've got you here to watch my interests now."

"It would be easier to do so if I knew who your enemies were," Mimi suggested.

"I know. I can give you no such help. Besides, I might unconsciously guide you falsely because of my prejudices. Bella Lucas was my enemy. She is dead, but things do not always end with death. Do you know where I've been to-day?"

"With Mr. Lucas, arranging for the funeral," Mimi ventured.

"That was soon finished. It's to be at Nice, early to-morrow. Directly that was settled I came back here and hid in a shed in the garden until the search party had gone. Then I watched my opportunity and slipped into the villa, unseen, by the servants' entrance and staircase. I've been in Bella Lucas's bedroom this afternoon, with the door locked, of course. I was looking for something. It was a waste of time."

Throughout, Eve had spoken in a detached tone, as if hope were remote.

Suddenly Mimi remembered the case in which she had placed the few trinkets.

"Mrs. Lucas's jewel-case was empty last evening," she stated, and explained the circumstances.

"Before she died!" Eve exclaimed with startled emphasis. "Mrs. Lucas kept other things besides jewels there," she added with a sigh.

And Mimi understood that those "other things" were what her employer had been looking for.

"Who else knew what she kept in the jewel-case? Her husband?"

Eve shook her head.

"He, least of all. Bella Lucas had a secretive and crud nature. As a child I fancy she was the type who would have pulled the wings off flies. It amused her to torment me. She held something that would wipe the dark shadow of dishonour from my life. But, because of a debt, she refused to clear my name. That's why I was in her bedroom to-day. I've been trying to pay her off for years."

"Blackmail is ugly. It entitles one to take unusual measures," Mimi replied.

"I must be fair to her. It wasn't exactly blackmail. When the debt had been wiped off, I think she would have given me what I wanted." There was no venom in Eve's calm words. "But you will see that—had my search been successful to-day—I had much to gain by her death."

"Which was medically certified to be caused by heart failure," the French girl supplemented.

"A lie masked by truth, Mimi. What else do people die of? Suicide, natural causes, accident, murder; in them all the heart must fail. It is fortunate for me that her end occurred in the Casino. The officials naturally don't want any publicity that would arise if murder or suicide were suspected. If there is any doubt at Monte Carlo, it is always given in favour of death from natural causes."

"And there was a doubt in this case?"

A haunted expression rose in Eve's eyes.

"I think Bella Lucas was murdered, Mimi. By whom, I do not know. But if ever a doubt is raised, suspicion will most likely rest on me. And if that packet falls into any hands but mine, my motive will seem obvious."

XII. TONY'S DISCOVERY

Tuesday evening.

MIMI was silent after Eve had spoken those fateful words. Scruples were warring with loyalty within her. Was Bella Lucas's murderer to escape punishment and be free to commit further crimes, so that no shadow should fall on Eve Daventry's life?

Yet how could she, herself a stranger in this house, hope to discover the criminal—knowing nothing of his motive—and still spare the woman who was her employer and whose interests she had promised to safeguard?

Broodingly, she weighed up the situation, so engrossed that she was unaware that Eve had rung the bell until the summons was answered by the housekeeper.

"You want me, my lady?" the woman asked, with a sidelong glance at the French girl.

Lady Daventry nodded.

"Will you please pack all Mrs. Lucas's things, Mrs. Warren? I would rather you did it than one of the maids."

"Certainly, my lady. I will do it this evening. You look very exhausted. Can I get you anything? A glass of sherry and a few biscuits?" The housekeeper's face showed concern.

"Thank you." Eve gave a tired smile of appreciation. "That would be excellent. I've had no luncheon."

"I'll get it for you myself," Mrs. Warren offered.

"I wonder no one else thought of it, seeing how worn out you look," she added, casting a bitter eye in Mimi's direction.

"You see, Mimi," Eve remarked as the woman went out, "she's a dragon with a kind heart." Presently when the sherry was brought she said: "Don't touch Mr. Lucas's room, Mrs. Warren. He is staying in Nice to-night and will not be back until after the funeral."

"Very good, my lady. Please drink your sherry," she urged, and went away.

A little colour flushed Eve Daventry's white cheeks as she sipped the wine.

"Mrs. Lucas and John Caryll were talking confidentially together after dinner last night, Mimi. She had just had angry words with me. It was before we all went to the Casino. I wonder what she said to him. It's queer: I'm sure she was angry about something. Did he seem different in speaking of me this morning?"

"No, madame," Mimi replied honestly, but her memory flashed back to the sound of drawers being opened in the study a moment before she entered and found John Caryll there alone, reading a newspaper. Of what use to disturb Eve by telling her of the incident?

"I'm nervous," Eve explained. "One imagines all sorts of stupid things then."

"Where is the false necklace, madame?"

Before Eve could reply the telephone bell jangled. "It is Mr. Lucas, speaking from Nice," Mimi said, and handed over the receiver.

"I won't come to the funeral, if you don't wish me to," Eve agreed over the wire. "Robert, Bella's jewels were not in her case before we went to the Casino, Mimi says. Did you take them?" she asked. She stared at the girl after the conversation was ended.

"Mr. Lucas says that he has not touched that case for months and his wife always carried the key. Mimi, who took those jewels and the packet?"

"I don't know, madame, but," she added boldly, "I heard Mr. Armitage tell you that he took Mrs. Lucas's pearls in the Casino. It was to prevent someone else from doing so. Probably he knew that there was an imitation necklace ready to be substituted."

"You may be right," Eve agreed warily, but offered no further explanation.

The door from the corridor was slung open with force and Tony Daventry entered, his mobile face alight with anger. Behind him followed the Austrian woman.

"Look at this, Eve!" he said explosively, and poured a mass of bracelets, rings, and necklaces on to the desk from a handkerchief that he carried. "Isn't this Bella Lucas's stuff?"

Eve examined the jewellery.

"Yes," she declared. "I recognize several of these things, don't you, Hester?" she asked the Austrian.

"Unofficially I do, but—"—the Baroness waved a hand—"I decline to be drawn into any complications," she said guardedly.

"I don't see how any can arise if nothing is missing," Eve replied in cold tones. "Where and when did you find them, Tony?"

"A minute ago in my dressing-table drawer!" he exclaimed. "And if I get the person who put them there, he'll be a hospital case with the screens round. It's lucky for me that Hester was there when I found them. She wanted a book on roulette systems, and on our way up to dress for dinner I ran into my room to get it. She was standing near me when I pulled open the drawer. There this little lot was, right on top of a pile of handkerchiefs. A nice time I'd have had if those French coppers had come across them when they searched the house."

The butler came in with a pile of letters as Tony finished speaking.

"Did those men search Mr. Tony's bedroom?" Eve asked him.

"Yes, my lady, and very thoroughly too." The manservant's habitually impassive face expressed annoyance at the incident.

"Were you near them when they opened my handkerchief drawer?" Tony demanded.

"Beside them, sir. I never let the blighters—I beg your ladyship's pardon—out of my sight for a second in case they played any American frame-up tricks."

Tony grinned.

"Good for you, Oswell. Was any of this junk—"—he pointed to the pile of jewels—"—in that drawer then?" The butler shook his head.

"No, sir; I'm quite certain," he stated. "The men took everything out, including the drawer, and even looked behind it."

"Thank you, Oswell. Lock all these jewels up with the pearls," Lady Daventry said, and dismissed the man. She turned to her stepson. "That clears you entirely, Tony," she said. "It was an extraordinary trick for anyone to have played on you. Have you any idea who did it?"

Tony set his jaw and nodded.

"A darned sound idea. If you hear fireworks, keep out of the way or you'll hear words Shakespeare never even thought of. Come on, Hester,"—he caught the Baroness's arm—"do a quick change for once and I'll mix you a special cocktail to celebrate my near escape from jail."

The woman gave a ripple of laughter. "You couldn't have been arrested because jewellery was found in your drawer, silly boy."

"Oh, couldn't I? Those detective merchants wanted to find Bella Lucas's pearls, didn't they? If they'd found her jewellery—and everybody here could identify it—in my possession, they'd say I'd had the necklace too." He pushed her towards the door. "Buck up."

Eve checked him from following the Austrian woman.

"One minute, Tony." She hesitated. "Was any thing else belonging to Mrs. Lucas, besides the jewels, in your drawer? I mean, passport, bank-book, letters or a blue envelope?" Her voice was a little breathless.

"Not a thing but that mess of gew-gaws," Tony declared. "Sorry I went off the deep end and upset you, Eve," he added over his shoulder.

Eve Daventry raised her eyebrows when Tony had gone.

"Has this mysterious affair made things better or worse?" she asked her companion.

"At least the jewels are safe," Mimi compromised.

"Is someone now trying to incriminate Tony instead of me?" Eve asked. "Or is it to be my turn next? Mimi, where is that blue envelope that I need so much?"

"I don't know, madame, but I will certainly try to find out."

Eve glanced at her watch and rose with a sigh.

"I must dress. It is only a bare half-hour to dinner. Go and get some fresh air you poor child, after being imprisoned here all day."

"The French are not so habituated to air as the English; madame. I will walk a little in the garden if I may. I am very quick at my toilette. You wish me to dine here?"

"No, with us, please. We shan't be a very festive party, and without you we shall only be three women—the Baroness, Jill Caryll and myself. If you're going out, will you post these letters that you have written? The post-box is a few yards down the hill."

It was dark when Mimi hurried along the drive and out through the gates. The road was newly made and as yet had no lamps.

She posted the letters and turned back, stumbling a little on the rough surface.

Suddenly a hand touched her arm, and the figure of a man loomed beside her, a mere shadow against the black wind-swept sky.

"Please do not be alarmed, mademoiselle," a voice, said deprecatingly. "It is I, Guido. I recognized you as you came out by the light over the gates."

"What do you want?" Mimi asked him.

"You were so kind yesterday at the Hotel Napoli in telling poor Madame Lucas that I did not spill the wine on her dress. I wish to thank you a thousand times."

"It was nothing, Guido. But you didn't come here now for that," Mimi observed shrewdly.

"No, mademoiselle. I am afraid to call at the Villa where no one likes me. When is the funeral of my poor lady?"

"Mr. Lucas wishes the ceremony to be private. It is to be at Nice," Mimi told him.

"Of course I should not have intruded personally. Madame Lucas was not only generous, but she trusted me. I wished to make a little prayer in my church for her," Guido explained humbly.

"Then do so to-morrow morning. I cannot tell you the hour. You say that Mrs. Lucas trusted you. In what way? Please tell me, Guido. It might be important."

He looked up at the lamp and bit his lip undecidedly for a moment.

"Mademoiselle, you did me a service and I would like to repay you. But I cannot betray a confidence of my dead client. In any other way I should be only too happy to help you. This is my address." He handed Mimi a card. "*Au 'voir*, mademoiselles"

With a sweeping wave of his, hat and a low bow, the gigolo left her.

XIII. DIAMOND CUT DIAMOND

Tuesday evening.

SOME of the house guests were already dressed and drinking cocktails in the hall as Mimi hurried in and ran upstairs. On the way, she met Jill coming down.

"You've only ten minutes before dinner," the latter warned her.

"I won't be late," Mimi promised. "Here's your fur."

Well before the gong sounded she had changed into her black lace evening frock.

Draping the Chinese wrap round her shoulders, her eye caught the end of a Turkish cigarette in her ash-tray. With a frown she picked it up: she had not smoked any of that brand recently.

Someone had been in her room for several minutes, and had made no secret of the fact, for the tray contained a considerable amount of ash. Lady Daventry and Jill disliked any cigarettes but Virginian, she knew.

On her way downstairs she went into the study.

Eve was stooping over something that lay on the floor. It was the imitation necklace. Raising a heavy paper weight she crushed the pearls to fragments.

"Horrible things," she said with a shiver. "I feel that they partly caused the tragedy."

"Or formed a convenient excuse for it," Mimi said quietly.

She waited for Eve to precede her and then on an impulse turned back to the study. Taking a small empty tin, she thrust into it the tiny pungent-smelling sponge that was still lying amongst the fragments of the broken scent bottle.

Dinner passed more smoothly than Eve Daventry had anticipated. Tony at the far end of the table kept his section of the party in good spirits, while Mimi and Glen Armitage, who were sitting opposite one another, kept up a fire of raillery that filled awkward pauses.

Dessert had been served when Van Godchen senior chose a momentary silence to lift up his enormous voice and remind the party of that which they wished to forget.

"We are to-night here nine, I zee," he boomed, "and last night we were ten. How comes it, when two are gone?" he demanded, counting heads with an obviously puzzled air. Unconscious of his gaff he blundered on. "Mr. Lucas is not here and the poor lady—"

"I am so small that you forget me, monsieur," Mimi broke in. "Last night I dined upstairs, in the study where you saw me to-day. How did you like I your trip to Nice?"

Eve gave her a grateful look as the conversation drifted into less disturbing channels.

But Van Godchen had not yet said his piece to his satisfaction. Presently he turned to John Caryll.

"You are even now zitting where the poor. Mrs. Lucas was last night," he observed.

Caryll made no reply.

"What of it?" Glen Armitage said. "Somebody must sit there."

Van Godchen ignored the pertinent interruption to his slow-moving train of thought.

"You spoke a leedle with Mrs. Lucas after dinner last night, Mr. Caryll. Did she zay she felt ill?"

"No," Caryll snapped curtly, and passed a dish of peaches to his hostess.

"When one is angry, of course one forgets the leedle matter of health," pursued the Hollander with bland vigour.

"I don't know what you're talking about," Caryll said in tones of icy distinctness. "Mrs. Lucas appeared perfectly well when we exchanged a few remarks about our different systems at roulette."

"Zo! You have a system! It is not your first visit to Monte Carlo then." Van Godchen's eyes were not so heavy as his voice.

"Roulette is played in other parts of the world," Caryll told him evenly.

"You shall tell me about your travels another day," Van Godchen promised with the benign manner of royalty granting an audience "Now I wish to speak of Mrs. Lucas not when you and she exchanged the few remarks on roulette, but when she refused to give you the photograph you asked for. She was very angry, I heard. And you looked at her as now you look at me."

John Caryll averted his eyes and busied himself with cracking a walnut.

"I don't know whether you've good imagination or poor eyesight," he informed the Hollander.

"It was in the garden near the shrubbery at exactly a quarter over nine o'clock last night," stated Van Godchen. "You say you will have the photograph or—"

"Speaking of photographs, Jill," Glen's voice rang out with sharp determination, "I'm going to snap you to-morrow at ten ack-emma, so be prepared and don't put me off with drivelling excuses about old clothes. This room's like a furnace. Let's go to the billiard-room. Couldn't we have coffee there, Eve?"

"Why not?"Eve said easily. "Perhaps Mr. Caryll would like to take you on and then Tony."

"Shall we not be rather a crowd in the billiard-room.?" Mimi asked. "If you like, madame, Jill and I will play bridge with the Hollanders."

"You'll save my reason if you can manage it," Eve murmured gratefully.

There was apparently no difficulty. The Van Godchens and Jill drifted off to the lounge with a little deft shepherding by Mimi.

Jill gave her friend an amused glance.

"Oh dear, 'zon' has found his tongue and come all over sentimental! He wants me to go in the garden and look at the moon."

"There isn't one yet," observed Mimi dryly, "but for heaven's sake go and pretend there is. I don't want to play bridge."

A while later when the elder Hollander had obligingly gone to sleep, Mimi went to the billiard-room. Glen and Tony were having an argument that seemed likely to last a while.

She ran up to the second floor, and lighting a cigarette, entered Glen Armitage's room. Swiftly she searched the various pieces of luggage and furniture, pausing at intervals to tap the end off her cigarette into an empty ash-tray.

One small item brought a gleam of interest to her eyes. Smearing a touch of lipstick on the butt of her cigarette, she crushed it out and left it in the tray.

Two minutes later she strolled nonchalantly into the billiard-room.

"All well?" inquired Eve, who was seated beside John Caryll watching the younger men play.

"Monsieur Van Godchen is singing in his sleep very nicely," Mimi told her. "His son and Jill are in the garden looking for the moon. They should be there some time."

"Van Godchen been asleep long?" asked Caryll in an indifferent tone.

"Ever since we went into the lounge," Mimi answered artlessly. "He sponged up a big drink, closed his eyes and opened his mouth." But she did not mention that the Hollander had asked several leading questions about John Caryll. They, were questions that she had parried skilfully, but which nevertheless caused her to wonder.

Glen halted before making his stroke and glanced at Mimi.

"And where have you been wandering since you left the sleeping beauty?" he sang out.

A ripple of laughter broke from the girl.

"I smoked one little cigarette and then I joined you in here. *Tout simple!*"

"Very simple," he said, and hurried up to his room; In a few moments he put his head round the door of the billiard-room.

"I want a walk," he said abruptly. "Will you come, Mimi?

Glen's manner was hard and definite, as though he had arrived at a sudden decision and wished to act upon it.

"Run along," urged Lady Daventry. "You've been indoors all day." Adding warningly to the man, "Try to be amiable for once, Glen. She's tired."

"Mimi can look after herself," he retorted, and stalked out after the French girl.

Neither of them spoke as they walked along the drive and turned up the hill. A hundred yards or so above the villa was a small plateau, set with pine trees, overlooking the bay.

Glen drew in a long breath as they stood looking across the twinkling lights of the town to the sea.

"I feel like that too," Mimi said, as if he had voiced his thoughts. "One can breathe freely here."

"Is it the Villa Lorne or us—all of us?" he demanded.

"I don't know, but I am glad to be away for a little moment. Perhaps it is that all the people there are at war in their minds, and one feels the tension."

Armitage nodded.

"Maybe. However, that's not what I've brought you here for. Never mind the secretary stuff: why are you in the villa?"

"Why are you there, monsieur?"

"Right; we'll agree not to answer that question. Are you going to trust me?"

"Have I had any cause to do so?" Mimi asked pointedly.

"No, you haven't," he admitted. "We've each tried to out-bluff the other. I've got a lot of good cards in hand, my girl."

"Poker is my favourite game, monsieur. Your cards lose value if I know what they are."

"You don't," he said confidently.

"You searched my room before dinner and found nothing interesting. If you had, you would not have left your cigarette-end to tell me of your visit."

"I see that you repaid my call and achieved the same result," he observed.

"Pardon. I searched your room when Van Godchen slept and found—"

"You found what?" he demanded sharply.

Mimi shook her forefinger to and fro.

"Oh no, monsieur, You forget we are playing poker. But there is one card that possibly you will expose, for your own safety, because you took the necklace from Mrs. Lucas in the Casino."

"So you know that, do you?"

"Yes. You took it and placed it in the side pocket of your dinner jacket."

"How the deuce do you know I put it there? You were fifteen or twenty yards away and I was in the midst of our crowd."

"The thief could not have taken it from you otherwise. Who was he?"

"I don't know," Glen confessed. "When you showed me what you'd found in the Casino settee, I thought you'd taken it from my pocket! Knowing that the necklace you found was an imitation I hid in Mrs. Lucas's room later on to see if the thief would come there, searching for the real one."

"And did he?" Mimi inquired.

"After a short trip, shadow, we have now come back to Dr. Jekyll and Mrs. Hyde." Glen's tone resumed its mocking note. "So you see I do hold a card or so more than you imagined."

"You placed the jewels in Tony's drawer," Mimi asserted. "He showed me a card on which was written, 'Take this as a warning.' I found cards of that size in your room to-night. Also, I found this."

The girl drew something from her bag and held it up for him to see. It was a bottle of aromatic vinegar.

"I know that you took Lady Daventry's bottle from Mrs. Lucas last night, monsieur."

With an angry exclamation, the man snatched it from her and tossed it far into the pine trees.

"Fools rush in where angels fear to tread,'" he said scornfully, and walked away alone.

XIV: REPERCUSSIONS

Wednesday noon.

AT noon next day Eve Daventry sat in her study, engaged with an unexpected visitor.

Mr. Naylor was a tall, sparely built man probably in the early fifties, but his smooth pallid face with its pale protruding eyes was unmarked by lines of age, temper or humour. His thin hair, pasted closely to his head, resembled a shiny skull cap of a nondescript shade. His lips were scarcely visible in that straight slit which served him for a mouth. His narrow, well-kept hands remained motionless on his knees, almost as if he had no use for them.

As Eve regarded him she was reminded of a dry glistening bone. Mr. Naylor's brain, however, was very much alive.

"I still don't understand why you came from London," she said. "Nor how you did so in such a short time. Mrs. Lucas only died the night before last."

"We will take your points consecutively, Lady Daventry. I received a cable yesterday morning informing me of your guest's death. I came at once travelling by air from London to Cannes; from the latter town I motored here."

Eve Daventry's brow wrinkled in surprise.

"I sent no cable," she declared.

"That is immaterial. I should have come directly I read the account in the newspapers; a delay of twenty-four hours perhaps."

Mr. Naylor's frigid statement aroused a flash of annoyance in Eve's blue eyes.

"Your explanation of this visit seems a trifle vague. Why have you, my late husband's lawyer, come here suddenly because one of my guests has died?"

"I have other clients than the late Sir Neale Daventry," was the lawyer's frigid reply. He gave a short cough. "When will Mrs. Lucas's funeral take place?"

Eve had been waiting for that question.

"It took place an hour ago," she informed him, and was pleased to see that he was nonplussed.

"Indeed!" he commented. "Where?"

"In Nice. Her husband wished the ceremony to be private. And now, Mr. Naylor, I trust you will excuse me from further discussion of this painful topic. I have explained how, where and when it happened, and what the doctors certified."

"Quite so, Lady Daventry. There remains, however, the matter of Mrs. Lucas's pearl necklace which you tell me disappeared."

"It is no longer missing."

"Where was it found?"

"That surely concerns only Mr. Robert Lucas." Eve's tone was composed, but her heart was beating wildly at the memory of Mimi's discovery of the pearls in her drawer. "It is now together with Mrs. Lucas's jewels, locked in the safe in my butler's pantry."

"Who has the key?"

"He has."

"Please ring for him," requested the lawyer. Oswell looked inquiringly at his mistress when he entered.

"Mr. Naylor wishes to ask you some questions, I think, Oswell," she told him, and picked up a letter with an air of withdrawing from the conversation.

"I have no questions to ask you," the lawyer stated "I merely want the key of the safe."

Receiving an assenting nod from Lady Daventry, the butler took a key from his bunch and handed it to the lawyer.

Mr. Naylor placed it in his pocket.

"You may go," he told the man.

Although not one of the three persons present had shown by voice or gesture that there was any friction the butler was conscious of it. Conscious, too, that his mistress was powerless but resentful. In his own way now he managed, in one apparently normal question, to convey his allegiance to his mistress and bland disregard for Mr. Naylor.

"The most valuable of the house silver is locked up each night and taken out each morning. Will your ladyship please instruct Mr. Naylor what she wishes done?"

"Unless you are an early riser," Eve suggested dryly to the lawyer when Oswell had gone, "it might be simpler for you to take out the jewels if you wish to hold yourself responsible for them until Mr. Lucas returns."

"When do you expect him?"

"I have no idea. Possibly to-day. Oswell, I am sure, will be as relieved as I shall be for you to take charge of the things. Why you should trouble to do so is beyond me."

The lawyer rose.

"I will lock the jewels and pearl necklace in my despatch-case."

"As you like everything to be on a business footing, I shall be glad if you will give me a receipt for them," Eve said formally. "The butler will show you your room. Luncheon is at one o'clock, dinner at eight. Please ring if you require anything."

"Lady Daventry, your attitude proves that you do not realize that there might yet be danger to one of your household should Mrs. Lucas's death prove to be other than a natural one. Awkward facts have a habit of cropping up. I intend to remain here until that contingency has ceased to exist."

"I see. I should like to know, please, who sent you that cable," she said authoritatively as he walked towards the door.

The cold pale eyes looked at her as if their owner were reflecting.

"It was signed 'Glen Armitage,'" he replied, and left her.

*   *   *   *   *

At noon that day a car driven by Tony Daventry pulled up on the Moyenne Corniche.

"This is where you all get out and look at the view," he ordered his passengers. They consisted of Mr. John Caryll, Jill and Mimi.

Obediently they stood on the cliff edge, while Tony indicated the various points of interest in the panorama far below them.

"That's Cap Ferrat and—take care, sir." He grabbed John Caryll's arm and pulled him back. "This dry soil is treacherous."

Caryll laughed.

"Don't worry about me, my lad. It's my lucky day. I had a much nearer shave this morning and got away all right."

"What happened?" asked Jill in alarm.

"Some fellow was potting rooks behind the villa. I was waiting for you girls in the drive while Tony got the car out. A shot whizzed past my ear."

"You were not hurt, monsieur?" questioned Mimi.

"Not a bit, but I hope the chap won't mistake me for a target another time when his aim might be better."

*   *   *   *   *

At noon that day, at the gates of the big cemetery at Nice, Robert Lucas was about to step into the vehicle that had brought him there.

"Dismiss your taxi, Robert," urged a woman's voice. "I'll drive you."

"You, Hester!" he exclaimed in a startled tone, swinging round to face Baroness Pertzoff.

"Yes, I. Don't argue. Get into the car."

With skilful hands she guided the powerful coupé round the curves that led down to the sea.

"Where are you going?" he asked, as she turned left and drove along the Promenade des Anglais. Not to Monte Carlo, please."

"We're going to my flat at Mont Boron," she told him. "My tenants left yesterday so it might not be very tidy, but we can have luncheon and talk there in peace. My old housekeeper is preparing some food for us."

"What is there to talk about?" the man asked drearily.

"A great deal," she rapped back. "Pull yourself together, Robert. You can't delude me into thinking that you're grieving for Bella."

"I'm human enough to regret her tragic end."

"I don't regret it, so long as it doesn't have unpleasant repercussions. If you must be cowardly, at least you can be honest. Bella's death is so great a relief that as yet I can scarcely realize it."

The man's face looked drawn and haggard as he stared blindly ahead, absorbed in the secret misery of his thoughts.

In a few minutes his companion ran the car inside the gates of a large house.

"Come along," she said, leading the way through a wide tiled hall and up flights of marble stairs.

"I didn't know you had a flat here," the man remarked as he gazed round the spacious room she showed him into. "Why don't you live in it?"

"It amuses me to let it furnished and be free to go where I like. It amuses me also to come here in retreat, at times and forget the Baroness Pertzoff and all the stupid people she knows. In this place I am Hester Taranova, and the few friends I receive here are mostly those who worked with me on the stage years ago."

A note of sadness hovered in her voice.

Lucas studied her thoughtfully. Her auburn hair, magnificent eyes and tall commanding figure would have marked her out as a woman of unusual type apart from her supreme powers as an actress.

"Why did you marry Baron Pertzoff and give up the profession you loved, Hester?" he asked. "If you'd wanted a title, you could have had your pick of a dozen, and kept your career. Yet you chose an elderly diplomat and, until he died, had to share his dull narrow circle of acquaintances who deplored rather than praised your talents."

"I married Pertzoff, Robert, as you married Bella, for security and because of fear. You made a mess of Bella's investments and to stop her reproaches you married her. I was afraid of age forcing me into a drab background. Hence Pertzoff and a title. After marriage though, the resemblance between you and me ceased. I did not cheat my husband," she said clearly.

"You've chosen a good day to bully me," he remarked in bitter accents. "is that why you dragged me here?"

"No, I brought you here to warn you. At the Villa Lorne, I feel as if someone is always spying and listening. Robert, you've been a coward ever since—"

He held up his hand to check her.

"Stop! Don't talk about that now, please," he begged. "There are limits to my endurance to-day."

"Very well. We'll leave that out for the moment. Who is John Caryll?"

"How should I know? A rich American who is paying Eve to chaperon his niece."

"Rich, he may be; American, I doubt. Educated Americans don't employ the accent of Western cowboys at times and forget it at others. My mother was an American, remember. Someone shot at Caryll as he stood in the drive at eleven o'clock this morning. The bullet missed him."

Lucas sat up stiffly.

"You're sure of this?"

"Quite. I was on my balcony. A minute later I went downstairs and spoke to him on my way to the garage. He did not mention the narrow escape he had had, but in the most casual manner he asked where everybody was on this lovely morning, and" —Hester smiled oddly—" in my most casual manner I told him."

"And was everyone in the villa?

"Everyone; except you, who were in Nice, and Tony, who was in the Villa Lorne garage." Hester paused with deliberate effect. "That's all, Robert. I'm sorry for you and I've warned you. Passion can make us brave, cowardly or criminal. Eve is a marvellous shot. If she fears Caryll knows too much—"

Lucas buried his face in his hands.

"Stop!" he cried. "Perhaps it's better that I do not return to the villa."

"Oh yes, you will," the woman asserted. "I'm going to drive you back immediately we've had luncheon. Don't be a fool, Robert. You can't go anywhere else now or you might be suspected of things you'd never have the courage to do. Bella's will, when it is read, might have startling results. You'd better prepare yourself for them. She was saturated with a desire for revenge; revenge that doesn't begin and end with you."

"Do you know who drew up her will?"

"Yes: Naylor, the Daventry family lawyer. I told Glen Armitage to cable to him."

The man looked puzzled.

"But what has it to do with you?" he asked.

Hester smiled faintly.

"Bella had a pretty strong hold over me too. I'd like to know the worst as soon as possible."

XV. CONCERNING TONY DAVENTRY

Wednesday afternoon.

"CAN I speak to you a minute privately, my lady?" Eve Daventry was about to go down to luncheon when the housekeeper made this unusual request.

"Of course, Mrs. Warren. Come in."

The woman closed the study door and stood before her mistress, obviously uncertain how to broach the object of this visit.

"Anything wrong with the staff?" Eve inquired. Mrs. Warren shook her head.

"No. It's Mr. Tony," she said unexpectedly. An amused twinkle flashed in Eve's eyes.

"Not frogs in a guest's bed again, I hope," she remarked, referring to an incident of a few weeks, ago.

The housekeeper hesitated.

"His pranks make me nervous, my lady. It worries me and I can't do my work properly for fear of what he'll do next."

"I'll speak to him very seriously," Eve promised, wondering whether the woman was ill or merely making a fuss about a trifle. "Tell me, why do you complain so often about him? You were here when he was a motherless baby, and one would think that you would naturally be fond of him."

"I'm only a glorified servant," was the housekeeper's sullen answer. "Why should I be fond of a mischievous spoilt boy? He ought to be earning his living instead of wasting his time down here, upsetting people who've got to work. If Sir Neale was too hard, you're too much the other way, if you'll allow me to say so, my lady."

"I do not allow you to say so, Mrs. Warren," Eve replied dryly, "but as you have expressed your views so freely, and have been here so long, it is only fair to Mr. Tony that you should hear my views. That smash in the 'plane he was piloting last October has finished him for the career he wanted. The specialist wished him to have at least several months' rest. That is why he is here. When we return to London shortly he is going into a motor engineering firm. Are you satisfied?"

"Thank you for telling me this, my lady." The woman twisted her hands. "You've been very good to him. All the same, I wish you'd send him to London now. I've got a lot of responsibility on my hands in this house and Mr. Tony's tricks prey on my mind and upset me."

Eve studied the housekeeper for a moment.

"We have all been upset by Mrs. Lucas's death," she said kindly. "Try to be calm and get more rest and fresh air. Would you like any extra help for the staff?"

"There's plenty of servants,"—Mrs. Warren's tone was stubborn—"though I must say I don't care for that new French secretary."

Eve rose and moved towards the door.

"That is one thing you certainly must not say, Mrs. Warren," she coldly corrected. "I will see that Mr. Tony does not disturb you again."

Five minutes later she sat at the head of the luncheon table, serene and gracious as always. Her plain pale blue linen frock, unflattering to many wearers, enhanced the proud classic beauty of her face, with its sapphire eyes and shining crown of fair hair.

"Had a nice morning, Jill?" she asked.

"Marvellous, thank you," the girl replied. "Tony drove us over the Moyenne Corniche to Nice, and back by the lower road."

If Tony had been at Nice that morning he certainly had not been able to worry Mrs. Warren then, Eve thought. She glanced at her stepson, who rolled his eyes inquiringly at the bent head of the lawyer beside him.

Eve answered her stepson's unspoken question. "Mr. Naylor has come to see me on business. He flew from London to Cannes."

Glen Armitage gave her an oblique look.

"Quite a 'flip'!" he observed, and turned to the lawyer. "Trade quiet your way?"

Mr. Naylor fixed him with a frigid eye.

"I believe that things commercially are improving, Mr. Armitage."

"I gathered that from the newspapers," Glen retorted. "I was referring to things legally, not commercially. Your hurried journey indicates that you were very, very busy or very, very quiet. You'll be a great comfort to Lady Daventry; she's worse than I am at figures."

Mimi leaned across the table.

"Pardon monsieur, but it is my job to make the addings-up for Lady Daventry," she remarked, "though never shall I learn, to write the figure seven in the English way without a little tail through it. It will not disturb you when you check the accounts, I trust," she added, her dark eyes resting appealingly on the lawyer as if her future happiness depended on his reply.

"I am a lawyer and not an accountant, mademoiselle." His stiff countenance relaxed to the vestige of a gallant smile. "But in any case, I am sure that your figures would be quite legible to me should I need to check them."

Mimi pressed her hand to her chest.

"I respire again," she said fervently, and amid general laughter contrived to make a face at Glen Armitage.

"So do I," echoed Eve Daventry softly.

From the far end of the table the elder Hollander took a header into the conversation.

"This morning we went to Nice and returned by the autobus, my zon and I. We zat on the fine promenade an hour. There is much to zee there." He raised his voice. "The Baroness Pertzoff drives well her nice car. It was kind of her to take poor Mr. Lucas for an airing. He must be sad so soon after his wife's funeral. They are not here for luncheon, I zee."

Glen twisted round in his chair and gazed in rapt admiration at Van Godchen.

"My word, you're as good as a detective. How, doth the little busy bee, etc. Lady Daventry, and I will have to be careful if we want to escape your eagle eye."

"Shut up, Glen," broke from Tony angrily. "The Baroness and Lucas don't need anyone's permission if they choose to feed elsewhere."

"Always the sweet little peacemaker!" commented Glen. "I seem to have said the wrong thing again. What shall I do now?"

"Eat your luncheon," Mimi advised. "If you make your mouth very full, all will be quite well."

Again Eve's eyes went to her gratefully.

"Would any of you care to go for a drive this afternoon?" she invited her guests. "The large car is at your disposal, and Tony might take Glen with Jill and Mimi."

"No, no, madame," Mimi said. "This afternoon I work, please, or you will give me the bag for being lazy."

"'Sack' is the word, if you must show off your vocabulary," Glen remarked caustically. He turned to Jill. "Like a run?" he asked in a languid manner.

"Very much." She responded in the same fashion, but her glance held amusement.

Tony glared at Glen.

"Might I act as chauffeur?"

"Yes, if you behave yourself, my lad. Jill and I will be ready in half an hour. Bring the car round." Van Godchen junior found his tongue suddenly.

"You have not forgotten, Miss Jill, that you promised me the honour—"

Jill stopped him with a smile.

"Mr. Van Godchen is going to drive me to Cap Ferrat, thank you, Mr. Armitage," she said sweetly. Tony chuckled.

"Ask her why, Glen, my precious," he urged.

"All right," was the irritated reply. "Why?"

"Because Mr. Van Godchen doesn't talk too much," Jill told him quietly. "There are several other reasons, but I think that one will do."

The elder Van Godchen beamed amiably upon Jill's uncle.

"While my zon and your niece take the leedle drive, shall you and I take the leedle walk, Mr. Caryll? I do not talk too much either, because it is sometimes good to listen."

Caryll fingered his collar as if he were seeking a way to escape from the invitation. His eye fell upon the lawyer.

"Perhaps Mr. Naylor would like to join us in a stroll," he suggested.

The idea was promptly turned down by the lawyer's statement that he had business in Monte Carlo that afternoon.

"Tony, I want you a moment, please," Eve said to her stepson as they left the dining-room.

His eyes danced with fun when they were in the study alone.

"What's the betting, Eve, that I don't make Glen eat humble pie before the day's over? He's insufferable. Did he send for that wizened rat of a lawyer? If so—"

Eve held up her hand.

"Stop, please, Tony. You worry me far more than Glen does. I'm always afraid what you'll do next. You're upsetting the staff badly. Don't you think you're fit enough to go back to London and begin your job?"

Tony stared at her, apparently startled to seriousness.

"Not yet, Eve. I hate cut-and-dried work. Perhaps I had an outlaw ancestor who comes out in my blood and gets me into mischief." He frowned quickly. "I know. It's that old hag Warren; she's always had her knife in me ever since I was a kid and stole coppers from her purse."

"She's neither very old nor a hag," Eve said soberly. "I hate to hold a rod over you, Tony, but if you annoy her in any way again, I must send you back to London and force you to earn your living by cutting off the allowance I give you."

He kissed her cheek lightly.

"You simply couldn't do it, my adorable tender-hearted stepmother. And to prove I'm right, you're going to write me a pretty little cheque now, darling. I owe Glen a bit, confound him, and the beast reminded me of it."

Eve sighed. Scenes with Tony usually ended in this fashion. She was too weak, too conscious of the unfairness of his father's will for combat, and Tony used better weapons than quarrelling to win his battles.

"How much?"she asked, opening her cheque-book.

"Better make it three hundred."

"A very moderate amount for you!" she said with a smile. "That's under five pounds." He grinned cheerfully.

"Not francs, Eve, my angel. Three hundred pounds, please. I'll change 'em fast enough."

XVI. A Warning From Glen

Wednesday afternoon.

"HERE'S the money you lent me, and I hope you choke for telling the world about it two days ago."

Tony banged a pile of notes down and was walking out of the lounge when Glen called him back.

"Hi, young 'un. Not so fast. I'll count these first." Tony crammed his hands in his pockets as if he felt they were safer there.

"I once heard that it takes a well-bred man to be a first-class cad," he rasped.

"Are you referring to me or, yourself?" inquired Glen. He flicked the wad of money contemptuously. "I might wonder where you got this if I were not certain that you'd scrounged it from Eve."

"I don't begrudge her a penny, but after all she did get it from my father, didn't she?"

"And you're leeching her by your sweet loving little ways! Tony, you're a nasty stink in my nostrils." Glen flung back his head and gave a harsh laugh. "A nice pair, aren't we? All the same, perhaps I at least have the courage to be honest in this nest of crookedness. Excepting the staff, is there one person in this villa who is not playing a part?"

"You can leave my stepmother off, the list, anyhow."

"I wish I could," Glen sighed. "Unfortunately Eve is playing a part only too well. I should know why if she were less clever."

"Mimi and Jill are frank enough," Tony asserted.

"About as frank as you are! They're delightful girls, both of 'em, but rather different from what they appear to be. And what do you make of our dear Austrian Baroness and her sudden solicitude for Robert Lucas! She and

Bella Lucas hated each other. As for Lucas, he's in a terrible funk, and it's not because he's lost his wife."

Tony lighted a cigarette.

"You've torn 'em all to pieces now except Jill's uncle and the Van Godchens," he observed. "Got anything against them?"

"A whale of a lot." Glen's tone was vehement. "I'm inclined to like Robert Caryll—not the genial mask he offers, but the pukka hard-as-granite man who knows what he wants and means to get it."

"And what is it he wants, Glen?" Tony inquired smoothly.

"I'd give something to find out. Concerning the Hollanders: there's deadly cunning, if not malice, underlying that old man's apparently blundering remarks, unless I'm much mistaken. His son is a milder type, possibly harmless, still—" Glen's lips tightened to an obstinate line.

"You've a personal grudge against him, haven't you?" Tony stabbed slyly. "He's making good running with Jill, so no wonder, you're peeved. She's by way of being her uncle's heiress, and as you seem to need money so badly that you have to call in your loan to me in public, you must be feeling a bit bruised."

A danger-signal flashed in Glen Armitage's eyes, but beyond that his languid cynical expression did not change.

"If things get too bad I can always follow your example and draw on Eve," he murmured.

"So that's your game!" Tony's face crimsoned with rage.

"I'll try most things once. I say, you and I are having a cosy chat, aren't we? We'll be telling each other all our girlie secrets soon, where I get my stays and where you get your fake pearls and—" Glen's tormenting voice stopped as Tony stepped forward and hit him a crashing blow on the chin.

Caught unawares, he slid backwards and fell heavily on to the parquet floor.

A moment or so later, two doors at opposite ends of the room were opened almost simultaneously, and Lady Daventry and Mrs. Warren approached the scene of the conflict as if they were actors responding to their respective cues.

The housekeeper licked her dry lips as her beady eyes darted from Glen to Tony.

"You see, my lady—" she began tremblingly.

"Be quiet and do as I say, Tony," muttered Glen under his breath. In a louder tone he remarked casually, "We're testing out my favourite ju-jitsu against Tony's preference for straight pugilism, Eve."

"Your theory seems to have a flaw in it." Eve's words were calm, but her face had paled.

"Not a bit of it," Glen assured her. "I foolishly stood on the slippery parquet." He moved on to the Persian rug while he was speaking. "Now then, Tony, we'll have another go and see how this works out. Flit me with the same force as before," he ordered. "Come on. Don't be afraid," he taunted, as his opponent appeared to hesitate.

Temper, always easily stirred in Tony Daventry, flared up again at the sneer. With all his strength he drove his clenched fist at Glen's jaw.

A second later he gave a yelp of pain. In a lightning flash his arm had been twisted upwards behind his back, and was being held at an intolerable angle in a grip like a steel vice.

"Hope I've proved my point to your satisfaction." Glen's tone was silky, but his glance challenged his victim.

"You've proved something," Tony growled savagely. "Let me go." He rubbed his wrist for a moment as Glen released it and then stalked out of the room.

"Yon tiger-cub is getting out of hand," Glen observed lightly to Eve. He cocked an inquiring eyebrow at the housekeeper. "Enjoyed the show, Mrs. Warren?"

The woman swallowed and, bending down, straightened the rug.

"No, sir, I didn't. This room isn't the place for a boxing match. I heard a thud and thought Mr. Tony and you were quarrelling."

"A 'thud' doesn't exactly indicate a quarrel," Glen told her, "if that was all you heard."

Mrs. Warren stood silently for a moment and then withdrew.

"Don't go, please, Glen," Eve said when the woman had gone. "I've two questions to ask you."

"Fire ahead. May I say that your ladyship looks particularly attractive in that gown and with your usually calm bored expression warmed by wrath. Good phrase that: warmed by wrath. Go on."

"Why were you and Tony quarrelling?" she demanded.

"My dear, don't ask absurd questions to which you know the answer. Tony and I are always at sworn enmity. At times it dies down slightly and then I have to stir it to briskness. Life would be unbearable if he and I were polite to one another. To-day's scrap was the result of my energetic efforts. He responded marvellously, as you observed."

"Glen, you're a fiend when you're malicious."

"What was the second question?"

"Why did you cable to Naylor and tell him that Bella Lucas had died suddenly?"

"H'm, I'll admit at first sight that it seems a trifle hard for me to have 'wished' that dried cod-fish into our happy home life. But can I help it that you have such a frozen ass for a lawyer?"

"Why did you send for him?" Eve persisted. Glen Armitage looked at her gravely.

"Because, believe me or believe me not, Eve, I think you're in more danger than you realize. The tragedy of Bella Lucas is a beginning, not an end of trouble, and I thought it was as well for you to have that death's head of a lawyer handy. Also there's another reason that you'll know soon enough."

"I suppose you think Naylor will be a great help to me," she said bitterly.

"About as much as a vulture is over a carcass." Glen's eyes grew stern. "Things are nearly boiling. Naylor's presence may hasten the process indirectly. When that happens—and if this tension exists much longer somebody will go mad—Naylor will come in useful to pick the flesh from the bones. Then we shall see what's underneath. I was always interested in anatomy."

"In human vivisection, too," she retorted. "What business is it of yours? If you hate me so much, why not go away?"

"I hate fools. Whereas knaves are often delightful people, fools are merely irritating. As for going away, why should I? I pay a monthly cheque for the privilege of being one of dear chic Lady Daventry's *sub rosa* lodgers. If you want to put the price up, say so frankly."

She winced at his brutal speech.

"I begged you to stay purely as my guest, Glen."

"And thereby have my lips sealed, or open them only to emit polite sychophantic phrases. No, thanks, I'll pay and be free. But as for pushing me out now that the balloon promises to go up shortly, you can't be so unfeeling! Especially when the balloon is likely to be a full-sized 'Blimp.'"

"All right," she agreed wearily. "Stay and torture me if it amuses you. I think I shall persuade Tony to go back to London if there is likely to be more trouble here."

Glen stared at her, obviously startled, then he controlled himself.

"Don't do that," he implored. "I couldn't bear life here without that little pet. He has such taking ways, hasn't he? You poor blind idiot!" Under his breath he whistled tunelessly. "Hope Jill and young Van Godchen are enjoying their excursion. I can picture him solemnly reading Baedeker to her."

"I'm afraid he's rather a dull companion," Eve replied. "You admire Jill very much, don't you, Glen?"

"Immensely. She's as sweet as she looks, and hasn't so much to conceal as everybody else here."

Eve puckered her brow anxiously.

"You think she is hiding something?"

"Undoubtedly, but if it will comfort you to know, I'm sure that Jill's baby secret doesn't seriously affect your cares or interests. It's a little private deceit that's been thrust upon her, I suspect. She doesn't like it, but she can't avoid it."

Eve bit her lip in alarm.

"Is it connected with her uncle?" she asked a little breathlessly.

"Most probably. Jill is too simple and straightforward to be able to conceal anything from that astute old bird, who says he's an American and her uncle."

"Of course he's her uncle. Why else should he bring her here openly for me to act as her chaperon if there was a sordid liaison."

"There isn't," Glen assured her. "You can cross that idea right out of your mind if I unconsciously put it there. If Caryll had that notion, he wouldn't have brought her here. It would have been unnecessary. The Riviera has many faults, but it's not self-righteous or interfering about other people's affairs. Still, my bet is that he's not her uncle, so watch your step, if you're counting John Caryll as a genial nouveau-riche, eager to give his niece a leg-up in the social world."

"I've noticed that he tries occasionally to speak with an English accent."

"The other way about. He unconsciously reverts to English. Which shows pretty plainly that he's not had much previous experience in whatever game he's playing. What d'you know about him, Eve?"

"Very little, really," she replied in a puzzled fashion.

"Of course, one doesn't ask personal questions, but if ever the subject of his past life crops up, he appears to talk frankly, switches off to another subject in the most natural manner, and afterwards you realize that you're no whit wiser. It doesn't matter, of course. I'm not at all curious."

"It might matter, so I'll give you a break. He owns huge tinned fruit factories in California called 'Caryll's Canned something or other.' Once a year he goes there for a visit and that's all. Jill was earning her living in London. After an expensive cruise, Caryll brought her here. That's the works, so far as I know."

"How did you know?" Eve asked pointedly.

"Oh, by snooping round," Glen replied in an airy tone. "Luckily for me your guests hoard their letters. I've got a lot of good work waiting for me in the other rooms."

"Glen, how can you stoop to such mean vulgar tricks?"

"Easily. It seems to come natural to one of my foul tastes." His eyes narrowed to warning slits. "I'll have to stoop much lower and work much faster though, if I'm to prevent your fair profile from being rubbed in the dust."

"You are doing this for me?" Eve's voice rose on a note of surprise.

"No," he told her tersely. "For myself principally. I like to see the wheels go round. Also, if I can keep Jill from being drawn into any unsavoury mess, I shall. If you benefit from my research work, so much the better for you. I seem to have opened my mouth pretty wide, don't I? By the way, where's your 'shadow'?"

"If you mean my secretary, she's in the study."

"I'm glad to hear it. Mimi's too hot on my heels for my liking: it rather cramps my method of nosing round." Glen wheeled swiftly. "Speak of—angels, here she is! Hello, shadow, d'you want me?"

"Never, I think, monsieur," Mimi retorted pleasantly. Turning to Eve, she said, "Mr. Lucas has come, madame, and would like to see you."

XVII. Vignettes

Wednesday evening.

IT was seven o'clock when John Caryll tapped at Jill's door that evening.

"Enjoyed your trip to Cap Ferrat?" he asked.

"Very much, thank you, uncle." Jill had learnt her lesson by this time. "Franz Van Godchen was most informative." Her lip twitched with amusement.

"What did he talk about?"

"Chiefly of things I'd already read in the guide book. On Cap St. Jean he became historical and reeled off facts about the tower, the quaint little church and the huge statue of the Madonna. He must have learnt it by heart."

Caryll, however, was not wholly satisfied.

"And on the return journey, what happened?"

Jill laughed.

"He was rather sentimental in his stiff, formal way: I think his brain must have been starched when he was a baby."

"Did he ask any personal questions?"

The girl puckered her brow.

"His questions were chiefly about my visit here, where and how long I'd been in America, and if I'd seen your factories in California. I gave vague replies—he would have thought it odd if I hadn't. Don't worry," she said gently. "I was very careful, uncle."

"You're a good child, Jill. I'm sorry to have to drag you into my affairs, but I'd have no excuse to be here without you."

"Couldn't you have come here alone? I believe that some of the other guests pay."

"They are old acquaintances of Lady Daventry's. I'm a stranger, and she is sharp enough to realize that a man of my type would obviously choose an hotel. With you here, everything is easy."

"I wonder what object the Hollanders had in coming to this villa?" Jill observed. "They've been here some time; they rarely gamble, or dance, and I'm sure they've done no sight-seeing. My escort must have read up all about cap Ferrat for my benefit. I asked him if he liked Cap Antibes and he said he'd never been to Italy!"

"That's queer. Antibes is between Nice and Cannes."

"Then I had real fun," Jill went on. "You noticed Eze, that ruined mountain village we saw on our drive this morning. It stands on the edge of the cliff above the main road, only a few miles from Monte Carlo."

Caryll nodded.

"I know it. A deserted spot, centuries old."

"I asked Franz Van Godchen if the shops at Eze were as large as at Nice. He said they were, but a little more expensive, probably!"

Caryll patted her shoulder.

"You're smarter than I thought, Jill. Put on your pretty red frock and look your best then you might be able to tempt Franz to talk."

*   *   *   *   *

At half-past seven Glen Armitage was alone in the billiard-room, practising a difficult shot. He looked up as a man in the forties with weary haggard eyes entered.

"Hello, Lucas," Glen greeted him. "Like a game? There's nearly half an hour to dinner. We're both dressed."

Lucas shook his head.

"My hand's not steady enough: nerves all shot to pieces. Why did you send that cable to Naylor? He was not my wife's legal representative."

Glen laid his cue down and approached the older man.

"Sorry, Lucas, but I've got a shock for you. Naylor is your wife's lawyer."

An expression of bewilderment crossed Lucas's face.

"I had no idea of this," he said slowly. "Bella was very secretive. When did she tell you?"

"She didn't. I found out the night she died. You went off early next morning to get the doctors' certificate, or I should have told you instead of telling Hester Pertzoff. It seemed wise to get Naylor here at once."

"Does Eve know?" Lucas asked.

"That Naylor drew up Bella's will recently? No. And I'm sure old codfish has not mentioned his real reason for coming."

"You are sure that Naylor made the will?"

"Yes. Three months ago. This proves it." Glen pulled a letter from his pocket. "The envelope was not sealed."

Lucas scanned the communication swiftly.

"Thanks," he said. "How did you get hold of it?"

"I was looking in Bella's room for something else, which incidentally, I didn't find, and came across this letter. Bella's clutch on you was pretty fierce, old lad."

Lucas nodded.

"Yes. She never forgot or forgave anything," he replied reminiscently. "To see her running round with that gigolo these past weeks one wouldn't credit her implacable mind, bent on the last ounce of vengeance."

"Naylor will read her will after dinner this evening, I expect," Glen remarked. "Would you like me to be present or not?"

"Please come," Lucas said emphatically. "I may need you badly. By the way, Eve's entertaining to-night. An informal dance after dinner."

Glen raised his eyebrows.

"Rather bad taste on her part so soon after Bella's death," he commented.

"Not at all. It didn't happen here, and Eve has a duty to Caryll and Jill," Lucas reminded him.

*   *   *   *   *

It was nearly eight o'clock when Tony Daventry saw the Hollanders and Naylor talking together in the hall.

"I am hongry," announced Van Godchen senior solemnly as the young man approached.

"Bear up. You'll have your nosebag in a minute or two," Tony promised. "Better not eat too much though, because we're throwing a party to-night and you'll all have to dance."

"I do not dance," the lawyer stated.

"Well, to-night's your chance to learn," Tony assured him. "There's a hefty wench coming who'll take you on. She's good-hearted and patient with beginners."

Mr. Naylor showed cold annoyance at the flippant suggestion.

"I shall dance myself certainly," roared the old Hollander. "Yet it is very zudden, this ball."

"Eve and I telephoned round to people after tea. It's more amusing that way," Tony told him. Franz Van Godchen exchanged a glance with his father.

"The sun has given me a bad headache," he remarked.

Tony slapped him on the shoulder and laughed.

"That's a rotten excuse, Franz. We don't get sun hot enough on the Riviera in February to incapacitate strong men, do we, Mr. Caryll?" he asked, as the latter strolled up.

"It hasn't done me any noticeable damage yet," Caryll agreed.

Van Godchen senior turned to the newcomer.

"My zon is not strong, Mr. Caryll. We are in Monte Carlo for his health. A weak heart my Franz has. I Therefore we live very calmly here; no egzitements, no egscursions. Just a leedle walk between our meals, you understand."

Caryll understood perfectly. Franz had evidently reported his conversation with Jill about Eze, and Van Godchen was clumsily endeavouring to excuse the mistake.

"Look here, Mr. Caryll," exclaimed Tony, who saw his prey slipping from his grasp if Franz is well enough to eat his dinner, he's well enough to dance, isn't he?"

"It seems a fair argument," John Caryll remarked easily. "There's the gong and here come the ladies."

"And very beautiful they look," commented the older Hollander with admiration.

Arm-in-arm, the two girls, Jill in red and Mimi in black, walked slowly down the wide staircase, their faces alight with animated conversation.

Behind them, grave and impressive, came Eve and Baroness Pertzoff; the former in a gown of shimmering blue and silver brocade, the latter in purple velvet that audaciously defied her mass of red hair.

Even the lawyer relaxed sufficiently to make an obvious comment.

"A remarkable contrast in types," he murmured.

The men looked from Jill's lovely radiance to, Mimi's piquant charm; from Eve's serene classic beauty to the vivid Austrian with her dominating personality.

"For a 'has-been' the Pertzoff still looks pretty powerful," muttered Tony irrepressibly to John Caryll. "I'll bet she'd have had Nero on leash if she'd lived in his time."

Eve's cool musical voice prevented any answer that he might have made. Her amused glance drifted from one to another in the group of men to which had now been added Glen and Robert Lucas.

"Seven men to four women!" she said. "Three of us must take two partners."

"If you dine, you dance," Tony firmly warned the young Hollander.

Franz shrugged his shoulders and turned to his hostess.

"I beg you will excuse me, Lady Daventry, if I retire. My head is rather bad." He made her a stiff bow and walked to the staircase. "I cannot dance tonight."

"Thought you said it was his heart. Now apparently it's his head and his feet," Tony remarked to the father of the invalid.

"My zon is delicate," thundered Van Godchen in anger. "If our gracious hostess permits him to retire, what will you?"

"What indeed?" Tony demanded mischievously. Eve silenced him with a stern glance and called the butler.

"Send a light meal up to Mr. Franz Van Godchen's room, Oswell; and some champagne also," she ordered.

Tony drew Jill's arm though his.

"Now let me get this recipe straight," he said. "One drive in the sun with you, one headache, dinner in bed and a private binge. That's how you avoid a dance."

"I wonder why," observed Glen who was close behind.

"Perhaps he has the corns," suggested Mimi, who also inwardly wondered why.

XVIII. Bella Lucas's Will

Wednesday evening.

TONY was obviously at the top of his form during dinner. He teased everyone in turn, made outrageous sallies and performed a number of conjuring tricks with various articles.

"You are quick with the fingers," commented the Hollander, smoothing his ruffled hair from which Tony had produced coins. "How comes it?"

"Inherited the talent from my parents," Tony said airily. "My mother was a pianist and my father a pickpocket."

From the opposite end of the table Eve watched him with growing dismay. Tony was drinking more than usual, and she was afraid where his effrontery would lead him.

Her eyes sought those of Glen Armitage appealingly, but received no aid from that source. Beyond a hardening of his mouth, Glen took no notice.

Outside in the hall stood Mrs. Warren. She caught the butler as he came out of the dining-room.

"What's all the roars of laughter about?" she demanded.

"Mr. Tony's got 'em good and proper," Oswell told her. "He's had about a quart of champagne and if nobody stops him there'll be trouble here to-night. Her ladyship looks quite upset."

"Well she might be," the housekeeper declared.

"He ought to be packed off to London. I told her so to-day. There's something horrible about this, place."

The butler placed an ice pudding on a salver and poised it high on one hand as though it were an offering for the gods.

"You've got the jitters about Mr. Tony. He's a bit high-spirited, that's all," Oswell said firmly.

"Have a cup of strong tea and put some gin it." Adding to himself as he went back to his post, "If you haven't done too much of that already."

He passed round the table, serving the guests deftly.

"How's the invalid, Oswell?" Tony sang out.

"Quite comfortable, I believe, sir," the butler replied without pausing in his task.

Glen Armitage was the last to be served. He seized the chance to ask Oswell a question under his breath concerning Franz's dinner.

"Consommé, salmon, cold chicken, an ice and champagne, sir," was the murmured reply.

"Serve coffee in here, Oswell, and have the rugs rolled up in the lounge, please," Eve ordered.

"Sling the furniture well back, too," requested Tony, "or we shall bark our shins when the lights go out."

"You dance in the dark?" came from Jill in astonished accents.

"Not all the time, of course," Tony replied. "We put the lights out as a surprise at odd moments. It's great sport. Gives you a chance to kiss your partner or pinch her bracelet, according to your taste and opportunity."

"You think it is wise, these surprise dances?" demanded Van Godchen solemnly of his hostess.

"Why not?" she inquired, a little piqued at his tone. "It's done everywhere nowadays. A twilight waltz is quite usual. You were here when we had them previously."

A little later in the hall, as visitors began to arrive, Eve spoke anxiously to Mimi.

"Try, to keep Tony near you," she begged. "He is in one of his mad moods. I must see that Jill has a good time."

Mimi nodded.

"I understand. Maybe he will wish to wring my neck, but no matter, I shall stick closely to him."

Coming downstairs was Van Godchen.

"I have been up to wish good night to my zon and now return to dance," he informed Eve ponderously, and passed into the lounge.

"After that kind permission, we might turn on the radio," Glen remarked. "You use the gramophone for the surprise dances, don't you? Who's going to switch off the lights?"

"Mr. Lucas offers to do that," Eve answered. "Naturally he won't dance, but he'll see to the lights and music in the library. Tell him we're ready, will you?"

Lucas was arranging a pile of records when Glen strolled in.

"Turn on the radio, Lucas. Van Godchen's kissed his son good night and is now going to honour the floor with his feet. He reminded me of a benign elephant just now."

"How many seconds shall I allow for the lights to be off in the twilight waltz?" Lucas asked.

"I don't know. Five, ten, perhaps twenty. Use your own judgment. There's a switch that controls all the lounge lights in the hall."

"Oswell showed it to me. He'll be busy seeing to the buffet supper. I say, Glen, it's odd that Naylor hasn't mentioned Bella's will to me. He had ample chance after dinner."

"Perhaps he thinks this is not a fitting moment," Glen said with a grin. "Too much levity! My hat, Lucas, he little knows how superficial that levity is. I hear that that red-headed Jezebel waylaid you at Nice to-day. She didn't waste much time."

"Don't call her that. She is unconventional."

"All right," Glen interrupted. "Don't explain. We'll say the Baroness Pertzoff is warm-hearted and leave it at that. That's a good tune. I'll go and foot it with the genial soul. Bye-bye. Let me know if Naylor drops in on you."

Glen stood in the entrance to the lounge and watched the crowd for a while. No longer was there a deficit of women, he thought. Eve Daventry was very popular and her impromptu invitations had brought a rich harvest.

Rich was the right word, he decided, observing the exquisite gowns and jewellery that were in evidence. Jill Caryll was undoubtedly a success. Her eyes sparkled as she floated past in the arms of a handsome Italian count, one of the most eligible bachelors on the Côte d'Azur.

Mimi was in a corner, apparently teaching Tony some intricate step. Glen hoped the lesson would last for some time.

He smiled as Van Godchen's heavy form moved past. The Hollander was fulfilling his threat to dance, and his arm now, encircled a South American woman of reputed wealth

The music stopped and Van Godchen led his partner to a seat and, with a bow, left her. Swinging from the woman neck on a slender platinum chain, Glen noticed an enormous ruby which flamed against her amber gown.

"That's a gorgeous bit of colour," he pointed out to Eve, who had paused near him.

"Yes. It makes all the necklaces and bracelets here look tawdry," she replied. "It's terribly hot, Glen. Couldn't we have the French windows open?"

The man obeyed her. On the way back he stopped for a word with the owner of the ruby, complimenting her for her good taste in wearing no other trinket to detract from its beauty.

"I can't very well, Mr. Armitage;" she replied. "It's so huge that it seems to dwarf my other jewellery. I love it, but it's rather a curse because it's so heavy." She raised the stone and placed it in his hand. "Feel the weight."

"Be careful the chain doesn't snap," he said, "This ruby must be worth a fortune."

"That depends on what one assesses a fortune at," she replied with a smile "Still, it is valuable and was once in a royal Turkish crown, I believe. My late husband bought it years ago, but I've only recently worn it when large stones became fashionable."

Glen performed a few duty dances and then strolled back to the library.

"We're in for a thunderstorm," he remarked to Lucas, "and I shan't be sorry when it starts. I envy you your job."

"I haven't one for the moment," the older man told him. "There's a good programme on the radio and I'm letting it run. Eve doesn't want the twilight dance for an hour."

He frowned as Naylor appeared in the doorway accompanied by Baroness Pertzoff.

"It is not a particularly suitable moment, Mr. Lucas," the lawyer began, "but I am anxious to discharge my duties as soon as possible. Lady Daventry has given me permission to use her study, where it will be quiet. Will you kindly follow me there?"

"You were not aware that I had drawn up a recent will for your late wife?" Mr. Naylor inquired, when they were seated in the room on the first floor.

Lucas caught a warning glance from Glen and acted upon it.

"She did not mention it to me," he parried. "As you are Lady Daventry's lawyer, I imagined that you were here on her business."

"Quite so," the lawyer commented in a brittle tone. "I have requested Baroness Pertzoff to remain here during the reading of the document, which is very brief."

The Austrian woman leaned forward.

"This is no business of mine, Robert, and I can't say Mr. Naylor wishes me to be here. I think for you to decide."

Lucas smiled faintly. "What does it matter, Hester? A will isn't any secret. Stay by all means."

The lawyer unfolded the document and began to read.

It was indeed brief; it was also startling. The Baroness stared in surprise.

"Is that all?" she demanded. "Is it legal?"

The lawyer bowed. "That is all, and the will is perfectly legal as no other one has been discovered."

The Austrian woman's eyes burned with indignation. "It's iniquitous, Robert," she declared. "I had no idea of this. Bella and I shared an active dislike one another, and now this—" She flicked the document contemptuously.

"Don't worry," Lucas said calmly. "Bella had a right to do as she pleased."

The woman pressed back the waves of her tawny hair.

"I am to inherit everything," she murmured perplexedly.

"There are two important conditions, Baroness," put in the lawyer.

"Let me read it myself," she demanded in her rich, vibrating voice. Herr eyes glanced through the sentences, picking the salient points.

"I, Isabel Lucas—to Hester Pertzoff—everything I possess. Two conditions: Hester Pertzoff must demand payment of two debts due to me of which she knows, and must preserve all letters and photographs that are now my property."

"You know of these debts and wishes to which my late client refers, Baroness?" inquired the lawyer.

The woman gazed at him blankly for a moment.

"I? Yes, I suppose I do. I must think this over and write to you later, Mr. Naylor." She rose, and without a glance at the other two men, went from the room.

Lucas's face was expressionless.

"It's a bit of an anti-climax, but I must see to the music," he said evenly. "Lady Daventry is depending on me. It's about time for the twilight affair, isn't it, Glen?"

His companion looked at his watch.

"Yes. Come along. What about you, Mr. Naylor?"

"I shall take a short walk and then retire," the lawyer replied. No wonder Mrs. Lucas had left her husband nothing, he reflected with disgust. The fellow seemed void of all sense of correct behaviour. Turning on radios indeed for a dance when his wife had only been buried that morning!

"Sorry, old man," Glen said curtly as he and Lucas went downstairs.

Lucas gave a short laugh.

"It's those cruel ironical conditions. I can't repay the money to the estate and I'm terrified that the purpose for which I needed it will come out. You guessed, of course, that I was one of the debtors?"

Glen nodded.

"Who's the other?" he demanded.

Before Lucas could reply there came a shout, from the hall.

"Hi, you two," yelled Tony. "We're waiting for the lights out stuff. Go to it, Mr. Lucas. And you," —he caught Glen's arm—"get back to the lounge, my lad, and do a spot of work with your feet. Jill's asked where you were. She's keeping this dance for you."

XIX. Shots in the Dark

Wednesday night.

JILL'S eyes had the happy light of a child at a party when Glen reached her.

"I hope you don't mind being my partner," she said shyly. "Tony wanted this dance, but he's so full of nonsense that—" She broke off. "You see I've been to no modern affairs like this. What happens when the lights go out? Do we stand still?"

Glen regarded her with mock solemnity.

"A wise man blessed with a charming partner rarely wastes those precious seconds," he assured her, "but a still wiser man would be content to wait until—"

"Until the lights went on again," Jill said, and smiled. "I was a fool to be nervous, but really, Tony has been rather impossible. He's been letting off parlour fireworks. Can't you smell them?"

An angry gleam flashed in the man's face.

"I'll have to teach that pup another lesson. They're dangerous with all these flimsy dresses," he declared. He took the girl in his arms as the strains of a waltz floated softly into the room. Eve was dancing with a dark-haired Italian officer; Hester Pertzoff, with Tony; talking to him animatedly as if the episode of a few moments ago in the study had passed from her mind. Glen was recalled from his thoughts by Jill's voice.

"I had one dance with Mr. Van Godchen," she said. "He was terribly thorough! He tramped firmly down the room and whirled me round violently at the corners."

"I 'done him wrong' in comparing him to a benign elephant," Glen remarked. "He more closely resembles a hippopotamus. Look at him now."

In the square embrasure of one of the open windows reclined the Hollander in an armchair, feet extended, hands crossed on his rotund stomach, eyes closed. His mouth was half open and deep rhythmic snores came from the vast expanse of his chest.

"At any rate, he danced, which was more than his son did," Jill remarked. "Oh!" she exclaimed as all the lights went out.

Soft laughter and shufflings were heard above the music in the darkness. Then brilliance again flooded the sparkling scene.

"Not too bad, was it?" asked Glen.

"It was fun." Jill's answer was a little tremulous. "There's uncle, dancing with the lady who has the wonderful ruby. I somehow thought the music would stop, too, during the twilight waltz."

"Lucas couldn't manage that single-handed. The gramophone's in the library and the switch in the hall. Oswell's busy in the kitchen, I expect. Hello, here we go again," Glen said as again the room was plunged into blackness. "Don't be alarmed," he added as a heavy roll of thunder was heard. "There's a peach of a storm rolling up."

A few seconds later the lights flashed on, and across Baroness Pertzoff's shoulder, Tony made an impish face at them. Close behind was Mimi, regarding him anxiously, and evidently uninterested in the stolid Frenchman who was her companion.

"Mimi's a clever kid," Glen said rather grudgingly. "She's positively tracking Tony, and her poor partner doesn't realize it."

"But why is she doing it?" Jill asked in surprise, while another long roll of thunder rumbled nearer in deafening peals, and rain streamed down noisily.

"Because—" Glen changed his sentence as this time the lights and music went out. "Jill my sweet, I love you. You're not frightened now are you?" he whispered. His arms held her, tightly while a terrific crash shook the house and a streak of lightning threw the room into an unearthly glare.

The girl shivered. During that thunder-clap there had come a sharp crack, and a smothered cry from somewhere in the room.

"What was that?" she asked in alarm.

"I don't know," Glen said slowly. "Don't be uneasy. Lucas ought to switch on." Holding Jill's hand, he guided her to the wall. "Stay there a minute, darling. I'll see what's wrong," he urged.

"Lights, please, Lucas," he called in incisive tones across the darkness of the room.

"They're out everywhere," came back Lucas's answer.

"Perhaps the storm has affected the wires." It was John Caryll who spoke.

"Something was due to happen in this house," Tony Daventry said, and gave a high-pitched laugh.

Eve checked him.

"This is no moment to be funny, Tony," she warned.

"I strike a match," Van Godchen's deep voice boomed placidly. A tiny spurt of flame showed him to be still seated in the armchair by the window. It died away, leaving the room by comparison in denser blackness.

Overhead another more violent peal of thunder banged its clamorous way through the air, rumbling on in sullen, anger for tense seconds.

And then Oswell appeared in the doorway bearing two lighted candles.

A sigh of relief went through, the weighted silence of the room.

"I'm afraid a main fuse has gone, my lady," he said calmly. "I'll see to it at once."

"Thank you, Oswell."

"If your ladyship prefers to go into the dining-room, supper is quite ready. The maids have put extra candles there."

He placed those he had brought on a table where their soft glow shed small circles of light in the immediate radius, the corners of the spacious lounge still remaining in shadowed gloom.

The guests crowded round, trying to appear cool or amused at the incident, yet inwardly keyed up with the conviction that something odd had happened.

One man voiced his fear frankly.

"I heard a sharp crack," he said. "It sounded like backfiring—a shot. It couldn't have been in here, of course."

Glen Armitage gave him a cold glance.

"We all appear to be here and unharmed." His eyes scanned the room rapidly. One person was missing! Veiling his anxiety, he marshalled the entire company into the dining-room where a dozen or more candies lighted up a buffet table.

"You all right, Jill?" he asked of the girl beside him.

She nodded gravely.

"Tony looks very white, Glen, and where is Baroness Pertzoff? That crack was a shot. I saw the flash. It was near where she was standing with Tony. Please go and look for her," she entreated.

Snatching a candle, Glen hurried into the hall and across to the library.

He started as a hand touched his arm. Mimi stood beside him, and spoke in an undertone.

"Come with me, monsieur."

She guided him to a small room used as a butler's pantry.

"In here, please," she said. Locking the door behind her she pointed to a figure clad in purple velvet, sitting in a shabby armchair. It was Hester Pertzoff. Her eyes were closed, cheeks of an ashen hue beneath grotesque patches of rouge. One hand was pressing a towel to her left shoulder. The heavy lids lifted as Mimi and Glen came towards her.

"Why did you bring him?" she demanded. "I gave you my orders, girl."

"Mimi had no choice. I was searching for you," Glen explained. "What has happened?"

"Somebody shot me," Hester replied tersely.

"Stay with her," Mimi said. "I will get dressings. The wound is not serious. *Ma foi*, but madame is brave."

Hester Pertzoff raised an imperious hand.

"Stop! You will tell Lady Daventry that the storm has affected my nerves. I felt faint you understand, and have retired."

"I understand," Mimi replied.

Glen sat down on the table beside the woman and took her hand in his.

"I admire your courage, Hester," he said, "but aren't you making a mistake? You must let me call up a doctor. You can give him what explanation you wish, but surely if someone shot at you you don't want him to escape unpunished."

"Be quiet, fool," she muttered savagely. "You're babbling about things of which you know nothing. That French chit helped me to this room and says she can dress the wound. I nursed in Austria during the war and know what to do, if she doesn't."

Glen gazed at her with exasperated admiration.

"An attempt has been made upon your life. It's fine of you to try to avoid a scandal for Eve's sake," he said.

"'Eve!'" Hester Pertzoff laughed harshly. "Why should I protect her? Listen, you heard the lawyer read that will to-night; you know there are two debtors to Bella's estate, that Robert Lucas is one of them. He has therefore—in the eyes of the law—a good reason for wishing me dead."

"Good heavens! You mean that Lucas shot you?"

"In the eyes of the law he'd be suspected. He's pressed for money. If I were out of the way he'd have no debt to pay. For all I know the estate might revert to him."

Glen cupped his chin in his hands and stared at her.

"Of course," he exclaimed. "He had the opportunity and his motive is clear, though I'd never have believed it of him. What are you going to do?"

"Nothing."

"Nothing?" the man echoed blankly. "In the name of fortune, why?"

"Because, you poor blind idiot, I love Robert Lucas, and have done so for years. He doesn't know, but Bella knew." The woman's lips curved bitterly. "He's too much in love with someone else to notice my existence. Do you want to know who she is?"

Glen frowned.

"No," he said shortly. "That's Lucas's private affair, and not yours or mine."

"You're talking like an immature public-schoolboy!" she jeered. "All sense of honour and the old school tie. I'm an actress of not over-refined birth, accustomed to life and emotions in the raw. There comes a time when you can't smother strong feelings any longer under a veil of refinement. That's what is causing most of the trouble in the Villa Lorne."

She pressed the towel more closely to her shoulder and winced.

"Robert Lucas is a weak cowed mortal," she went on. "I don't know why I love him, any more than I understand why he loves that cold beautiful iceberg."

"You can't mean Eve?" the man exclaimed in astonishment.

Hester sneered.

"I'm glad you recognize the description. Of course it's Eve. You're fond of her yourself, aren't you?"

"Not in that way," Glen said definitely.

Hester Pertzoff looked at him under her blackened lashes.

"That's just a bit of luck for you, my boy," she said meaningly.

"Why?"

"Because Eve is the other person who'll have to pay up. She owed Bella a pretty considerable sum of money, besides—"

"That will do," Glen rasped. "Eve has suffered enough in the past."

"She also has a strong motive, you see, for wishing me out of the way," persisted Hester.

"Nonsense. You've no grounds for such a wild accusation."

"Haven't I?" The woman drew a small revolver from under a fold of her dress. "Do you recognize this? It is Eve's gun. Yesterday I saw it in a drawer in the library. It was dropped on my foot after the shot."

"Lucas was in the library alone to-night," Glen reminded her. He had more chance to get hold of it than Eve."

"The revolver might have been taken before then. You'd better be silent about this business, Glen Armitage. You want to shield Eve, and I intend to shield Robert Lucas. The odds are very delicately balanced, but if the truth comes out, I warn you I shall weight the scales against Eve. Ah!" she exclaimed as Mimi entered with a tray of dressings and bowl of hot water, "you've been a long time."

"I had to find iodine and bandages. It was not easy with only a candle," Mimi told her as she bared the woman's shoulder. "There are the lights at last."

Hester twisted her head round and examined the wound in an impersonal manner.

"As I said, it's not serious," she pronounced. "A clean flesh wound, bullet's passed right through. Better look for it in the lounge while the mob are having supper, Glen." She turned to Mimi. "Now then, girl, get on with this job quickly and then I'll go to bed. Bolt the door after Mr. Armitage."

Mimi slipped close to Glen as he passed her.

"The person who fired had a small electric torch, monsieur. I saw the tiny pencil of light a moment before. The shot that wounded Baroness Pertzoff's shoulder first passed through the sleeve of Mr. Tony's coat."

"A rotten poor aim!" Glen commented.

"It depends what his aim was," the girl said dryly.

"Perhaps it was to distract attention; perhaps to fix blame on someone else."

XX. A Frustrated Burglary

Wednesday night.

GLEN encountered Tony at the foot of the stairs. "Where are you going?" he demanded, catching the younger man by the shoulder.

Tony shook himself free irritably.

"I'm not going anywhere. I've been to change my collar. Any objection?"

"Were you hurt?"

"Hurt! Heaven bless my soul! Is the man mad?" Tony exclaimed. "It's hard if a fellow can't change a wilted collar without your permission. Who d'you think you are in this house?"

Glen glanced at Tony's clothes thoughtfully.

"You're lucky to have two 'tail' coats," he remarked. "Now if I'd had a bullet through my sleeve I'd have been reduced to a dinner-jacket if I'd wanted to keep the job quiet."

Tony scowled at him.

"So you know all about that, do you?"

"Not all, unfortunately, but quite a bit." Glen's eyes narrowed. "Tony, where were Eve and her partner when the shooting was going on? And where exactly were you and Hester Pertzoff?"

"We were all four pretty close to the door which leads into the hall." Tony opened the door of the empty lounge and indicated the spot where he had been standing. "Just about here. I wanted to keep the business quiet for Eve's sake as I wasn't hurt. Lucky I'd been messing about with the parlour fireworks earlier or people might have noticed the smell of gunpowder. Have you any idea who fired at me?"

Glen ignored the question. Apparently Tony had no idea that Baroness Pertzoff had been injured.

"Were you holding Hester Pertzoff when the gun went off?" he asked.

"No. She's too hefty a handful to hang on to. When the lights and music stopped I stood clear, ready to grab a pretty girl if I could find one in the darkness," Tony declared, unabashed. "Then the shot hit my sleeve, and by the time Oswell brought the candles Hester had vanished. Piqued, I suppose, because I didn't try to kiss her! Those old birds are vain as peacocks."

"I wouldn't call Hester vain," Glen observed. "She's gone to bed; the storm has upset her, I hear." As he spoke he remembered another member of the party who had retired earlier in the evening.

Leaving, abruptly, he went upstairs to Franz Van Godchen's room. A light was shining beneath the door. Tapping once, Glen entered.

The young Hollander was sitting up in bed, reading. "How's the headache?" inquired Glen.

"Thank you, a little better," Van Godchen reported. "My reading-lamp went out a while ago. I thought perhaps the bulb had gone, but after a time the light came on again."

"A fuse went, I believe," Glen explained. "That's really why I came up. Thought you might have been uneasy, what with the storm and the lights going out."

"No I was not alarmed," Franz replied adding politely, "though it is good of you to come up."

"Not at all. What about dinner?"

"It was so excellent that I'm ashamed to say I ate it all," Franz owned naïvely. "You see, Mr. Armitage, my head was not very bad, but my dancing is. So I preferred to come to bed rather than make a fool of myself."

The explanation amused Glen. He glanced at the windows which were immediately above the lounge. "Did you hear any queer sounds during the thunderstorm?"

Franz shook his head.

"No. The air seems cooler now. Has it rained at all?"

"There's been one heavy shower; I think it's over." Glen strolled across the room. He unlatched the shutters and stepping on to the narrow balcony, looked up at the sky. "Yes, it's fine now," he said. "Good night."

Jill was seated with John Caryll when Glen entered the dining-room.

"I've been visiting the sick," he informed her. "Poor Franz is better but—he won't be well enough to take you on another excursion to-morrow."

"Oh! Did he say so?" Jill asked.

"No, I said so." Glen's tone was definite.

John Caryll turned an eye of mock severity upon him.

"Is this young man bullying you, Jill?" he demanded.

The girl smiled.

"A little, but I can bear it."

Glen took a sandwich from her plate.

"You'll have to, my child," he said firmly. "You're likely to be having a lot of it from now onwards. I'm going to marry you, so you'd better start learning obedience right away. I'd hate to become a wife-beater."

Mr. Caryll's lips twitched.

"Don't I, as Jill's uncle, have any say in the matter?"

Glen looked at him significantly.

"No," he said in a low tone. Adding gaily, "But you might congratulate me and wish Jill happiness." The older man flushed.

"I do, most sincerely," he answered, after a moment's silence. "I'd like a chat with you to-morrow, Glen."

"Whenever you wish, sir." There was a note of respect in Glen's voice that had not been there before.

He rose as a woman came up to him. It was the South American widow.

"Can I speak to you alone, Mr. Armitage?" she asked a little tremulously.

Glen took her out to the hall.

"We shan't be disturbed here, Mrs. Kellner," he told her.

Half-way down the staircase stood Mimi, having just taken the Baroness to her room. She drew back when she saw Glen and his companion.

Mrs. Kellner pulled aside the gauze scarf she wore.

"My ruby has gone; chain and all," she stated. Glen caught his breath.

"Have you any idea where and when you lost it," he asked.

A disturbed expression crossed the woman's face.

"It must have happened during the twilight dance when the lights were out," she said diffidently.

Glen offered her a cigarette and they lighted up before he spoke again.

"Any particular reason for thinking so, Mrs. Kellner?"

"Yes. I noticed my ruby before the dance. When the lights and the music stopped I remember my scarf seemed to catch in something, and I drew it round my shoulders more closely. There it remained until a moment ago when an English girl exclaimed that she'd lost her bracelet. Then I saw that my ruby had gone and at once came to you."

Glen assumed an indifference that he was far from feeling.

"Was this girl's bracelet valuable?"

Mrs. Kellner smiled ruefully.

"Not at all. She says it's merely a pretty coral thing that matched her dress. She is not greatly concerned and I am trying not to be. What can we do about it, Mr. Armitage?"

What indeed, thought Glen with sinking spirits. Mrs. Kellner was standing with her back to the staircase. Suddenly he caught sight of Mimi half-way, up, signalling to him to be silent. As he gazed at her she vanished, and he saw her pass along the corridor.

"First we will have the lounge thoroughly searched while everyone is at supper," he told Mrs. Kellner, speaking slowly to gain time. "And if nothing comes of that, every room and every person shall also be searched.

No one of course must leave the house until your ruby is found."

"I'm terribly sorry," she murmured. "Naturally I want to recover my stone, but I wish it hadn't been lost here."

"You're extraordinarily nice about it," he observed, scanning the landing impatiently. "Most people would have made a ghastly scene and"—he laughed bitterly—"wanted to call in the police and arrest the lot of us."

"I couldn't possibly do that." Mrs. Kellner's tone was emphatic. "Not only do I admire Lady Daventry very much, but she was once extremely kind to me. My husband killed himself rather than be arrested for his share in some gigantic swindle. That was two years ago in Rio. All my supposed friends deserted me. Eve Daventry, who was staying there and had only met me once, stood by me through that dreadful time. We have been friends ever since. Now do you understand that I would not pain her in any way?"

"Perfectly," Glen said. From the head of the stairs Mimi again signalled.

"Will you leave this affair to me, Mrs. Kellner? I suggest that you go into the dining-room. Say nothing about your loss for the moment. I'll search the lounge at once."

Directly Mrs. Kellner had gone, Mimi ran downstairs and joined him.

"Well?" he demanded eagerly.

She tossed a coral bangle into his hand.

"A so cheap bracelet when a valuable ruby has been stolen!" Her eyes shone with angry tears. "Where did you find it?"

"In the pocket of Tony Daventry's coat: the one he has just taken off. I heard what Mrs. Kellner said and guessed." Mimi stamped her foot with rage "I hate this house. There is something horrible about it. Where are you going?" she asked quickly as Glen swung round on his heel.

"To get that ruby from Tony, even if I have to choke the life out of the young scoundrel."

Mimi nodded scornfully.

"And you call yourself clever, monsieur!" she taunted. "Tell me, if you stole two things, one valuable, one *rien du tout*," she pointed to the bracelet, "would you leave the rubbish in a coat in your room so that all the world could prove that you were the thief? Come! we will look in the lounge, but we shall not find the ruby, I think."

Meticulously thy searched the floor and furniture, submitting every ornament and picture to a close scrutiny.

"Nothing!" exclaimed Glen in despair.

"The bullet," reported Mimi. "It is embedded in the wall."

Glen stared at the wall where a bullet was plainly visible. With a penknife he dug it out and placed it in his pocket.

"Put it away safely," the girl warned. Remember, it was Lady Daventry's revolver that was used."

"If I only knew who used it!"

"You may, sooner than you think, monsieur."

"Was the thief the person who fired the shot?" he asked.

"Did the hand that killed Mrs. Lucas also take her pearls?" she retorted. "*Ma foi*, but your brain is of a stupidity at times."

"Somebody else meant to steal those pearls and I forestalled him," was Glen's reply.

"Even so, a thief does not risk his neck by shooting if he can get what he wants otherwise."

Glen flung out his arms with a hopeless gesture.

"Phew! Let's get a breath of air in the garden," he said, "before I face Mrs. Kellner with the dismal truth."

The storm had cleared the atmosphere, and myriads of stars now twinkled in the night sky.

"Hi! Haven't you any sense?" Glen said in an exasperated tone as Mimi left the gravel path and ran swiftly across the wet grass. "Your slippers will be soaked."

"*N'imorte.* I want to see what this is."

Inside the empty lounge she opened a crumpled piece of tissue paper.

"I found this in the middle of the lawn," she said. "It was not there before the twilight dance. I should have noticed it when I went out to see if it was raining."

"Some find!" Glen said cynically. He peered at it a moment. "Hello! There are specks of gold on it, near the edges."

"Yes, yes," Mimi agreed impatiently. "A gold leaf has been on that paper; the kind of thing that gilders use." She pressed her hand to her face. "Now where—Oh, come with me quickly. We mustn't waste a second."

Together they hurried across the ball to the wide staircase. Half-way up, in the recess where Mimi had paused when Glen was talking to Mrs. Kellner, was a narrow marble shelf fixed to the wall, and above it a huge mirror in an ornate gilded frame.

"Lift me up," she whispered breathlessly.

Standing on the marble shelf, Glen watched while the girl's slim fingers moved over the embossed gilt scrolls of flowers and leaves.

At last she touched the rounded centre of a monstrous sunflower, pressed it tentatively and glanced at her finger. It was shining as if it had been gilded!

With a deft twist she wrenched off the middle of the flower, which resembled a flattened tangerine orange. After a moment's manipulation she replaced it and jumped lightly down.

"Is that all?" demanded Glen disappointedly. She opened her hand and disclosed the ruby. "How did you guess it was there?" he asked in puzzled tones as they went down to the hall. Mimi gave a soft ripple of laughter.

"Because, monsieur, I use my eyes and remember what I see. There is no other gilt frame in the house.

Lady Daventry dislikes them, she said, and had them put away. This mirror, however, was a fixture."

"Will you give Mrs. Kellner her stone and explain that you found it?" Mimi shook her head.

"No. You must give it to her and say nothing, nothing at all. Tell her to place it in her bag. The chain is gone. As for the coral bangle, I will give it back to its owner and say I picked it up in the hall."

The man grinned.

"Are you aware that you've squashed a burglary? There's absolutely nothing left of it."

"Except a lump of newly gilded putty that was quite soft," Mimi said quietly. "The thief will still think it has a ruby core and that Mrs. Kellner has not yet noticed her loss."

XXI. The Trap

Wednesday, midnight.

THE last of the guests invited for the dance had gone, Oswell had locked the doors and windows, and most of the house-party had retired.

Tony kissed his stepmother's cheek lightly as she lingered in the hall talking to Lucas and Glen Armitage.

"Good night, Eve It's been a rare lark, eh?" he said with a yawn. "I'm off to bed."

"A rare lark, indeed," commented Glen as he watched Tony take the stairs three at a time.

"You don't make much allowance for youth, do you?" Eve remarked with a wan smile. She held out her hand invitingly to Mimi who came from the lounge. "Come to my study for a moment if you're not too tired."

The French girl's eyes sparkled with alertness

"Tired? *Pas du tout*, madame. My English certainly is worn through, but not all your dreadful verbs and tensions are scrambled, but I can still talk with fluency, is it not so, monsieur?" she demanded of Glen.

"I've never known you when you couldn't," he retorted, "but I won't say that you are always intelligible."

"Don't squabble, children," Eve Daventry put in. "I've had as much anxiety as I want. Why, Mimi, what's the matter?" she asked as the girl sank on a stair and buried her face in her hands.

"I must preserve my thoughts for an important question," was Mimi's solemn answer. "To be laughed at for mistakes is only a hurt to my pride, but to be not intelligible in my sentences might be serious. Mr. Lucas, you speak French?"

"Very little and very badly," he confessed.

"Ah!" Mimi groaned, and concentrated once more. "It is this," she said in a moment, addressing him. "When the electricity failed during the dance, why did you stop the music and what did you do, please?"

"I was startled and switched off the gramophone instantly," Lucas explained. "Then, as I walked across the library I heard a shot—though I wasn't sure it was a shot at the time—a moment before I reached the hall."

"You saw nobody there?" questioned the girl.

"It was pitch dark; I couldn't. Next, Glen called out for lights. After that Oswell came from the kitchen with two candles and the maids took others into the dining-room. Also Mrs. Warren ran out to know what was wrong."

"And what was wrong?" the girl pursued.

"I'm afraid I'm no electrician," Mr. Lucas told her. "Oswell said a fuse had gone."

"Where does the meter rest?"

Glen answered that question. He indicated a door which was adjacent to the door of the lounge. "Down there in the cellar," he replied. "There is another exit by steps near the kitchen somewhere. I've gone down this way many times, but I've never used the other steps at all. Do you want to investigate now, Miss Sherlock Holmes?"

"No, no. That can wait." Mimi relapsed into thought again and sighed. "Mr. Lucas, were you in the hall from the moment after the shot until the guests had gone into the dining-room? It is intelligent that question, yes?" she demanded in triumph.

"Perfectly intelligent," he agreed gravely. "Yes, I was there, facing the lounge doorway."

"And the candles brought by Oswell gave a little light into the hall?"

"They did. Also the dining-room door was open."

"Then you could see clearly anyone who went upstairs?" There was an earnestness in her tone that caused Lucas to respond in the same manner.

"I could have seen clearly had anyone gone upstairs," he corrected. "No one did so."

"You are sure? Not even one of us now here, for instance?"

"No one went up—or down, then," he affirmed steadily. "Everyone trooped out of the lounge into the dining-room."

"Excepting Mr. Armitage and Baroness Pertzoff," reminded Mimi. "And also myself."

"That is so, but neither of you went upstairs."

"Tony went up to change his—collar some time later," Glen reminded her.

"Thank you," she said reflectively. "Oswell told me that Mrs. Warren, two maids and himself were busy in the kitchen, or carrying supper and candles into the dining-room."

Lucas nodded.

"They were running to and fro all the time I was there," he agreed. "There was a gas jet in the kitchen so they were better, off than we were."

"Mr. Naylor was out walking. He came in long afterwards," Mimi stated. "So Mr. Franz Van Godchen was the only person upstairs."

Glen broke into the conversation.

"Franz was in bed and dressed in pyjamas when I saw him a couple of minutes later. He couldn't have come downstairs in that garb. The French windows were open to the garden but the lounge is a very lofty room," Glen continued, "and although there are balconies above, it would be practically impossible for anyone to climb up from the grounds. The walls between the windows are covered with a fragile creeper which wouldn't bear the weight of a cat, and not a leaf is disturbed."

"Yet," Mimi said in an undertone to Glen as they went upstairs, "that ruby could not have walked alone to its hiding-place half-way up the stairs. Oh, la, la, it is very puzzling. One is quite defeated, yes?"

"You made a fortunate guess about the ruby," Glen replied cynically, "but guessing doesn't help you now, shadow. Your luck's out."

Mimi made a despairing gesture.

"All hope is gone," she sighed, but her eyes held a demure expression that Glen did not notice. "*Bone nuit, messieurs,*" she added, and followed Lady Daventry into the study.

Directly the door was closed, it was as if Eve's mask of easy composure dropped from her, showing her face to be white and harassed.

"Mimi," she whispered, glancing timidly round the room, "I'm beaten, frightened."

"No, no," Mimi reassured her. "You are tired and a little worried." She laid her hand on Eve's arm. "All goes quite well; perhaps better than you think."

"All has gone better than I dared hope after this ghastly evening, thanks to you."

"Why am I here if it is not to be of some service to you?" demanded the girl. "By a lucky guess, as Mr. Armitage said, I saved you anxiety by finding the ruby."

"You have no idea about finding out who stole it?" Eve inquired quickly.

Was there something a little furtive in that question, Mimi pondered. Did she fear that Tony was the culprit?

"How can I?" she parried. "The thief has covered his tracks very cleverly." And she was sure Eve was relieved by that answer. "There have been other—losses of jewels here; in this villa, I mean. Could you tell me if the circumstances were by chance the same as to-night?"

"Who has been talking to you?" Eve demanded wildly. "Forgive me, Mimi I'm a little overwrought. You may as well know the truth. Yes, in each case the jewellery was lost, during a twilight dance. I was mad, to risk having one to-night"

Mimi slid her arm through that of the older woman and drew her towards the bedroom.

"Please rest, and forget everything, madame," she begged. "Has your maid gone to bed?"

"Yes. I rarely keep Felice up after midnight. It's half-past one now."

"Then to-night I will be Felice," Mimi said. "Once I acted as personal maid to a French countess for a while." She did not add that the woman had proved to be a famous spy. "Oh! How drôle she looked after her toilette was made for the night, and her beautiful hair was on the table!"

Without a break she poured out a stream of amusing reminiscences, and was rewarded by seeing the strained look fade from Eve's face.

"Thank you," Eve murmured gratefully when Mimi tucked her into bed as if she had been a child. "You're terribly kind to me. I feel better already."

"I also feel much better—because we have been speaking French," Mimi said with feeling. "And it is not kindness to do something which I like. When I do not enjoy my job, I change it."

The woman smiled. "It was only three days ago that you told me you were strong and knew your work!"

"Only three days ago, madame."

"So much has happened since then that it seems years, but I have proved the truth of your words. You're a loyal little friend."

Mimi looked at her beseechingly.

"I will try to give you even more proof of my loyalty, dear madame. Then perhaps you will trust me completely. Until then I cannot help you as much as I wish."

Eve's beautiful eyes were shadowed by pain as she gazed abstractedly across the room.

"Suppose, Mimi, that you had thrust some horrible things into a trunk and locked them up, hoping to forget their existence. Would you willingly drag them out into the light and, seeing them again, be tortured by memories of the past?"

"Yes," said Mimi stoutly. "I would bring them out and destroy them. Putting the lid on a full ashbin will not prevent the smell. One must empty the tin and have it disinfected, lest someone else should pull off the lid. Good night, madame; sleep well. I will switch off the lights in the corridor."

She sped lightly up to her room and put on a pair of soft felt slippers and dressing-gown, in the pocket of which she slipped an electric torch.

There was not a moment to lose in devising some ingenious method to trap the thief. All she could manage was a simple trick, old as the hills. She prayed it might work.

Her feet made no sound as they crept down through the now darkened house to the kitchen quarters where the furnace was. In a few minutes she was back, stopping half-way up the staircase near the gilt mirror to perform a curious task.

Then she went to bed, and slept calmly, having resolved to awake at a certain hour.

*   *   *   *   *

It was still dark when Mimi roused and opened her door. She started at a faint sound, as if some object had rolled along a parquet floor. It was certainly not in her room, however, she decided, and stepped into the corridor.

The hall clock struck five as her feet moved silently down the thickly covered stairs, keeping well to one side of them. It was a sombre carpet, patterned in brown and black, for which at the moment she was thankful.

At the bend of the staircase by the gilt mirror she paused and flashed her torch up cautiously. The orange-like centre of the giant sunflower was there apparently untouched.

But the mouse had been in the trap! On the marble slab were black smudges caused by the soot which she had spread on the floor.

Stooping close to the carpet, she scanned the stairs, going slowly upwards. Here and there on the treads were even fainter black marks, scarcely discernible in the patterned carpet. When they became invisible, she picked up the trail by touching the carpet with her fingers.

Where would it lead her, she wondered anxiously, as she reached the top of the staircase.

She let the small smudges of black guide her along the corridor until they ended sharply outside a bedroom door. Intent on not losing the trail, she had not noticed how many rooms she had passed.

To whose door had these tell-tale marks led her? And why was she, who had dared much in her life, afraid to learn the truth now? For a chill of dread gripped her, urging her to postpone knowledge until her mind had adjusted itself to face stark facts.

Still crouching, she stared at the floor in the pale glimmer of dawn that peeped slantingly through the shuttered corridor windows. Directly she raised her eyes she would know whose room this was; know, too, that its occupant was not only responsible for more robberies than Mrs. Kellner's ruby, but possibly for the murder of Mrs. Lucas.

And then, what? She would need wisdom and courage to act justly *after* she knew, and the icy trembling of her limbs told her that she possessed neither. Was it through mere tiredness, or was it caused by the ominous atmosphere of this unhappy household?

Setting her lips firmly, she drew herself up and raised her torch.

She was outside Tony Daventry's room.

XXII. Two on the Stairs

Thursday, 5 a.m.

FOR a moment Mimi stood motionless, stunned mentally by the force of this discovery.

Gradually she sorted the different information concerning Tony Daventry that she had acquired. The early quarrels with his father, who had died leaving everything to Eve, were explained now. Tony had probably been a thief then.

The charming and affectionate manners he showed his stepmother were nothing but the cheap duplicity of a rogue. Eve was easy to dupe in her kindly credulous belief in human nature.

Tony had everything to gain by playing the role of an irresponsible, high-spirited boy whose mischief was harmless and lovable.

In the Villa Lorne he not only had free board and lodging and the run of Eve's money, as the counterfoils of her cheque-book had proved, but a fine field for his unlawful exploits amongst the wealthy guests who gathered there.

Hesitating how next to act, Mimi walked along the corridor as far as the Baroness Pertzoff's room. A light showed beneath the door.

Mimi turned the handle gently and entered.

"Can I get you anything?" she asked, seeing that the Austrian woman was awake.

"Yes. Give me my flask from the table. Brandy may not be the perfect medicine for a gunshot wound, but I mean to have some." The woman's brusque manner softened slightly. "It's decent of you to get up at this hour to see how an irritable patient was doing."

"It is nothing, Baroness. I often wake early." Mimi was too honest to wish for credit where none was due. "How is your arm?"

"Not too bad. I've had worse pain in far less comfortable circumstances."

"Have you any idea who fired the shot?" Mimi inquired.

Hester Pertzoff regarded her with a frown.

"Listen to me, girl. This is my business, and I don't choose to talk about it. Understand that."

Mimi's lips tightened to a determined line.

"For other people's safety, one must find out who attacked you," she insisted, robbed of caution by her fatigue.

"I see your point." The woman spoke with a disarming reasonableness. "You mean to try?" she asked sweetly.

"With all my power," Mimi replied in a dogged tone. Inwardly she was agreeably surprised at the woman's submission. "Already I have a clue which I mean to follow."

Hester sipped her drink musingly.

"I can't very well stop you, even if I wished," she observed in a casual manner. "How do you propose to find out? You're only a girl, remember, who surely can't do much against a criminal's cunning wits."

"What I have just discovered might have a connection with the revolver shots, or it might not. I mean to see."

Hester checked a yawn of apparent boredom.

"Clever child. You must tell me all about it another time," she murmured. "My head aches rather badly. Will you get me some eau-de-Cologne and a little cold water from the bathroom?"

Mimi collected the necessary articles and placed them on the side table.

"You look so tired, child, that I ought to be waiting on you," Hester remarked sympathetically. "Here, drink this," she added, giving Mimi her own half-finished glass of brandy and water. "You need it more than I. It may help you to sleep for an hour or two. It's only a quarter past five."

Mimi took the glass and drank obediently, too weary to resist the woman's dominance.

"One moment," Hester said. "Knock at Tony Daventry's room as you pass and ask him to take me out in his car at ten o'clock. Possibly I'll let a doctor see my arm."

"That is wise, Baroness." Mimi hesitated. "I don't like to disturb Mr. Tony so early." In her heart she wished to see Tony very much for a moment, but had had no idea how she could manage it. "I will deliver your, message with pleasure if you think he won't be annoyed with me."

"I'll write the message," Hester told her curtly, "then he can't blame you." She picked up her letter-case and scribbled rapidly in her bold writing, while Mimi stood at the foot of the bed. "I've written, 'Please take me to see a doctor in your car at ten o'clock this morning.' Give it to him and then go back to bed." She put the note into an envelope, sealed it and pressed the flap firmly. "Don't push it under the door. He might sleep late. Wake him.

Mimi's eyelids drooped with heaviness as she waited for Tony to answer her gentle knock, and she suppressed a yawn with difficulty. Three hours' sleep certainly had not been sufficient. Directly she had delivered this note, she would take the Baroness's advice. For one more minute, however, she must try to be alert.

The door opcncd and Tony appeared.

"What on earth—?" he began, and then after listening to her brief explanation, tore open the envelope.

She forced herself to vigilance as he switched on the light to read Hester's message.

Suddenly the drowsy veil that was fast creeping over her consciousness was lifted. Tony's fingers were glistening with gold.

Gazing at that revealing glitter, her glance fell on the paper he held. There was no time for her to read all the message before he crumpled it up, but of one thing she was sure: there was no word in it so long as "morning."

She repeated to herself what Hester said she had written. It was one long sentence. This definitely contained two. Before it slipped from her memory she must try, to pick out the stray words she had seen. One was "lounge," another—the last—"much" and in between something that looked like "cry knows," Which didn't make sense.

"All right," Tony said, and closed his door. Retracing her steps to reach the staircase, she pondered on the meaning of that message.

With a flash it was clear. The word was not "cry" but "spy." Hester had sent a warning to Tony:

"This spy knows too much," or something in that fashion.

Well, there was nothing to be done about it now, with her brain stupid for want of sleep.

She gave a frightened gasp as a voice came from the gloom.

"Quite a round of visits!" it remarked quietly. "But isn't it rather early for social calls?"

With a nervous, gesture she clicked on the light of her torch. Glen Armitage was sitting on the stairs, regarding her with an air of cynical amusement.

"I went to see if Baroness Pertzoff needed anything," she, answered dully.

"Devoted little nurse, I know that. I also know where you went previous to the Florence Nightingale act. By the way, I wish you'd used face powder instead of soot," he grumbled plaintively. "I've had no end of a job clearing up after your bit of fun."

The girl stared at him dazedly. Hester Pertzoff's message was forming into a pattern. "Come to the lounge. This spy knows too much." Yes, she was sure that was what Tony had read. It meant that Hester was mixed up with Tony's thefts, if not the murder of Bella Lucas. Yet who had fired that shot at Hester and Tony?

She glanced at Glen Armitage. Had he done it?

He must have been watching her movements, otherwise he would not be here now. Perhaps he too was in league with Tony and Hester.

A noise was singing in her ears, and the ground seemed to be whirling round.

"How did you know I was up?" she asked, grasping the stair rail for support.

"You played one trick with the soot, and I played another to see what you were up to. I placed a reel of thread on my floor, and tied one end to your handle. When you opened your door the reel danced round and woke me—Hello!" he exclaimed, as the girl's eyes closed and she swayed. "Are you ill?"

"Asleep," Mimi murmured, and collapsed in an inert heap.

Glen gathered her light form in his arms, and, focussing the flashlight so that he should not stumble, carried the girl up to her room.

Farther along the corridor a door opened and Jill, disturbed by the sound of soft voices, peeped out. She was in time to see the man, whom she had promised to marry only a few hours ago, lift Mimi and bear her to her room.

Mimi, whom she had trusted and liked so much! Glen, who had swept her into a world of happiness in that brief moment during the dance! Jill shivered with disgust at her own weakness in believing him to be sincere.

Why had she ever allowed herself to be trapped into coming to this horrible house? How could she get out of it? Apparently free as air, in reality she was a prisoner, chained to the will of John Caryll.

If she ran away now, she had barely enough money to pay her fare to London, nothing to live on when she arrived there, no job and no friends.

No, she had to stay and carry out her share of Caryll's strange bargain. Stay and face Glen Armitage, who must even now be laughing at his easy conquest.

Jill flung back her head: she had a winning card and, to save her pride, she would play it. He did not know that she had witnessed the scene with Mimi; he should not know.

To-morrow she would meet him with an amused cynicism that equalled his own, and allude to his proposal of the previous night as a jest. John Caryll would back her up. Convinced that she hated Glen, Jill put out the light and paradoxically cried herself to sleep.

XXIII. A Change of Mind

Thursday morning.

SOON after nine o'clock that morning Jill went to her uncle's room.

"Very well, Jill," John Caryll agreed, after she had stated her wishes. He rubbed his head in bewilderment. "It was sudden, of course, but I could have sworn that you liked this chap. You aren't the fickle or flirtatious type. What have you got against him? he demanded shrewdly.

"Nothing. Glen is an amusing companion, but one doesn't marry a man on that account," Jill declared stolidly, having rehearsed this excuse to herself. "Last night he rather rushed me. Since then I have had time to think."

Caryll regarded her wan face.

"The period of meditation doesn't seem to have been exactly a beauty treatment!" he commented. "You, look a sickly, object this morning. However, this is entirely your affair; and I'll tell Armitage that the deal is off so far as you're concerned."

"Thank you." Jill bit her lip nervously. "Please can we leave the Villa Lorne soon?" she pleaded. In an instant hardness sprang to Caryll's eyes.

"We leave when I am ready to do so," he stated, in a tone that brooked neither interference nor contradiction.

"Am I really necessary to your business, whatever it is?" she inquired. "I seem to be quite useless. You could easily stay here now that you know everyone, and let me go back to London and get a job as a secretary."

"You found it very easy to get one before you applied to me, didn't you?" he rapped back sarcastically. "No, my girl, your job's right here where I want you. Nobody will guess my plans while I've a pretty niece to tote round. Come in," he called as someone knocked on the door.

A maid entered with a note.

Caryll examined the envelope with a grin.

"I expect your poor suitor has written to fix an appointment, Jill," he remarked. "Got any idea how Glen guessed that I wasn't your uncle?"

"None," she said. "I've never discussed you with him. Please see what he says."

The man scanned the note, and looked at her in a puzzled fashion.

"So that's your game, is it? You're deeper than I thought, my girl, or more attractive than I realized. This isn't from Armitage. It's from Franz Van Godchen. A formal request to be allowed to pay his addresses to you! Well, well, who'd have believed that that bloodless young Hollander could be so human as to fall in love! You can't really care for such an icicle, Jill."

A wild idea crossed the girl's mind. Here indeed was an unexpected way to save her pride.

"I like Franz," she avowed. "He's—he's solid, and very well informed."

Caryll burst into a hearty laugh.

"Heaven bless my soul, so is Baedeker's guide. Women don't marry to be instructed. It would be simpler to go to a night school."

A flush rose to Jill's pale cheeks.

"I shall accept Franz," she said obstinately, with the inner feeling that nothing would induce her to become his wife. "After all, it will be a way of escape, and as you say, I've little chance of earning my living."

"As bad as all that, eh!" Caryll mused, watching her steadily. "Isn't it a bit mean to marry a man merely to get a roof and your board?"

"Thousands of women do and the marriages turn out very well."

"But they don't usually marry one man when they love another," he persisted astutely.

"It's easy to forget—I expect."

Caryll drummed his fingers on the arm of his chair.

"Jill," he said suddenly, "I'm not making you my heiress or any nonsense of that sort, because I might marry and raise a family yet. But I've already settled a sum of money upon you that will provide at least the independence you seem to crave. Now, knowing that, do you want to be engaged to this Van Godchen? Think carefully."

How else could she revenge herself on Glen? Jill reflected.

"Yes," she said aloud. "Although I can't thank you enough for your generous thought, uncle."

"Don't try," he snapped irritably. "You're every kind of a pig-headed fool. If you won't have Glen Armitage, at least you needn't have Van Godchen. I don't know what's come over you since last night. That little French girl has a level head, and you and she seem to be pretty good friends; go and talk it over with her."

Jill's cheeks crimsoned as she remembered the vision of Mimi being carried to her room by Glen last night.

"Oh no, no," she exclaimed quickly, and knew at once that John Caryll had divined something.

"I've business of my own to attend to," he rasped. "Until you can come to your wits, you're a hindrance instead of a help. I'll see neither Van Godchen nor Armitage. Now get out and leave me alone. I'm sick of neurotic people."

The girl went away, feeling that the bottom had dropped out of her world, leaving her friendless and forlorn.

Whatever John Caryll's purpose had been in bringing her here, the fact stood out that he was a man who had shown her unparalleled kindness and consideration, requiring apparently no service in return save the harmless farce of pretending that she was his niece. Even that, she thought, might have been to save her from any unpleasant comments.

She drifted into the garden, aimless and depressed, wishing with all her heart for Mimi's cheerful society.

She glanced up at the French girl's window, half hoping, half fearing to see that little figure in black. But the shutters were still closed, and again the incident of the night before darkened her memory.

A voice boomed across the lawn, calling her by name.

"My zon and I hope you will make the leedle egcursion with us to Sospel, Miss Jeel, this morning." The vast form of Mr. Van Godchen stood beside her, his face beaming kindly.

In her lonely state of mind she grasped at this invitation with nervous haste.

"Yes, I should, like to."

The man nodded.

"It is good. We will start at ten o'clock Where is everyone this morning? Not one person but you have I yet seen, though I hear an automobile pass up and down the drive early."

"I've seen no one either, except my uncle," Jill replied

"It must be pleasant to be rich as Mr. Caryll and travel where one wishes or stay here and do nothing. He is a millionaire, your uncle, and still a bachelor, I hear!"

"He is not yet married," Jill agreed, wondering if Van Godchen had mercenary ideas concerning her proposed alliance with Franz, "but he probably will be one day. He is not a millionaire. I am definitely not his heiress and I have no money at all."

The Hollander's countenance clouded to naïve disappointment.

"So! I am sorry. Money is good to have when one is young. I thought perhaps you had a dowry. Franz should have his chance. Your uncle will, I think, understand that. If not,"—Van Godchen spread his fat hands regretfully—" it will be a pity, for my zon is much attracted to you."

Jill choked back an inclination to laugh, and determined to warn John Caryll on no account to mention the money he had promised to settle upon her.

"I'm afraid, Mr. Van Godchen, that your son is worth more than my uncle can afford to pay for a husband for me," she said gravely. "I shall have to find a young man who will be content with a poor wife. Your son and I can, however, remain perfectly good friends and nothing more, so don't be anxious."

Van Godchen was obviously relieved.

"You are wonderful, Miss Jeel; so understanding of a father's feelings. We will say nothing to Franz of our little talk. If he proposes the marriage, you will refuse him?" he asked anxiously.

"I promise," Jill said, with twitching lips.

"Ah, then we make the leedle egscursion together, and Franz will never guess that his old father interfered."

It was an unexpected solution to Jill's problem. She would not be drawn into an engagement with Franz, and could still be in his company sufficiently to impress Glen Armitage.

There he was now, striding across the lawn towards her in his cool possessive way. Well, Jill decided, as she strolled to meet him, Glen should have his first lesson.

"Good morning," she remarked airily. "Will you tell Lady Daventry that I'm going for a drive with Franz and his father?"

"Why should I?" demanded Glen. "I'm not a page-boy." His eyes searched the garden as he spoke. "Where's Mimi?" he demanded abruptly.

Jill drew back as though he had struck her.

"Surely you're more likely to know that than I," she retorted with temper, forgetting her determination not to let Glen know that she had seen the incident on the stairs.

Apparently he read no such meaning into her words.

"I wish to heaven I did." His reply was fervent. "Run up and have a look at her room and tell me what you make of it, Jill. Buck up," he snapped as she made no movement.

"I have told you that I'm going out with Franz Van Godchen," she said deliberately. "If you want Mimi, go and find her yourself."

For a second Glen stared at her incredulously. Then: "Right. I will," he retorted, and swinging round, raced back to the house.

She heard him barking questions at Tony Daventry as she passed Tony's room, heard the reply.

"How should I know where Mimi is? Get out, Glen. I want to shave in peace."

Had he gone crazy for the French girl, Jill wondered as she put on her hat.

Going downstairs the mystery was explained. Eve Daventry was in the corridor with Glen.

"Hester Pertzoff and Mimi have gone away for a few days, Glen," she was telling him placidly. "They left early this morning. Why are you so agitated?

Glen grasped her arm.

"Is that the truth, Eve?"

Eve released herself with a laugh as she saw Jill.

"Of course," she replied lightly. "You seem to be piqued because my secretary didn't ask your permission."

"Piqued! Don't try to fool me, Eve. I won't stand for any more queer stuff in this house without—"

Eve made a warning gesture of silence.

"Hello, Jill," she called to the girl. "Off for a walk?"

A little awkwardly Jill explained where she was going, avoiding any glance in Glen's direction.

"Better take a warm coat if you're driving up the mountains," Eve advised.

"And hold Franz's hand if you're frightened at the hairpin bends," put in Glen mockingly. "By the way, Jill," he added in a serious manner, "is your uncle in his room? I want to have an important talk with him."

The girl's eyes gleamed with triumph; the enemy was delivered into her hands.

"He is, but there is no need for any important talk," she said with biting emphasis. "I have changed my mind completely."

"Good. I didn't think much of the one you had," Glen remarked pleasantly. "But apparently you and I are at cross purposes. I want to ask Mr. Caryll's opinion before I sell some Californian shares. Goodbye. You'll have a splendid time: there are lots of hairpin bends on that road. Franz should be hooked before noon with luck."

XXIV. Where is Mimi

Thursday morning.

"YOU'VE treated that girl abominably." Eve said a little later when she and Glen were in her study.

"Don't worry about my affairs. You can't manage your own," Glen informed her. "Now, where's this note you say Hester left for you?"

Eve passed it to him without a word.

> *Am taking Mimi away with me for a few days. My arm needs her attention. Sorry to rob you of your efficient little secretary, but feel sure you will understand.*
>
> *Hester Pertzoff.*

"And do you understand?" the man demanded, flinging the note on the desk contemptuously.

Eve bit her underlip.

"Hester is always a strange, impulsive creature. I suppose she is taking Mimi along as nurse because the shooting business is being kept quiet for my sake"

"Bilge! It's Mimi who is being kept quiet and you know it. By what right does Hester decoy your secretary away?"

"It's not 'decoying' if Mimi went of her own free will, Glen."

"In whose car did they go, and where?" the man demanded.

"You know as much as I. Probably Hester telephoned for a taxi. No one saw them leave the house. It must have been early."

"Before even the servants were up," was Glen's acid comment. "I want to know if Mimi went willingly."

Eve shrugged her shoulders.

"Well, don't let me hinder your investigations. It seems rather absurd, however, to imagine Mimi, with her clear brain and common sense, allowing herself to be kidnapped! Also, don't forget that she is strong and wiry, while Hester was handicapped by a bullet wound in her shoulder."

Glen pondered the point.

"That's true," he agreed at length.

And then his thoughts flashed to the incident of last night when Mimi had collapsed, asleep. She was undoubtedly heavily asleep when he had laid her on her bed and covered her with an eiderdown soon after five o'clock.

Would she have been sufficiently awake less than three hours afterwards to dress, pack a bag and go off with Hester Pertzoff? He doubted it, and knowing Mimi's capacity for loyalty, he was sure she would have left a note for Eve.

"Mimi left no message for you?" he asked.

Eve shook her head.

"There was nothing but Hester's note. Probably Mimi was very busy helping her to pack some things."

"Never mind the 'probable' part of it. I want certainties," Glen stated. "Where has Hester gone, or where is she most likely to be now?"

"I have no idea. Paris, Rome, Vienna; she is at home equally in each place, I should say."

Glen snatched at one word.

"Home! That might be it. Has she one?"

"If so, she has never told me where it is," Eve replied. "It's no use firing questions at me, Glen. Find another target."

"You bet I will," he snapped, and stalked angrily, in search of Robert Lucas.

Lucas was in the lounge talking to Naylor.

On the table lay a collection of jewels and a necklace of pearls.

"These," the lawyer was explaining as Glen entered the room, "now belong to Baroness Pertzoff by the will of your late wife."

"They appear to be all there so far as I can remember," Lucas said.

Mr. Naylor replaced them in his bag.

"As I am leaving for London immediately, I will deliver these to the Baroness."

"You'll have a job! "Glen remarked. "She's gone away."

Lucas stared at him in surprise.

"Where?"

"That's what I've come to ask you," was Glen's answer. He lighted a cigarette, watching Lucas closely all the while. "You met her in Nice immediately after your wife's funeral, didn't you?"

"By chance, yes."

"Nice is a pretty big place for a chance meeting, Lucas."

"Baroness Pertzoff was outside the cemetery," Lucas explained. "It was an unexpected act of good nature on her part. I was naturally surprised to see her. She offered to drive me back to Monte Carlo."

"You didn't reach here until late in the afternoon," Glen pursued.

Lucas smiled calmingly.

"Even a newly-made widower must eat, and it is surely permissible for him to offer luncheon to a lady," he suggested.

Mr. Naylor interrupted the conversation with a preliminary dry cough.

"If the Baroness is not here and her address unknown for the moment, I shall deposit these jewels in the bank, Mr. Lucas."

"Put them where you like," Lucas said firmly. They have brought enough trouble."

The lawyer gave a formal bow to both men and left them.

"Why are you badgering me with questions about Hester Pertzoff?" Lucas demanded hotly of Glen.

"I've good reasons. Where did you and she have luncheon? Her car was seen heading towards Monte. Carlo."

By the changed expression in Lucas's face, Glen Armitage knew that he was on the right track.

"Hester Pertzoff scorns poor food," he went on, "and there are few good restaurants once you leave Nice."

"I won't gratify your idle curiosity," Lucas said shortly.

"Perhaps you'll decide to open up when you hear that she has taken Mimi with her."

A frown crossed Lucas's face.

"Mimi went with her, you mean."

"I meant exactly what I said." Glen's voice held a steely quality. "I suspect that Mimi was drugged some time during the night and, in that state, was carried off by Hester. Who drugged her and where she has been taken, I've yet to find out, but I can guess why it happened. That little French girl had eyes and brains and was using both too well for the comfort of folk in this house."

"And what had Hester to hide?" Lucas studied his companion covertly as he put the question.

"If I'd known, I shouldn't have come to you," Glen said irritably. He added a chance shot. "Maybe she's acting as a red herring to draw scent from the real track."

Lucas smothered an imaginary yawn.

"It all sounds very mysterious, Glen. If it amuses you, go ahead. But"—there was a glint in his eyes that belied boredom—"probing into a minor concealment often discloses major secrets that were better hidden for the peace of many innocent people."

"I've not noticed much peace in the Villa Lorne," observed Glen caustically. "Are you one of the innocent people whose peace of mind might be disturbed if I dig too deeply?"

Lucas was silent for a moment.

"I should certainly be disturbed," he replied in a broken manner; "the more so because I am not innocent. It doesn't matter," he went on, as Glen murmured swift apologies. "I'm not guilty of murder. But that's about all there is to my credit."

Glen Armitage walked towards the door.

"To come back to my first question, Lucas, will you tell me if you can guess at any address to which Hester Pertzoff might have taken Mimi, or must I find out?"

"You must find out, Glen." The older man's voice had no hint of temper. "Though you might be well advised not to do so."

On the landing near Mimi's door Glen met the housekeeper.

"Mrs. Warren, come in here a minute, will you?" he asked, and led the way into the French girl's room. She followed in evident surprise.

"Lady Daventry isn't quite sure how long her secretary will be away with Baroness Pertzoff, and I thought you might be able to help her. Have a look round and see what clothes Miss Mimi has taken."

The housekeeper opened the drawers and wardrobe and glanced inside them.

"So that's where Miss Mimi has gone," she observed. "I knew nothing about it until the maid brought her tray at eight o'clock and found the room empty. She might have left a note for me."

"It was decided very hurriedly," Glen explained. "The Baroness is impulsive and wanted Miss Mimi to go away with her on business."

The woman finished her inspection.

"All her clothes, even her shoes, are here, so far as I can tell," she stated. "It looks as if she only intends to remain away for a day or two, as I don't think that much beside her dressing-gown seems to be missing."

"What about hats and coats?"

"They're in the wardrobe, sir. I've never seen any others, but she might have had some locked away in her other suitcase."

It was highly improbable, Glen reflected: Mimi would have had more respect for her garments than to leave them packed up.

"That's all, thank you, Mrs. Warren," he said.

Down in the hall he called the butler aside.

"What was wrong with the electricity last night, Oswell?"

"There was nothing wrong with it, sir." Oswell's tone was reserved.

Glen smiled.

"The lights went out."

"They did, sir. The main switch was turned off."

"Was it, indeed!" Glen's eyebrows shot up "Then the trick was played by someone who knew the house pretty well."

The butler nodded gravely.

"But those lights were off for several minutes!" Glen exclaimed. "It wouldn't have taken a second for you to turn the main switch on. Wasn't a fuse gone, Oswell?

"Yes, sir, but not in the sense that you mean. I found it on the floor. Someone had deliberately pulled out the whole plug that contains the fuse."

XXV. A Spy at Large

Thursday noon.

SEIZING the moment when the staff were at luncheon, Glen made a lightning inspection of Hester Pertzoff's bedroom.

He gained nothing by his efforts. Her wardrobes were overflowing with garments, and it was impossible to tell what had been taken.

An interview with Hester's extremely stupid Austrian maid was equally unfruitful, partly because the maid spoke no language but her own and Glen knew only a few words of it.

All he was sure of was that she had not seen her mistress since before dinner on the previous evening, and knew of no address to which she might have gone.

Considerably disappointed, Glen turned away.

Suddenly he thought of Hester's car. She could not easily have driven it with a wound in her right shoulder.

Inside the big garage he saw Eve's chauffeur. "Do you want your car, sir?" the man asked. "Yes, please, Fenton. By the way, when did the Baroness last use hers?"

"It's funny you asked that, sir. I've just been wondering myself. I cleaned it late yesterday and now it's splashed badly with rain and mud. Unless she took it out late last night, somebody must have had it out early this morning."

"She didn't use it last night," Glen replied. "What time were you here to-day?

"At a quarter to eight. The garage was locked as usual. Let me see." The man thought for a minute. "There was a heavy shower about half-past six this morning."

"H'm. Did you hear a car go down the drive about that time?"

"No, sir. My room's at the back of the villa and I had another nap after I heard the rain coming down. It's unlike the Baroness to get up at that hour. Do you suppose anybody else could have taken the car out?"

"If they did, they soon brought it back," Glen answered. "Any means of checking the mileage?"

"I have, sir. Ever since the Baroness accused me of using her car a month ago—though I never touched the thing—I've checked her speedometer each night. You'll find the figures written up there on the garage wall."

Glen compared them with those that were now registered on the dial;.

"A very short drive!" he remarked. "Six kilometres wouldn't take one very far."

"Excuse me, sir; six is for the double journey. That means only three kilometres for the outward trip."

"Of course. Where would three kilometres from this villa land one?"

Fenton did a little mental arithmetic.

"I can't be sure sir. Monte Carlo station is two and a quarter, the Casino barely two, and Monaco station about the same. Three kilometres is a bit beyond all those points. Just under two miles, isn't it?"

Glen nodded.

"Well, don't worry about it. Run my car out to the drive, will you?"

Glen's speedometer recorded both French and English distance. Carefully setting it, he drove down the hill to the town.

He found that Fenton's figures were correct on reaching the Casino, and for some time drove to different points in search of that missing three-quarters of a kilometre.

Shops would be closed at half-past six in the morning, and no trains from either station coincided with that time, even had the distance been correct.

Driving down the hill from the Casino, after once more looking at his speedometer, he had a thread of hope.

The harbour was exactly three kilometres from the Villa Lorne.

Gradually his mind linked up few details, and formed a significant chain. John Caryll had noticed Lucas by the harbour on the morning after Mrs. Lucas's death. And Lucas, in some subtle way, was hiding information concerning Hester Pertzoff, both concerning their meeting in Nice, and her extraordinary and secret departure with Mimi.

Also, Glen reflected, while Baroness Pertzoff's attitude towards Lucas had been cordial, Lucas had always seemed to avoid her.

The situation warranted a few inquiries at the harbour, although he had no evidence, save the speedometer, on which to base them.

After half a dozen futile attempts, he discovered an old sailor who said he had been there early that morning.

"Did a boat of any kind leave before eight o'clock?" Glen asked.

The sailor grinned.

"This is a harbour, m'sieur. Boats are coming and going all the time."

"Did you notice one which contained two friends of mine? They went on board early. A tall woman with auburn hair accompanied by a young girl in black."

"I saw no couple like that," declared the man. "There was a big red-headed woman in a fur cloak, but she only had an invalid child."

"How do you know it was an invalid?" Glen demanded eagerly.

"Because the lady's chauffeur carried it wrapped in a rug from the car right on board the boat. I could see him go down to the cabin so evidently the child was too ill to walk."

"What happened then?"

The sailor looked at him with an artful leer.

"I expect the lady tipped the chauffeur," he remarked pointedly, and paused. "Ah, *merci*, m'sieur," he added as Glen took the hint.

"Whose boat was it?"he asked.

The tip, however, did not loosen the sailor's tongue. He considered that was already earned.

"They can't be great friends of yours if you didn't know the child was ill, m'sieur," he said boldly, "nor the owner of the boat they went on."

"You'll get another ten francs when you answer my question," Glen told him.

That indeed was a language the sailor understood and responded to.

"It's a small cabin cruiser called *Anncel*. She's tied up here most of her time, and only fit for short trips. Belongs to an Austrian officer, I heard. I don't know his name, m'sieur."

"Where was the *Anncel* bound for?"

"I don't know, but she can't go far without provisions," the man surmised. "I met one of the crew at a bar last night. He said his master slept on board, but came ashore for his meals, so there wouldn't be food there fit for a lady and a sick child."

"Which port is it most likely they'll call at first? I've an important message for the lady."

"Why not try Nice harbour?"the sailor suggested. "It's only seventeen kilometres by road."

"Can you describe the car or chauffeur?"

"No, m'sieur. I think he was a young man though"

On the way back to his car Glen met John Caryll.

"Hello, Armitage. I thought I recognized your bus," the latter hailed him. "Been down on the quay? I often go there. It's far more fascinating than the Casino."

"Yes, it very interesting," Glen agreed. "Did you ever notice a craft there called the *Anncel*?"

Caryll's eyes narrowed curiously.

"I know most of them by sight. It's odd about that boat," he said.

"Why odd?"

"Somebody else from the Villa Lorne spent a long time staring at her. And she's nothing to look at either!"

"You mean Lucas," Glen suggested. "Is it particularly odd for a man to stroll down on the quay and look at a boat?"

"No, I often do it." John Caryll was silent for a moment. "But I can't imagine myself fixing my attention—and a furtive attention too—on a small Austrian craft the morning after my wife had died in tragic circumstances."

"That's decidedly queer," Glen reflected. "Was Lucas there long?"

"I saw him standing in the same position, half concealed in that archway,"—Caryll indicated the spot— "for more than an hour. How long he remained I can't say. Jill came along in the car and spotted me and I took her off to have luncheon."

"I remember," Glen said slowly. "Did you go down to the harbour later?"

"Yes. I left Jill in the Casino that afternoon. She thought I was playing at another table. Lucas wasn't on the quay then."

"Care to come to Nice now?" Glen invited on an impulse: "I want to see if the *Anncel* has gone there."

Caryll assented with a nod.

Not once did they mention the subject during that drive. It was as though each had said as much as he intended, and had no wish to discuss the matter further

At Nice harbour Glen stopped the car.

"I'll wait here if you prefer," Caryll said.

"No. Please come with me."

Again Caryll gave his characteristic nod of assent and followed, the younger man along the busy quay-side.

In a moment he gave an exclamation and pointed to a boat that was heading out to sea.

"I'm afraid you're too late, Armitage," he said. "There goes the *Anncel*."

The two men watched her as she headed east.

"Surely she can't be going back to Monte Carlo again!" Glen exclaimed. "Do you mind trying to find out, Caryll, while I make a few other inquiries?" He raced along the quay, stopping to ask likely people if they had noticed the pair for whom he was searching.

In about twenty minutes he rejoined his companion. "Any luck, Caryll?" he asked dejectedly.

"A kind of dock policeman thinks that the *Anncel* is returning to Monte Carlo. Don't ask me how he knows. The boat came in earlyish this morning, I learned from another source. Nobody noticed if any passengers disembarked, if that's what you want to know."

"I do," Glen said with emphasis. "I've had less luck than you. The big boat from Corsica came in with a huge crowd on board about the same time as the *Anncel*. That effectually covered up the trail I want to follow. I say," he added with a smile, "don't you wonder what all this stuff is leading to?"

"Not particularly, my lad," Caryll told him. "I've learnt to mind my own business and keep my mouth shut. This definitely isn't my business, so you needn't talk unless you wish to; or alternatively if you do talk, my mind will be a convenient blank on the subject if I'm asked."

"Thanks; I'll talk," Glen said briefly. "Mimi has been taken away forcibly by Baroness Pertzoff, I believe. I'm trying, to trace 'em."

"Any idea why the Pertzoff took her?"

"A pretty good one. Mimi's too shrewd for Hester's taste, I think."

Caryll brooded over that for a moment.

"Don"t answer this question unless you wish, Armitage. Care to tell me how long you've known Lady Daventry?"

"No. Sorry." Glen's tone was amiable but definite.

"It doesn't matter," Caryll replied with equal pleasantness. "I can play my own hand. Let's get back to the other matter. Tell me all you can about Hester's flight."

Glen gave him the details concisely, omitting to mention Mimi's strangely sleepy condition when he met her on the stairs, and substituting a surmise that she must have been drugged, otherwise she would not have gone.

"You're probably right," observed Caryll. "Well, I don't usually give away information when I've been refused it, but I'll make you a handsome present of this. I've reason to believe that Hester Pertzoff is in the pay of the Austrian secret service."

"It's decent of you to tell me, but does it affect this case?"

John Caryll looked grave.

"It might—very considerably," he replied. "Should Mimi be in the pay of her own country."

The suggestion staggered Glen Armitage.

"Let's get back go Monte Carlo before the *Anncel* docks there," he said urgently. "By the way, how did you find out that Hester was an Austrian spy?"

"While doing a little research work of my own affairs," replied Caryll. "Mrs. Lucas told me an hour or two before she died."

XXVI. Scotland Yard

Thursday afternoon.

TWO men strolled along the wide quay at Monte Carlo harbour talking casually, as the *Anncel* glided gracefully in and picked up her moorings.

They were still strolling, apparently engrossed in conversation, when a man in smart yachting attire left the boat and walked briskly along the quay.

"Time presses," murmured Glen to Caryll, as the newcomer approached them, "otherwise I'd prefer the indirect method of trailing the gentleman. Well, here goes," he added, and walked up to his quarry.

"You own the *Anncel*, I believe," he remarked.

The stranger, who was of the military type, looked at him haughtily.

"I do," he stated, "but I have not the honour of your acquaintance." His voice had a not unpleasant foreign accent.

"No," Glen agreed. "I have a message for Baroness Pertzoff. She was a guest at the villa where I am staying, and is now, I believe, on your boat."

"You are mistaken. I do not know the lady," the newcomer said frigidly, and with a formal bow walked on.

Glen looked after him with pursed lips.

"Like that, eh!" he remarked. "Things are more serious than I expected."

"Keep your eye on him in case he comes back," Caryll ordered. "I'll go on to his boat and see what a little bribery and corruption will do with the crew."

"They're probably Austrians. D'you speak that lingo?"

Caryll shook his head regretfully.

"I forgot that important obstacle. Can you?"

"One of the crew speaks French. He told my informant last night about his master having no meals on board," Glen replied.

"On your way then," urged the older man. "I'll whistle 'Annie Laurie' if the owner turns back. If I do, push off sharp. We don't want to be mixed up in any international complications! Boarding an Austrian officer's yacht against his wish, and pumping his crew for information he evidently desires to conceal, might have a nasty back-wash. Particularly if the gent can prove that his is a Government boat. I've no urge to be the target of a firing squad at dawn, and be planted as a spy."

"I'll be wary," Glen promised, and made for the *Anncel's* gangway.

His feet were barely on the deck when two powerfully-built sailors appeared at either side of him.

One look at their stolid faces assured him that bribes would be of no avail, and for strategy there was no time. The only thing was to see as much as he could before he was removed forcibly.

Sidestepping deftly, Glen dashed towards the small cabin and pulled open the door. It was empty. But lying on a cushioned bunk was a black rug fringed with green and white, a rug that belonged to Eve Daventry! This, in all probability, had covered Mimi when she was carried on board, and proved without doubt that someone from the Villa Lorne had been in the cabin.

"Mimi," he called. "Mimi!"

A clasp of steel tightened upon his arms, and he was drawn back to the gangway by the lusty guardians of the *Anncel*.

From the quay came Caryll's warning whistle. Ought he to regard that signal, or dare he attempt another dash back to the cabin in the hope of finding some clue to the girl's whereabouts?

A glance in Caryll's direction made him decide to retire in good order. Hurrying along the quay was a policeman, and behind him, at a more leisurely pace, followed the owner of the *Anncel*.

With a bound, Glen sprang off the boat, and sauntered towards the enemy in uniform.

"What were you doing on that yacht?"demanded the policeman.

Glen grinned disarmingly.

"I thought my sweetheart was onboard, officer," he said confidentially. "She isn't. It's the wrong boat! I'm so sorry."

He turned to the boat's owner, who by now was level with them, and addressed him in French for the policeman's benefit.

"Send back Lady Daventry's rug when you've finished with it, will you?" he requested pleasantly, and raising his hat, rejoined Caryll.

"A near shave!" quoth that individual severely.

"As all good shaves should be," Glen retorted, "Net gain of facts, one rug as mentioned. Not much, eh?"

"No." Caryll was silent for a moment. "Against that, there's a net gain of fact to the Austrian that we're hot on the trail."

"What passes for my brain may work better after a drink. The Hotel Napoli lounge should be quiet at this hour," Glen suggested as they got into the car.

"It seems a century since I met Lady Daventry there at her cocktail party, yet it's only four days ago." Caryll sighed. "A lot has happened in that short time. Jewels have been lost and found, Mrs. Lucas has died, and we've had quite a bit of shooting."

Glen cast a glance at Caryll sideways as he drove up the hill to the Casino.

"What do you mean by that? he asked.

"Not only the shot during the dance last night, Armitage. Don't forget somebody took a shot at me in daylight."

"Any reason why they should do so?" demanded the younger man bluntly.

Caryll's eyes twinkled.

"Haven't we a kind of pact against answering personal questions? I rather fancy you declined to tell me how long you had known Lady Daventry."

"I'll answer that when you tell me who you really are, Caryll, and what you're doing here."

"An American, rich if you like, doing Europe with his pretty niece. How will that do?"

"Not at all. You've done Europe before, and know Monte Carlo well, I'll swear. Jill isn't your niece and you're not an American."

Caryll gave a low amused chuckle.

"I have pretty big financial interests in America."

"And I've small financial interests in China, but I'm not Chinese," Glen retaliated. "You'll have to think up a better excuse than that."

"I'll see what a drink will do," temporized Caryll as the car, stopped outside the hotel.

As Glen had predicted, the lounge was indeed quiet, and very restful after the glare of the sun. They sat down close to the reception bureau and gave their order.

Near them a man and woman, obviously English, were seated. The woman's voice floated across to Glen clearly.

"Do ask if there is a note from Mimi, Tom. I can't understand why she didn't call or ring up."

Her husband, a grey-eyed, good-looking man of about forty, whose face held strength and humour, went across to the bureau and put the question.

"No, m'sieur," replied the clerk, handing him some letters. "Only this English mail which has just arrived."

"Ask if Mimi has telephoned," called out the woman. Her husband repeated her remark in excellent French.

"There is no telephone message for Monsieur or Madame Reynolds," the clerk told him.

"How far away is the Villa Lorne?"

"Do you hear that, Caryll?" asked Glen eagerly. "They must be friends of Mimi. I'm going to speak to them."

Waiting until the man rejoined his wife, Glen introduced himself as being a guest at the Villa Lorne "I heard you mention Mimi's name," he explained, beckoning to Caryll. "My friend is also at the Villa."

"My name is Reynolds," said the man, "and this is my wife. We have known Mimi for years. She always stays with us when she is in London. I can't understand why she hasn't come along to see us. This is Thursday. I wrote and told her we should be here yesterday afternoon."

His wife corrected him.

"No, Tom; you wanted to surprise her, so you said some friends would be here. Don't you remember?" Reynolds gave a rueful smile.

"You're quite right, dear. I asked her to telephone or call here about four o'clock yesterday."

"And you've heard nothing?"inquired Caryll.

"No," Reynolds answered. "It's most unlike her."

"Mimi is extremely punctilious," put in his wife, as if in defence of the French girl. "Had she known that my husband and I were here, she would have sent a message, however busy she was."

"She has been exceptionally busy," Glen told them. He turned to his companion. "Shall I shoot the works to Mr. and Mrs. Reynolds, Caryll?"

"Most decidedly," was the advice.

Glen looked at the French girl's friends with anxious eyes.

"Mimi vanished from the Villa Lorna about six-thirty this morning, and we have no idea where she is," he stated.

Reynolds exchanged an amused glance with his wife, and seemed not at all disturbed by the news.

"She'll be all right," he said reassuringly. "What her reason was, I don't know, but from long experience of that wise little minx, I'm sure it was a sound one."

"I'm afraid you don't understand," Glen said in worried tones. "She did not go of her own free will."

The genial expression slid from Reynolds' face and was replaced by one of alert keenness, as though he, a holiday maker, was suddenly faced with a job of stern work.

"I think you'd better tell me everything that has happened, Mr. Armitage," he said in crisp accents.

"And I think we'd better tell Mr. Armitage who you are, Tom," suggested his wife as she caught Glen's wary glance and realized that he was debating the wisdom of revealing what he knew to strangers. "My husband is Detective Inspector Reynolds, from New Scotland Yard. He had to go to Marseilles on business, and we're spending a few days here before returning to London."

XXVII. A Prisoner

Thursday morning.

THE splash of a wave as the boat made a sharp turn roused the girl lying under the black rug.

Eyes weighted with slumber, she gazed about the cabin. It required real effort to raise her wrist and see the time, but she succeeded, realizing at the same moment where she was. It was five minutes past seven in the morning, and she was at sea, and alone in this cabin.

She fought hard to remain awake, repeating these singular facts until they formed a little refrain to which the monotonous beat of the engine vamped an accompaniment.

"Alone at sea, and it's five minutes past seven," rang in her drugged brain, over and over again, lulling her back into deep sleep in spite of her struggle to regain consciousness.

It was to an entirely different scene that she awoke later. So different, that, for a while she fancied she must have had an extraordinarily vivid dream.

The hands of her watch pointed to half-past eleven, sunlight was filtering through the crevices of thick shutters, so she knew it was morning and not night. Also it must be the same day or her watch would have stopped.

She was lying on a bed, in a strange room, clad in her black dressing-gown and covered by a blanket.

An unusually spacious and lofty room, filled with enormous ornate furniture of a period which she recognized as being Louis the Fourteenth, or was it Fifteenth?

Ugly and uncomfortable, she decided drowsily, and felt herself nestling again into the pillow.

"Alone at sea, and it's five minutes past seven." She blinked at the shutters and wondered why that funny sentence came rhythmically to her mind.

Suddenly she flung back the covering and sprang to her feet resolutely as she recalled those few seconds of semi-consciousness in the boat.

The shutters were of the roll-down variety, similar to those used on jewellers' windows. Also, resembling jewellers' windows, they were padlocked at the bottom!

By peering through the tiny cracks, she caught a glimpse of sky and sea. She must be in some house on the edge of a cliff, for the sea was far below.

So much for the window. Perhaps she would fare better in another part of the house. She turned the handle of the massive door. It was locked.

Mimi's first instinct was to rattle the door angrily. She repressed the impulse. It offended her sense of dignity to let her captors know that she was at a disadvantage, also common sense assured her that anyone who had so cunningly contrived to get her here as a prisoner would not be foolish enough to release her at her wish.

There was one modern article in the room: a wash-hand basin with two taps. Modernity began and ended, however, at the tap marked "cold" which leaked, but she bathed her face and hands thankfully.

A search informed her that her jailors had not been thoughtful enough to bring her handbag, so her nose had to remain unpowdered.

In her dressing-gown pocket she discovered a carton of cigarettes and a packet of matches.

Lighting one, she sat down in the least uncomfortable of the immense armchairs and surveyed her quarters with a view to leaving them at the earliest opportunity.

Although that prospect did not appear to be immediate without a blacksmith's strength and tools, her spirits began to rise. She had been in far worse plights than this and had extricated herself by a measure of ingenuity.

The main thing was not to lose her poise, and so be at the mercy of those who had brought her here.

From past experience she had found that it was always a good trick to act in a manner least expected of her in the circumstances.

Her captors would anticipate rage, fear, a string of questions, perhaps even hysteria on her part. A dangerous little smile curved her firm lips as she decided that they were to be disappointed.

Why she had been brought here was childishly simple to guess: she was getting too near the truth for the peace of someone at the Villa Lorne.

Who the "someone" was would be solved the instant her door was opened. It might be Tony Daventry, Lucas, the Hollanders or Glen Armitage.

Where she was concerned her far more. Again she studied the vast gloomy room, seeking some clue to her whereabouts.

The drawers and wardrobe were empty. Blankets and sheets bore no name or initials. The place was as void of character as a museum, and of no interest to anyone save an admirer of Louis the something furniture.

Mimi made a face at the colossal glass chandelier and felt better for the gesture.

Once more her gaze dwelt lovingly on the wash-hand basin with the dripping tap, solitary emblem of twentieth-century life in this mausoleum. Having no noticeable urge to drown herself in the basin, she couldn't see how that was going to help her.

She drank a glass of water and discovered that she was humiliatingly hungry. If someone didn't come soon, she would be forced to make the first move by pulling the ancient bell rope that dangled beside the marble fireplace.

She had no idea of the length of the sea trip, as she had been asleep. Could she be somewhere on the coast of Italy?

The deep boom of a cannon came to her ears. Target practice from a battery or a man-of-war, she thought idly, and awaited the next explosion. No further sound broke the stillness.

Suddenly she sat erect and glanced at her watch. It was exactly noon. The next moment she broke into peals of merriment.

She was still laughing when she heard a key turn in the lock, and neither moved not checked her laughter when the door opened and Baroness Pertzoff entered the room.

Dressed in hat and fur cloak, her arm in a sling, she regarded the girl with obvious amazement.

"Don't be hysterical or frightened," she said anxiously. "You will not be harmed if you do as you are told."

"Hysterical! *Mon Dieu!*" exclaimed Mimi, and relapsed again into irrepressible mirth. "I am not afraid; I merely enjoy such a funny joke, Baroness. It is a pity that you cannot share it too. One day perhaps I will tell you. How is your arm?" she demanded coolly.

The Austrian woman frowned: she had been prepared for tears or anger. This laughter—and it was genuine, she knew—plus perfect composure was disconcerting.

"It throbs a little," she replied with reserve.

"You should have visited a doctor. However, bring me the dressings and I will bandage it for you. Don't forget, iodine and hot water also."

Hester Pertzoff was distinctly uneasy. Why had not Mimi humbly begged to be released? Instead, the girl had issued orders in a tone of authority, and calmly lighted another cigarette.

"You've slept late," Hester remarked, in an endeavour to ascertain what the girl's reactions were. Surely she must realize that she had been drugged.

"I probably needed rest. After many short nights, it often happens so," was the reply. "Will you kindly send me in some coffee and rolls. I'm hungry and want my breakfast."

"Luncheon is ready," Hester told her. "Come into the dining-room. You can eat with me."

"I can eat anywhere and anything," Mimi assured her earnestly. "Do you like ravioli? Me, I adore it. Also to follow, there is nothing to equal a tender escallop of veal, fried to a delicate brown in good butter."

Did the girl suspect nothing that she could prattle of her favourite dishes at such a time, Hester reflected. She gripped Mimi's arm, however, when the girl would have stood back politely to allow her to pass out first.

As they crossed a large dark hall, Mimi's senses were in full working order, and her eyes darted from side to side.

Ah! This was a flat, for no stairs were visible, and there was the front door, as big as a church portal and with heavy iron mountings on its surface. There was no sign of a telephone, but in spite of that, she was beginning to bubble over with cheerfulness.

If only she could get Hester out of the place on some pretext, the plan of escape already simmering in her brain might be feasible.

Meanwhile she could sense her hostess's growing agitation.

They ate in another vast room, served by a very deaf elderly woman with an expressionless face. Twice only did Hester address her in German, a brief remark concerning the food, spoken in loud carrying tones.

The old woman mumbled some reply. Not once did she look at the visitor, who, entirely at her ease in a dressing-gown and bedroom slippers, was making a hearty meal.

Mimi talked brightly of impersonal matters, complimented Hester on providing an excellent luncheon, and altogether behaved as if she were a charming guest content to stay in this pleasant household for ever.

"Your poor arm!" she exclaimed. "I am forgetting my work in your delightful company, Baroness. It should be dressed at once."

Rather sullenly Hester agreed, and raising her voice, shouted to the old woman to get hot water.

"We will go to my room," she told Mimi. "I have all the necessary things there."

Beside the large four-poster bed in that other room Mimi saw a telephone!

After one lightning glance at it she studiously kept her back to the instrument, concentrating her attention on the wound.

"It does not look very happy, your arm, madame." Her tone was grave. She mentioned one or two preparations, unlikely to be in the house, as being wise use. "Blood poisoning is painful and dangerous; we must avoid it."

For the first time Hester seemed nervous about her injury.

"Perhaps you are right," she admitted. "I will go to the chemist at once."

With a sudden flick Mimi sent a bandage rolling along the floor. She picked it up hastily, and in doing so, managed to see the number of the telephone which was inscribed on the dial.

Then, meekly she let Hester take her to her room and heard the key turned in the door.

XXVIII. The Rescue

Thursday afternoon.

When the door closed behind her, Mimi pressed her ear to the panel and listened intently. The telephone bell jangled from the room across the hall, and though not one word of the conversation audible, she was able to gather the result from orders shouted to the old woman.

"I have an engagement and some purchases to make. I cannot be back for an hour, perhaps two. On no account are you to unlock mademoiselle's door, understand? She has mental trouble and may do herself harm."

Evidently the woman promised obedience, for the heavy front door clanged presently.

Immediately as Hester had gone, Mimi made some preparations.

Tearing up a towel into strips, she took a thin rod from the wardrobe and rammed the pieces of linen down the hole in the wash-hand basin and into the overflow pipe. Then she turned the water on full and awaited developments.

Mental trouble, eh! she soliloquized with a grin as the water ran on to the parquet floor. Crazy people should do crazy things, so she was only living up to the role thrust upon her.

Curled up on the bed, smoking a cigarette, she watched the room gradually becoming flooded. Ah, now the fun would soon begin, she fancied, as a thin stream trickled beneath the door into the hall.

What would happen first? Would the old woman notice the water, or would the tenants from the flat below come up and complain?

Mimi felt totally indifferent. Her mind was busily seeking some forgotten duty, something that she had been asked to do days ago.

More practical matters, however, claimed her attention. She had neither clothes nor money, and knew of no one to whom she could telephone for either. Certainly not to the Villa Lorne. Too many of the party there were in league with Baroness Pertzoff. Lady Daventry she was sure was no instigator of this business. But she might be powerless to help, weighted as she was with the secret that Mimi had begged her to reveal.

And any one of the others might be Hester's confederate, only too willing to imprison Mimi still more closely.

What *was* that tantalizing thing she had been asked to do? Try as she would, it eluded her memory.

Action at last! Outside her door came a wail of despair, a frantic knocking on the panel and a flow of angry words in Austrian.

Stooping close to the keyhole, Mimi emitted one ear-piercing scream, calculated to rival a blast from a factory whistle.

There was no doubt that the old woman had heard, for a few moments later the key grated in the lock. The girl made rapidly for the huge wardrobe which stood close to the door, and dived inside it.

From-her hiding-place, she saw the woman enter the room.

"Mademoiselle," she cried, not seeing the girl. Then, mumbling and muttering, she pattered across the wet floor and bent over the wash-hand basin.

Silently Mimi slipped out of the wardrobe and through the open door, noticing regretfully that the woman had removed the key.

Now came the problem: should she open the front door and escape, clad as she was, or should she risk Hester's return being delayed and use the telephone?

A survey of her sopping dressing-gown and felt slippers made her decide on taking the longer chance.

In a flash she darted into Hester's bedroom and locked herself in. There was the telephone, but whom could she ask to help her out of her plight?

Jill, of course; she was a loyal type, and would betray no confidence.

She put through a call to the Villa Lorne at Monte Carlo, urging the operator to hurry. A maid's voice answered, and in reply to a request for Miss Caryll, said that she had that moment come in and was actually in the hall.

"This is Miss Caryll speaking," Mimi heard a second later.

"Jill, it's Mimi. Say nothing to anyone, and don't mention my name when you speak now, please."

"I have no wish to do so," was the icy reply. "Why have you rung me up?"

"Jill dear, don't you understand? I rang because you are my friend and—"

"You are entirely mistaken," Jill interrupted. "I am not interested in you, your movements or your associates," and hung up the receiver.

A shivering, little figure in a damp dressing-gown stared blankly at the instrument. Rarely had Mimi felt so deserted. What *was* she to do?

And then, by some odd trick of the brain, she recalled the forgotten duty. In that letter from her old friend Reynolds, he had asked her to ring up or call at the Hotel Napoli bureau yesterday at four o'clock; some friends would be there, he had written.

She did not know these people, it was true, and in any case they might be out. But friends of Mr. and Mrs. Reynolds would be friends to her.

The old woman was knocking furiously at Hester's door as the girl asked for the hotel number. It seemed ages before a man's voice came over the wire.

"'Allo, 'allo, Hotel Napoli, Monte Carlo."

"I had an appointment yesterday with some friends of Mr. and Mrs. Reynolds of London. Are they in now?" Mimi inquired breathlessly.

The man's voice seemed curiously eager as he demanded her name; still more eager when he heard it.

"One moment, Mademoiselle Mimi," he begged. "They are here and have been inquiring for you. Hold the line, please."

Laying down the receiver, the clerk beckened to Inspector and Mrs. Reynolds, who at that moment were talking to Glen Armitage and Caryll.

"*On vous demande au téléphone,*" the clerk told Reynolds in a discreet whisper. "*C'est Mademoiselle Mimi, monsieur.*"

Reynolds snatched up the instrument.

"Inspector Reynolds speaking, Mimi. My wife is close by. Don't worry, minx: we'll get you out of whatever mess you're in. Where are you?"

"Somewhere in Nice, in a large flat with water pouring out of my room and the front door," she replied. "I don't know the address and I've no clothes or money. The flat belongs to an Austrian named Baroness Pertzoff. She is out, but her housekeeper is in."

"Give the your telephone number quickly," Reynolds urged.

She repeated it carefully.

"Please hurry," she begged, "or they might hide me somewhere else before you arrive."

"I'll be there in half an hour," he promised. "Two men from the Villa Lorne are here hunting for you— Armitage and Caryll. Do you trust them?"

"I trust nobody but you and dear Madame Reynolds because—The housekeeper is coming," she whispered, and ending the call abruptly, hurried to the opposite side of the room.

The old woman made her entrance through a second door concealed by a screen which led into the bathroom.

With hard, strong hands, she seized the girl and shook her fiercely, murmuring imprecations. Mimi's strength in comparison was as fine wire in steel pliers.

Struggling, twisting, even the use of her teeth on the woman's arm, effected nothing more than a tighter grasp which was not relaxed until the girl was flung back into her sodden bedroom and the door was locked upon her.

The water had ceased to run. Turning the taps, she found that the woman had evidently turned it off at the main.

Mimi looked at her watch and began to work out her chances. Hester Pertzoff had left the flat nearly half an hour ago, and said that she might be away an hour or more. On the other side of the picture, Inspector Reynolds had a full half-hour's journey to Nice.

It was going to be a race between the inspector and Hester.

She paced the room restlessly.

$$\ast \qquad \ast \qquad \ast \qquad \ast \qquad \ast$$

Having got rid of Caryll and Glen Armitage, Reynolds ordered a fast car. By the time it arrived he had been through to the Nice telephone exchange and ascertained the address of the house from which Mimi had rung him up.

Bundling his wife into the car, he instructed the driver to hurry.

With a ruthless application of the brakes, the man halted the car at last.

Three at a time, Reynolds raced up the wide marble steps of a house on the edge of the cliff at Mont Boron. It was a block of flats. He scanned the name-plates on each landing. Half-way up the third flight, there was a suspicion of water on the stairs. The landing too was damp at one side.

A second later he was thundering on a massive door, beneath which a thin wet trickle still emerged.

The old woman opened it a few inches, and peered out cautiously. Reynolds thrust her aside. Entering the hall, he called Mimi's name. A moment later he had unlocked her door.

Carrying the quaintly clad little form downstairs, he lifted her into the car.

"Look after this 'baggage,' Agnes," he said with an assumption of sternness he was far from feeling. "I told you she'd get into mischief."

Curled up in the warmth of Mrs. Reynolds' fur coat, Mimi grinned at him happily.

"I might not have seen you two darlings otherwise," she replied.

"And now you'll go straight back to Paris and behave yourself," Reynolds informed her. "Your clothes can be sent to you by Lady Daventry."

"And now I will go straight back to the Villa Lorne," Mimi announced with determination. "I think everyone will be so pleased to see me, yes? Oh, la, la, shall I ever forget how I laughed this morning? You see, up to a certain moment I had no idea where I was imprisoned. It might have been in Italy or Corsica."

"What was that moment?"

"When I heard the gun from the Chateau! It is fired at noon," Mimi told him. "I've known its sound for years."

"Come back to the hotel with us first, and tell me all about the Villa Lorne happenings," urged Reynolds.

The inspector and his wife listened gravely while Mimi related the history of the past few days. It was past six o'clock when she finished.

"I'd like you to meet Lady Daventry and her guests," she said.

"Not as much as I would," observed Reynolds. "I'll send you back in a cab now, and we'll call on you at the villa in an hour. How's that?"

"Marvellous!" exclaimed the girl. "And if you are asked to dine, please stay."

"We certainly will," Reynolds promised.

*   *   *   *   *

In due course the inspector and his wife accepted Lady Daventry's warm invitation to stay to dinner that evening.

XXIX. MIMI RETURNS

Thursday afternoon.

"A BIT odd of that Scotland Yardman and his wife rushing off," commented Caryll as he and Glen drove away from the Hotel Napoli. "They appeared to be devoted to Mimi, and lapped up your story of her disappearance. I thought that inspector Reynolds would be full of bright ideas."

"If he is, perhaps he prefers to keep the secrets of his trade to himself," Glen replied.

"Perhaps he resented our amateur efforts at sleuthing."

"Well, we've been more zealous than effective, I'll admit, Caryll. I'd give a lot to know where that poor kid is. She's a gallant little creature."

Caryll glanced at him with a quiet smile.

"Are you addicted to these sudden interests, Glen? To-day you've got the Mimi complex pretty badly. Last night it was Jill. What went wrong there?"

Glen swerved round a corner, savagely.

"Everything," he ejaculated. "Daylight brought us both to our senses with a jerk."

"I see. Lucky for Mimi, rough on Jill. Even though she is not my niece, I have the same affection for her as if she were."

"If that is so, why don't you take her away from the Villa Lorne?" Glen suggested harshly. "It's a rotten atmosphere for a decent girl to be in. Hate, malice, cunning, robbery, attempted murder, sudden death. Get her out of it, Caryll, before anything worse happens."

"I've been used to managing my own affairs without advice or interference."

"Right. I'll remember that." Glen drove furiously up the hill and turned into the drive of the villa. "Is it agreed that we mention no word of our search?

Caryll nodded.

"Of course," he said curtly, and strode into the house.

Jill, coming from the lounge, met him in the hall. "I'm so glad to see you, uncle."

"That's very nice to hear," Caryll told her. "Had a good time with the Hollanders?

"Oh, that! There were fine views at Sospel. This afternoon Lady Daventry took me to a delightful party, and was terribly kind to me, although she looks very tired and worried. I like her so much, uncle; she seems to believe the best in everyone."

"That might stamp her as being a fool," Caryll said with a smile. "It's a pity to be too credulous, Jill. That's One of your faults."

"I'm being rapidly cured of it." There was a bitter tang in the girl's voice, and her grey eyes were wistful. "What have you been doing?"

"Motoring with Glen most of the day." The man watched her as he spoke.

"I suppose he said some horrid things about me."

"Your name was scarcely mentioned."

Jill winced visibly.

"Where did you go?"

"All round the place," Caryll fenced. "Here he comes; you can ask him about it. I'm going to look at the English papers." He called back across his shoulder. "Jill wants to know where we've been, Glen," he said, and walked off.

"I'm flattered," the young man replied woodenly.

"You needn't be," she retorted with spirit. "I'm not interested in you or your movements." A smile crept over her face. "I must have a very poor vocabulary. That's the second time to-day I've used that phrase."

Glen sat on the hall table and assumed a grieved expression.

"Poor old Franz! You don't mean to say that you've had a row with him already?"

"Certainly not. He's far too amiable and his manners are charming."

"I've noticed 'em. I go green with envy when I see him handle a teacup with his little finger cocked elegantly," Glen said. "If it wasn't Franz, who was the other poor swain you ticked off?"

"It wasn't a man." Jill paused and added distinctly, "It was Mimi."

The man jumped from the table and caught her wrist.

"Where is she?" he demanded eagerly.

Jill wrenched herself free.

"I neither know nor care. She had the impertinence to ring me up on the telephone, and began by giving me orders not to mention her call or her name when I spoke."

"Go on," the man rasped behind set teeth.

"That's all," Jill said airily. "I told her wasn't interested in her, her movements or her associates, and I rang off."

Glen made an exclamation and raised his eyes to the ceiling.

"You rang off!"

"Exactly."

"Did she say where she was, or with whom, or give you her telephone number?"

The girl's lip curved scornfully.

"She had no chance to do so. I took care of that by hanging up."

Glen's temper boiled over.

"You prize idiot!" he stormed. "I've been scouring the neighbourhood for hours trying to trace her and—you rang off! What time did she call you?"

"Just as I'd returned after luncheon and before I went out with Lady Daventry."

"Can't you be exact?"

"No; and why should I try to be?"

The man drew in a long breath.

"Because," he began in a quiet deadly tone; "Mimi is in danger, grave danger. She was evidently trying to get a message to you—her supposed friend. You failed her. Heaven only knows where she is now, but if anything happens to her, I should think you'd have a pretty troubled conscience—providing you possess one."

Had Glen stayed to see the effect of his words he might have regretted them. For Jill's grey eyes were blinded with sudden tears, and a sense of suffocating, panic made her tremble violently.

She went miserably to her room, and sinking on to a chair, buried her head in her hands and wept.

Tears were still streaming down her cheeks when the dressing bell sounded. She bathed her swollen eyelids and powdered carefully. It was bad enough to be smarting under the cruelty of Glen Armitage's lashing words; it would be far worse to give him the satisfaction of knowing how much they had hurt.

And all the while, a dreadful fear was gnawing at her heart. Suppose anything had happened to Mimi, she would for ever feel guilty, as Glen had said.

There was no doubt that he was serious; probably had good reason for being serious. The grim fact remained that out of purely personal revenge, she had refused to help Mimi when she was in danger.

White faced, and frightened, she walked slowly down the staircase to dinner—and saw Mimi!

Mimi, perfectly dressed from head to foot, gaily chattering to Glen with the rest of the guests gathered round her as if she were the centre of attraction.

Jill stared incredulously, and then, fear changed to frozen anger, she moved deliberately across the hall towards the group.

Tony Daventry and Franz Van Godchen, approaching from different angles, made a bee line and reached her side simultaneously. The little attention raised Jill's morale considerably as she glanced from one to the other of her good-looking cavaliers.

The Hollander raised her hand to his lips.

"May I have the pleasure of taking you to the Casino after dinner?" he inquired.

"Thanks. It would be great fun." Jill turned with a touch of coquetry and smiled at Tony.

"And may I have the pleasure—" Tony began in imitation of the Hollander's ponderous politeness. "Here, lass, have a cocktail," he suggested in his normal manner, and took two glasses from the tray which Oswell offered them.

Franz raised his glass to the girl.

"I drink to your health and happiness," he said.

"To you and your boy friend, Jill, whoever he is," was Tony's toast. "Now it's your turn, as we seem to be taking our drinks solemnly."

Jill lifted her glass with a laugh.

"Good luck and congratulations to Mimi and Glen."

Her clear tones caught Glen Armitage's ear, but he missed one word of her sentence, the final "and." It was an omission that totally altered the meaning for him. He gathered that Jill regretted her hasty words on the telephone, was holding out the olive branch, and wished him to know it by adding his name!

"Thanks, Jill," he said, walking towards her.

"Your anxiety seems to have had a happy ending," she observed.

"I'm much happier than I was when I saw you last," replied Glen.

"Naturally." Jill's eyes drifted across to Mimi's animated figure and back again to Glen. "One can understand a whole lot now and make allowances accordingly. Your anxiety for Mimi's welfare is understandable in the circumstances; you'll have to keep her on a shorter leash in future, Glen. You go a long way to meet trouble, don't you?"

"Meaning what?" he demanded.

"That Mimi was never for a moment in any danger," Jill rapped back with contempt, and turned away just as Reynolds and his wife joined the party.

"Of course, you must stay to dinner," Lady Daventry was saying. "Your little friend has been a great comfort to me. Ah, Mimi," she cried, drawing the French girl away from the circle of guests; "where have you been? I've worried terribly about you."

The French girl smiled tenderly at her.

"Dear madame, all is well. Don't ask me about it, now or ever. It is forgotten," she whispered, and went forward to her friends.

At which moment there appeared at the head of the stairs the Baroness Pertzoff.

She flung up her head with its riot of red curls, and assuming her usual air of magnificent arrogance, strolled down.

Engrossed with her thoughts, she moved towards the guests clustered round the log fire in the hall, without observing the little figure in their midst.

The guests parted to admit her, and she saw Mimi. The Baroness's brilliant eyes under their thickly painted lashes met the sparkling dark eyes of the French girl for a second. It was a glance of hate on the woman's side, of amusement on Mimi's. Then both turned away as if they had not seen each other.

XXX, A DINNER-PARTY

Thursday evening.

TO Inspector Reynolds that dinner-party resembled the first act of a play during which one became gradually familiar with the members of the cast. The brightest touch of humour, from his point of view, lay in the fact that he had been placed next to the Baroness at dinner.

Lady Daventry, for all her poise, was by no means a heartless society woman, he decided. He had seen shades of emotion in her sapphire eyes—anxiety, relief, and then tenderness with which she had met Mimi.

Every detail that the French girl had given him was not only recorded en bloc in his brain, but thanks to this occasion was being rapidly sorted into pigeonholes.

While on the one side of him sat Baroness Pertzoff, on the other was Mimi. The former monopolized a large portion of his time but during intervals of listening, Reynolds used his eyes shrewdly.

Tony Daventry was at the far end of the table, facing his stepmother. Restless, with bursts of wild merriment interspersed with patches of brooding depression, Tony was unaware that his moods were under the scrutiny of a Scotland Yard detective.

Opposite Reynolds, his wife sat between Robert Lucas and Van Godchen senior.

As usual when the Hollander spoke, the rest of the guests had perforce to listen.

"You are strangers to Monte Carlo, Mrs. Reynolds, you and your husband?" he inquired now in a voice that drowned all other conversation.

"We have been here before," that lady fenced calmly. There was a twinkle in her eyes that her husband knew well. She was being pumped for information and enjoying the process.

"You spend the winter on the Riviera perhaps?" Van Godchen continued.

"No, my husband's duties would prevent that even if we wished to do so."

"Ha!" The Hollander paused to find a fresh angle. "He is a lawyer perhaps."

"If so, he's kept his dark secret from me," Mrs. Reynolds answered. "His work is done in an office in London largely; he goes away occasionally on business, is fond of gardening and dogs, and we live in Highgate. Now tell me something about yourself, monsieur," she asked naïvely, with an air of having unfolded all her, past.

Reynolds concealed a smile, while the Hollander made a painstaking effort to do the same.

"I have a little property near Rotterdam," Van Godchen explained. "My zon was delicate so we come here"—he bowed towards his hostess—"at Lady Daventry's invitation, and are very comfortable. She has many guests, as you observe."

John Caryll cut into the conversation.

"It would be stupid to have empty rooms when one has many friends," he observed easily from his place at Eve's right.

Van Godchen transferred his attentions to Caryll.

"You and Lady Daventry are old friends?" he inquired. "I thought your charming niece said that you had not known her long."

Caryll smiled.

"My niece doesn't know all my friends."

The Hollander, baffled, contented himself with one last question addressed to the table in general.

"Is it not remarkable," he demanded, "that Mr. Caryll who is an American also speaks with an English accent at times, when—"

"'When he wishes," interrupted Reynolds with determination. "I am a Londoner, but"—he assumed a nasal drawl—"I guess, boss, I can give a purty good show as a Yank when I like."

The laughter which followed his successful imitation quenched Van Godchen.

"Thank goodness you've stopped that tiresome old man, Mr. Reynolds," observed Hester. "I was telling you about Vienna, wasn't I?"

"You were," he agreed, adding quietly, "May I say that I recognize you as the wonderful Hester Taranova whom I once saw act in Paris in '*Après Tout*.' You were marvellous. It was a grave loss to the stage when you left it. How could you desert our public?"

"I married and my husband wished me to retire," she replied, obviously gratified by Reynolds' compliment.

"You could bear to live on in Vienna after your brilliant career there?" he asked.

"We travelled a great deal. I still do so since his death."

A whisper reached Reynolds' ear from Mimi. "Find out where she was living six or seven years ago."

Dessert was on the table before he obtained that information from Hester's unwitting lips.

Not once did Glen Armitage and Caryll show any sign that they had met Mr. and Mrs. Reynolds at the Hotel Napoli that afternoon, nor did either man address him, as "Inspector," as Reynolds had feared.

Almost, save for Caryll's remark during dinner, had they avoided him, as if they wished their share in the quest for Mimi to be unknown to the others.

"Did anyone ask how and when you returned to the villa?" Reynolds inquired *sub rosa* of Mimi.

"Glen passed a comment before dinner, and I told him I had taken a day off to go on the busting. It is right, yes?"

"He probably understood," Reynolds said with a grin. "I know quite a lot about our dear Hester."

"Hush! Later," the girl warned as Lady Daventry rose. "We all go to the Casino at nine o'clock."

"And Hester has booked me for her escort," he retorted softly.

Left with the men, who drew their chairs together for a final glass of port, Reynolds had an opportunity to talk to Robert Lucas. He noted that, beneath that mask of calm geniality, the man's nerves were raw and jumpy.

Leading Lucas on, he learnt that he was a retired London stockbroker.

Van Godchen caught the phrase and leaned across the table.

"But you have made a little business since with the shares and not in London, I think," the Hollander said maliciously.

For some odd reason that was against his own interests, Reynolds felt pleased that Lucas was equal to the occasion.

"Is there any law against my doing so?" he inquired blandly. "You also, I expect, did business outside Rotterdam occasionally."

There was a blaze of anger in the Hollander's eyes.

"My business I may do where I will," he thundered.

"You also, Mr. Lucas, if it is not against any law." This time Van Godchen drew blood.

"And if ever I did business against the law, since when are you, a Hollander, the judge of an Englishman's conduct?" Lucas demanded hotly.

A sly expression crept over the old man's face. "But supposing that leedle business did not take place in England?" he asked in triumph.

Glen Armitage intervened with a yawn.

"Time, gentlemen, please," he drawled. "If we're going to break the bank we ought to be putting on our tippets." He stared hard at Franz Van Godchen. "Are you coming, or have you a stomach-ache or something?

"l am escorting Miss Jill," Franz announced in his precise accents. "I had a headache on the night of the dance," he added with emphasis.

"So you did, my lad," Glen agreed. "A mistake on my part. But you shouldn't walk about your bedroom with wet feet, no matter what kind of an ache you have. It's bad for your health and leaves nasty marks on the floor."

There was a pungency behind his casual manner that brought silence to the pair from Holland. It added one more link, too, to the chain the Scotland Yard man was slowly forging from the facts Mimi had given him.

Reynolds contrived to get a few words alone with her before they left the villa.

"Listen to me, young woman," he said sternly, "you've asked me to give you my unofficial help. Exactly what do you want me to do—track the murderer of Mrs. Lucas, always supposing she was murdered; find the thief who has been taking jewels; or get to the bottom of the intrigue that landed you a prisoner in Hester's flat to-day?

Mimi screwed up her forehead.

"Perhaps all of it," she suggested. "Really I care more for Lady Daventry's peace of mind than anything else. You see, she is not only beautiful to look at, but," she added plaintively, "she has a lovely inside."

"And that," the inspector observed in grieved tones, "comes from a conceited brat who boasts of her fluency in English! Well, well, we must see what we can do for the lady whose beauty and good heart have inspired such affection in you. It's a shame to tease you in the circumstances. If I'd been through a day of kidnapping and escape such as you have, I doubt if I'd be intelligent in my own language. I'll see you through as best I can—unofficially, mind. Who's old hatchet-face at the back of the hall?"

The girl wheeled round.

"That is Mrs. Warren, the housekeeper. She doesn't like me, nor anyone else much, excepting Lady Daventry."

Reynolds beckoned to his wife.

"Agnes, go over and sweeten that old acid-drop. She's the housekeeper. Do the motherly act and ask her to be kind to our poor little orphaned lamb when we go back to England. I'll give you a minute's start and join you. I like to meet all the household pets in this establishment."

Under Mrs. Reynolds' tactful management, the housekeeper had thawed considerably when Reynolds strolled across.

His wife gave him a useful cue.

"I've been telling Mrs. Warren that it must be a lonely life here for her, an Englishwoman," she remarked.

"It is that, sir," the housekeeper agreed. "Hemmed in, as you may say, by a pack of foreigners. I couldn't bear it but for her ladyship; there's nothing I wouldn't do for her."

"And there's nothing—" Reynolds suddenly changed his mind and altered the end of his sentence—"so rare and excellent as a faithful servant," he told her. "Tom, it isn't like you to be sententious," his wife remarked in a puzzled manner a little later. "You were going to say, 'And there's nothing Mimi wouldn't do either for Lady Daventry,' weren't you?"

"Witch!" said Reynolds, and laughed.

"Why didn't you say it?"

"Because, my dear, I had a funny little hunch. You're kind enough to call it my intuition. Let it go at that. Get your cloak. They're ready to start. Whom would you like as an escort?"

Mrs. Reynolds glanced at the party reflectively.

"If there's a chance," she replied, "I think I'd like to have Mr. Lucas. He might talk, if I am quietly sympathetic and not too eager."

"I'll fix it," her husband promised. "And remember this. You'll have to work fast. We leave for London the day after to-morrow."

XXXI, AN ECHO FROM THE PAST

Wednesday afternoon.

RATHER more than twenty-four hours before that dinner-party in Monte Carlo, Bill Staines entered the brightly lighted bar of the Red Lion hostelry in Pimlico.

"Hello, Bill!" a well-known voice called out from behind the counter. "You're early. What's up?"

"Everything," he said dejectedly, climbing on to a vacant stool.

The plump pretty blonde surveyed him for a moment, as if weighing up what she could do about it.

"Whisky's what you need," she diagnosed, and measured off a double. "Mop it up. You'll feel better afterwards, no matter what's wrong."

Bill pushed it away.

"Sorry, kid, but half a pint of bitter will have to be my little lot. I've got to go easy. My job's bust up to-day."

"Nonsense," the girl said. "You'll jolly well have that on me, job or no job. Finish it and tell me what's come unstuck. You look like death warmed up. Getting the sack's nothing."

"I've been on the dole once and dread going back" Bill Staines sipped the drink as if he meant to make it last a long while. "I didn't exactly get the sack, Al. My boss has hit a spot of bad luck and can't afford to keep a chauffeur."

"You're a good driver. You'll soon get work with your references, and I'm all right here."

"It took me over a year to get this job," he said gloomily. "Besides, it'll delay our getting married and having that little pub in the country. My luck's been out ever since I left Mr. Lucas. He was a corker, Al, though his old woman was a regular hell-cat."

"Funny thing you mentioned him," the girl remarked "I read a bit in the paper about a Mrs. Lucas dying sudden, in Monte Carlo Casino of all places!"

"Go on! I'll bet there was a rare scene. It ain't likely to be her though. Plenty of Lucases about." The barmaid searched under the counter and producing a newspaper, pointed to a paragraph. Bill Staines read it and frowned.

"It is her; at least, he's called Robert Lucas." He stared at the newspaper for a moment. "I wonder what'll happen now," he said thoughtfully. "Poor old guv'ner. I'd like to see him again."

Al leaned across to him.

"Wasn't there something queer that time you was abroad with him?" she asked.

Bill's lips tightened. " No," he said shortly.

"Oh yes, there was," Al persisted. "I'm beginning to remember now. You and me met for the first time just as you'd landed home from some foreign place with a funny name. "You'd left him, and though you had plenty of cash, you looked awful and told me there'd been some kind of a bother. What was the fuss about?"

"Forget it. I'd probably been seasick on the boat." Bill's tone was distinctly irritable. "Let's talk of something else. Been to the movies this week?" He tucked the paper into his pocket as he spoke.

"No. Let's go to-morrow. It's my night off. I've got a couple of passes."

The man avoided her eyes.

"Sorry, kid. I can't."

"Why?" she demanded suspiciously. "Your boss never wants you after six."

"I may have to go and see about another job." His manner was evasive. "Look, there's a crowd coming in. You'll be busy for a long time, so I think I'll go home. My bad luck's given me a headache."

"It's not your bad luck but the bad news in the paper that's upset you, if you asked me."

"I haven't asked you," he retorted, "and I told you I didn't want to talk about it. Can't you leave a chap alone, Al?"

"I certainly can for a long time and never notice he wasn't there!" the girl snapped, and went to attend to another customer.

Bill Staines wandered home to his lodgings, his mind disturbed by memories in which neither Al nor his lost job played any part.

Alone in his room, he pulled out the newspaper and re-read the short account of the sudden death of Mrs. Robert Lucas. The paper was a day old, he noticed, and felt an illogical grudge against Al for not observing it sooner. Still, there might be more about it in a paper of a later date.

Going down to the kitchen, he asked his landlady for the day's journal. There was nothing in it, however, of special interest.

"What do you want to find, Bill?" his landlady inquired. "You look white as a ghost."

The chauffeur decided to take her partially into his confidence.

"I believe my old guv'ner's lost his wife, and I want to be sure before I send him a letter of sympathy," he explained. He'd lodged with "Ma" Parker for many years, and knew she had a keen eye for any sensational news. "Got any of yesterday's papers?"

The woman placed a plate of hot sausages before him.

"No; I use a lot now to light the fires. Eat your tea while I think. It's been waiting an hour for you. I read something about Mrs. Robert Lucas." She related what he already knew, adding, "And this afternoon I saw in some paper that she died natural and was to be buried at Nice. Her husband was a retired stockbroker, it said. That's him you always call the guv'ner, isn't it?"

Bill nodded, and ate his meal moodily.

"Lost my job, Ma," he announced. "My boss has got to cut down expenses. I'll have to find cheaper digs."

"Nonsense. You'll stay here and pay what you can," Mrs. Parker told him briskly. "After all these years I'd miss the sound of your great feet clumpin' about the house. I ain't the sentimental kind, but a few shillings a week isn't going to make me lose a good lodger. Besides, you might come in handy again to throw out another 'drunk' for me like you did last week. At sixty-odd, with no man of my own about, it's nice to feel there's a decent chap in the place if there's any trouble. So you'll stay and not feel under any obligation to me. Got that into your thick head?"

Bill grinned into her hard, rugged face.

"Thanks, Ma."

Mrs. Parker watched him in silence until he had finished his food, conscious of the fact that his thoughts were elsewhere; extremely worried thoughts if she was any judge.

"You're bothered what to do about this Lucas business, ain't you?" she asked at last.

The man nodded.

"I'd go to him at once," she advised: "Have you forgotten you told me all about it at the time?"

"Yes, I had," Bill confessed.

"Well, I haven't. Don't worry. I know how to keep my mouth shut. I've never told a soul and am not likely to. Ever spoken to Al of it?"

"Never. I was too darned glad to forget. But she remembered the name and gave me the paper. And," he said bitterly, "she remembered I looked funny and had said there'd been a spot of bother when I was abroad. That's all, but it was enough. I got away quick and came home before she wanted to know any more."

"Al can't do any harm even if she tried," the woman said wisely. "She asked me a lot of questions once when she was here. But, bless my soul, I'd got such a bad memory that day "—she winked at Bill—" that I couldn't recall you'd even been abroad!"

"You're a good sport." The man sighed. "I wish I hadn't been such a funk years ago. My nerves went all to pieces with that horrible business, and I couldn't sleep."

"You weren't driving a car for Mr. Lucas then, were you?"

"When they were in England I was. Then when they were going abroad, the guv'ner asked me to act as his valet on the trip. He'd got pots of money at that time, and though he could have afforded a smart chap, he said he'd rather have me. The guv'ner liked me and he knew I liked him. There was very little for me to do, he never made work for anybody. When we stopped at that island he hired a car and I drove. I felt I was earning my wages then, at least."

"You earned 'em all right, by what you went through," Mrs. Parker stated. "What started it all, Bill?

"Well rightly speaking, I suppose it was his meeting that girl on the trip out. She was the loveliest thing you ever set eyes on, and nice, too. None of your haughty manners about her. You can't blame the guv'ner for falling head over ears in love with her."

"Did she lead him on?"

"Never," the man said emphatically. "He didn't want no leading. He used to follow her about like a devoted dog, thankful if she gave him a kind word. She was sweet to everybody, even to me. I don't believe she ever noticed what was happening to him."

"Most girls would have," Mrs. Parker objected.

"I dare say, but she was going out to marry that bloke and was crazy with happiness."

"I wonder Mrs. Lucas didn't stop the affair."

"She would have fast enough, but she was terribly seasick, and never left her cabin for the first week. It was too late then. The guv'ner had got it so badly that I don't believe he even remembered he'd got a missus until she started raging at him."

"How did you come to know Mrs. Lucas quarrelled with her husband about this girl?"

"I was in his state-room, laying out his clothes and talking to him, when in came the old vixen—I can't help it Ma, even if she is dead. She called him a lot of filthy names he didn't deserve, and nagged him about her money."

"You ought to have gone out and left 'em alone, Bill," Mrs. Parker, said reprovingly. "I was in good service with gentry and know what's what."

"So do I," the man retorted. "It was darned awkward. I tried to go, but the guv'ner caught my arm and said, 'I want you to stay, Staines. Mrs. Lucas can say what she likes about me, but if she makes one false accusation against an innocent girl's character, I shall not be responsible for my actions. If you want to prevent murder, you'd better stay.' So I stayed. Why he didn't throttle her then and there, I don't know. Perhaps I helped to keep him quiet."

"Is he the hot-tempered, violent kind?"

Bill brought his hand down with a bang.

"The guv'ner? No. He's the calmest, best-tempered man in the world naturally, but who could stand injustice and lies? She was threatening to go to this girl's fiancé directly they landed and tell him what she said had happened. A low intrigue going on behind her back and with her money, was her words."

"And was it her money?"

The man screwed up his forehead dubiously.

"I don't rightly know all about that. From what I could make out after that row, she was a rich widow before the guv'ner knew her. He became her stockbroker. Some investments must have gone wrong. Anyhow, I recollect, during the quarrel, that she accused him of losing a fortune for her by his stupidity, if not worse. And for once he hit back and said she'd still plenty and he'd been punished enough by marrying her. He offered to go back to his business and make money and repay her. She scoffed and said she'd bought him as a compensation for her losses, and meant to have him handy for a companion. If only he'd done her in then!" Bill said with a groan.

"It couldn't have been worse than what he went through after."

"Did Mrs. Lucas keep her threat to tell the girl's fiancé?"

"I don't know. Anyhow, the fiancé was shot a few days after we landed, and the girl was found standing with the gun in her hand beside him, half-dazed. She was arrested and tried, but got off, as you know. And I bolted home like a coward. I'll never get those ghastly weeks before the trial out of my head."

"What became of the girl?"

"She was nearly off her head, even after she was acquitted. I heard that some old barrister with a title married her. As for the guv'ner, he seemed to turn into stone."

"The lawyers must have cost a lot," Mrs. Parker, observed reflectively. "Had the girl any money?"

"Not a dime. Her fiancé had paid her fare out, we heard at the trial." Bill gnawed his under-lip. "There was an Austrian woman with a lot of red hair mixed up in the business some way. How, I could never make head nor tail of. She was an actress, I fancy. I can't think of her name."

Mrs. Parker pursed her mouth scornfully.

"I never did hold with actresses; always playing a part, I says, whether they're off the stage or on. Why exactly did you run away, Bill? The trial was over and they couldn't arrest that girl again. Do you think she actually murdered her young man?"

"I'm positive she didn't," he stated, and for the very good reason that I know who did. And that's why I bolted. The guv'ner knew I was going. It's because of what he said that I'm worried now. 'Get out of the mess, quick, Staines, or your nerves'll smash up and you'll say more than you intend to. But, if anything ever happens to my wife, for Heaven's sake, wherever you are, come back or I may be in serious trouble.' That's what he said."

Mrs. Parker nodded.

"I remember; you told me the night you come back when you was all in. That's why I say, you've got to go to him now."

"You're right, Ma. I'll get off to-morrow." The woman looked at the clock and rose.

"What's the matter with now?" she demanded. "I'll pack your bag. There's plenty of time for you to catch the boat-train at Victoria and cross this evening."

"Shall I cable to him?" the man asked uncertainly, conceding her the right to decision in his confused state of mind.

"No. Just get to Monte Carlo as fast as you can," advised Mrs. Parker. "The newspapers said the Lucases were staying at the Villa Lorne. Take a cab there, and good luck."

XXXII, IN THE CASINO

Thursday evening.

BILL STAINES reached the Villa Lorne on Thursday evening and learned that Mr. Lucas and the entire house-party had just gone to the Casino.

"They might not be home until long after midnight," the butler explained. "Would you like to leave a message for Mr. Lucas, or will you call and see him to-morrow?"

Bill was distinctly nonplussed by this unexpected set-back.

"I particularly wanted to see him to-night," he said. "He doesn't expect me, but when I read about Mrs. Lucas's death, I came at once. My name's Staines, Bill Staines. I was his chauffeur and valet years ago. I don't want any money out of him or anything like that. But"— Bill twisted his hat awkwardly—"well—I'd do anything for the guv'ner."

Oswell was a sound judge of human nature; the man's simple statement had an honest ring.

"If you've been travelling since last night, you must be tired out. Come into the housekeeper's room and I'll get you some tea," he suggested. "You can decide later whether you'll wait for Mr. Lucas."

"Thank you, mate," Bill said gratefully. "But I don't want to keep you up."

"I shan't be going to bed myself until they come back," Oswell told him. "You'll be company for me. How's old London looking?"

"Pretty damp and foggy when I left last night. I come all of a hop. I s'pose it's warmer down here though it's only February, Mr.—" Bill paused inquiringly.

"Oswell's my name—without the Mister," was the reply. "Well, it's better than England by day, but the nights are cold. I always say the Riviera sun's all glitter and no warmth in the winter. Her ladyship will be going back to England shortly, and I shan't be sorry. Bring your bag. You can come through the front hall; everybody's out."

"Sorry I didn't know the French for back entrance to tell the cabby," Bill apologized with a grin. "Big place you've got here. Does the master keep much company?"

"'Her ladyship's a young widow. Her husband was an elderly gent and died three years ago, just before I came. Yes, we've several guests, but there's plenty of staff to do the work. Like to see the reception-rooms?"

"You bet I would." Bill put his bag down and followed Oswell, feeling decidedly, more cheerful.

"This is the lounge," the butler said, after they had visited the library and dining-room. "There's a photograph of my mistress," he remarked, indicating a large silver-framed portrait.

Bill stepped nearer to examine it. He drew in his breath with a sharp exclamation as he looked at the dazzling beauty of the pictured face.

The butler mistook the sound for one of awe.

"Lady Daventry's a remarkably beautiful woman," he said proudly.

"Yes." Bill continued to gaze at the photograph in a dazed fashion. "Her name's Lady Daventry, you said."

"It is, but she could change it any time she liked," Oswell answered with a smile. "Half the men she meets fall in love with her. Unfortunately she doesn't seem interested in them. I'd like to see her married and happy. She can't be more than thirty."

"Not that," Bill thought, reckoning up the years mentally.

Oswell led the way to a room at the back of the hall and opened a door. The housekeeper looked up as they entered.

"Mrs. Warren, this is Staines," the butler introduced. "He was once Mr. Lucas's chauffeur and has just arrived from London to see his old master on urgent business. I'm going to get him some sandwiches while he's waiting."

The housekeeper was in an amiable mood and welcomed the stranger with unusual cordiality.

"Burgess hasn't gone to bed yet, Mr. Oswell," she remarked "Tell her to lay a tray and give you the cold beef. Sandwiches are no good after a long journey." She turned to Bill and told him to take a chair near the fire. "I always have one here evenings, though it's only logs. Give me good old England and a Christian coal fire, instead of central heating."

"You don't like the Riviera, ma'am."

"No, I don't," Mrs. Warren replied fiercely. "People should stay in their own country, particularly young men." Her fingers tightened on the linen she was mending. "There wouldn't have been no trouble here if folks had stayed in England. Sudden death and such like. Why, you're buried so quick here that the breath's hardly out of your body."

Bill checked an impulse to say he hadn't yet suffered from that inconvenience, but feared Mrs. Warren might think he was a bit too "fresh".

"I expect the guv'ner's wife—I mean Mrs. Lucas— dying so sudden, upset you a good deal," he ventured.

"What do you know about it?" she demanded.

"Nothing, except two or three lines in the London papers, ma'am."

"Then why are you here?"

Bill hastily brought forth once more his plea of business. It sounded a trifle vague. Mrs. Warren mercifully reverted to her former theme that young men should stay in their own country.

"A bit of travel broadens the mind," he suggested when she paused for breath.

"Where have you travelled to get that idea?" came back her sharp question.

It put the man on his guard. His life abroad was the last topic that he wished to discuss.

"Once I toured round France for a few months with the guv'ner and Mrs. Lucas," he said warily.

"How long ago was that?"

Advancing the year of that tour considerably, Bill saw the look of interest in his movements fade from the housekeeper's face.

"For the life of me I can't see what business you've got with Mr. Lucas," she said tartly. "When a man's just lost his wife, it doesn't seem decent to bother him."

It was on the edge of Bill's tongue to observe that a man in the depths of grief would not have gone to a Casino. The butler's entry with a substantially laden supper-tray saved the situation.

"Where are you going to sleep?" asked Oswell, when the chauffeur had finished his meal.

"I hadn't thought about that, mate," Bill owned.

"Well, by the time Mr. Lucas returns and you've had a talk, it will be very late, and this villa's a goodish walk from the town." Oswell decided to pass the buck to the housekeeper. "What about it, Mrs. Warren?"

The housekeeper studied Bill Staines from head to foot slowly. Apparently the inspection satisfied her.

"He can have the room next to you, Mr. Oswell. It's all ready. Her ladyship would wish you to sleep here if I think fit. I'm going to bed now. Good night."

Bill murmured his thanks. He relapsed into his thoughts as the butler, after giving him a brief account of Mrs. Lucas's death, settled down to read a newspaper.

What would the guv'ner want him to do? Bill wondered. The thought nagged at his brain. He forced his mind into another channel by endeavouring to picture the Casino which he had never seen. Probably Mr. Lucas was even now talking to that beautiful woman, who the butler had said was Lady Daventry, and whom Bill had known long ago in such tragic circumstances.

*   *   *   *

At that very moment Mr. Lucas was doing precisely what his late chauffeur imagined.

"Who are your new guests, Eve?" Lucas asked as they strolled through the gambling-room.

"You mean Mr. and Mrs. Reynolds? They're friends of Mimi; staying at the Hotel Napoli for a few days," Eve Daventry replied. "I like them both so much. It's a pleasure to meet really nice people, isn't it?"

"All your geese are swans." Lucas smiled at her. "I've had no chance to talk much to Reynolds, but his wife seems to be a charming woman. She has two rare qualities: a pleasant voice and the ability to listen. In fact, now I come to think of it, she did more listening than talking. Going to play a while?" he asked as they paused at a crowded roulette table.

Eve shook her head.

"I can't concentrate on gambling when—" She left her sentence unfinished, but the man understood.

Pulling a hundred-franc note from his pocket, he pushed it into her hand.

"Don't try to concentrate. Throw this down anywhere," he urged. "If it wins we'll divide the loot. It might be a good omen that the luck has turned for us."

Without a second's hesitation, she placed it on red.

"An even chance isn't adventurous enough," Lucas reproved her.

"Anyhow, it's won. Here's your capital. I'll play with our winnings."

Again she tried an even chance with success, next tossing both notes on to one of the dozens. That stake also bore fruit.

"Do I stop now, Robert?" she asked.

"Certainly not. Risk a number. It's a thirty-five to one chance and worth while."

"I'd hate to lose now," she said in an undertone. "I feel, as you said, that it might be an omen."

The ball dropped into a socket as she spoke.

"There, zero has turned up," she went on. "I'm so glad I didn't play that coup. Hold your breath. I'm going to back my age"

She placed one of her winning plaques on the number twenty-nine. They watched the ball as it swung round, at first rapidly, then slowly, hovering, as if undecided which number it preferred.

"It's going to be seven. I can't look," she said, and deliberately turned away.

"*Vingt-neuf, noir, impair et passe,*" sang out the croupier in impassive tones.

"You've won!" Lucas exclaimed. A curious expression of relief and joy rose to his eyes. "Collect your winnings, and please don't play again to-night, Eve."

"Nothing would induce me to," she assured him. "Let's sit down and divide it up. What a pile!" Her hands were full of plaques of different values. She poured them on to her lap as they withdrew to one of the corner lounges, which happened to be empty.

"A very pretty bit of work," he said when they had counted the amount. "Less tips, you've won roughly about forty pounds in English money, Eve."

Her face sparkled with animation.

"I've gained much more than that," she declared. "My morale seems to have gone up with a bound. Oh!" her voice rose on a note of dismay, "we're on the same seat where your wife was taken ill!"

Lucas calmed her.

"What does it matter? That's over and finished. Hello!" he exclaimed, "the party is coming in a bunch. Try to get rid of 'em. I'll cash these chips and come back."

Eve Daventry glanced from one to the other of the guests she knew too well for her peace of mind. Van Godchen senior and Mr. Caryll were on either side of Baroness Pertzoff, whose stormy, face indicated trouble.

"A terrible time!" Hester declaimed with a despairing gesture. "I won over six thousand francs and then I lost it all."

"What a pity you did not stop when you had so much," Eve observed with less tact than usual. "Still, you are no worse off than when you started."

"You were always a timid fool at gambling," retorted Hester irritably. She swung around to Van Godchen. "I play boldly; small stakes do not amuse me. I prefer to plunge."

From behind her came a clear voice.

"To-day seems to be your unlucky day, Baroness," Mimi remarked steadily. It was the first time that evening that she had directly addressed the woman from whom she had escaped only a few hours ago.

The implication underlying her words roused Hester to visible anger. She muttered something to John Caryll, but his attention was riveted on a slight maneuver that Mimi was carrying out.

Apparently without pre-organized plan, the guests were taking up various positions. Glen Armitage moved close to the settee with Lucas near him. Mrs. Reynolds sat down next to Lady Daventry, so that Glen and Lucas were standing on either side.

Around them in a semicircle were Caryll, the Baroness Pertzoff, Van Godchen, Tony and the tall commanding figure of Inspector Reynolds beside Mimi.

"Where were Jill Caryll and Franz Van Godchen?" Reynolds asked the French girl in an undertone.

"They were not here when it happened," Mimi told him. "All the others with one exception, are in the same positions, with your wife where Mrs. Lucas sat."

"Right. We'll proceed. Watch closely and try to remember," he urged, and gave a faint signal to his wife.

Instantly Mrs. Reynolds rose, and swaying a little, pressed her hand to her head.

"The heat," she exclaimed feebly. "I feel faint."

Eve, sitting immediately behind, held out her scent bottle for someone to pass to Mrs. Reynolds.

It was taken from her hand by the nearest person and given to the seemingly fainting woman.

Mrs. Reynolds took it, inhaled deeply, and then, still grasping the bottle, appeared to collapse in Lucas's arms, with Glen lending his support.

Together the two men helped her to the couch, where she sank down. The scent bottle was no longer in her hand.

"And there, I believe, the reconstruction ends," Reynolds whispered to the French girl "Did it work?"

"Perfectly. I remembered everything," she replied. Someone else also remembered, for Hester Pertzoff took Van Godchen's arm.

"Let's go. They've actually enacted what occurred on the night when Mrs. Lucas died!" she said with a sneer. "I presume the morbid performance is for the benefit of Mr. and Mrs. Reynolds. It's appallingly bad taste."

"You feel better, Mrs. Reynolds?" inquired John Caryll.

"Thank you, yes," she replied. "The scent bottle was most refreshing. What good Samaritan gave it to me?"

"I did." Caryll's eyes twinkled. He glanced across at Inspector Reynolds. "Was that what you wanted to know?"

"That was it," agreed Reynolds calmly. "Only you took someone else's place to-night by arrangement." He turned to Lady Daventry. "Tell me," he said in an undertone, "how and where did you meet the Van Godchens and Baroness Pertzoff?

"They were staying on an island. I knew them before Sir Neale Daventry married me," she replied. "Come back to the villa now and I will tell you about it."

XXXIII, Under the Moon

Thursday night.

GLEN ARMITAGE, leaving the Casino with Mimi caught sight of Jill in the Atrium. Grasping her by the elbow, he forced her along at a smart pace towards the glass doors, followed by the French girl.

Outside on the path, Glen paused and looked about him with a frown.

"Too many people here," he announced, tightening his grip on Jill. "Where can we go, Mimi, to have a nice healthy row without being disturbed?"

"The Terrace might be quiet, monsieur"

"That's the idea. On we go." Glen twisted his captive around and hustled her down by the side of the Casino. "There!" he said in triumph, as they reached an empty seat "I've been spoiling for this quarrel all day, Jill, but I haven't had any time to waste on you. Sit down, young woman."

"Don't let my dislike of both you and Mimi hinder your plans." Jill said icily.

"Of course I won't," Glen assured her. "Now then, I don't care two hoots about your imaginary grievance against me, but for Mimi's sake I intend to straighten out this business—"

Jill threw back her head and laughed.

"Naturally it would be for her sake!"

Mimi lent forward.

"Jill, tell me when you first felt angry with me," she said in an earnest tone.

"On the stairs at five o'clock this morning," Jill stated. "Hearing voices, I looked out of my door in time to see Glen carrying you to your room. Isn't that enough?"

"More than enough," Mimi answered pityingly, "if what you assumed had been true." She looked across at Glen. "You see, Jill had good reason."

"I suppose so," he admitted. "But why in the name of fortune didn't you tell me what you'd seen, Jill? Don't hide behind your wounded pride or whatever it's called. Be frank."

"Very well, I will," she retorted. "I was hurt, and wanted to hurt you both in return, and I couldn't bear any smooth false explanations. You pretended that Mimi was in danger when I told you I'd cut off her telephone call; it was simply because you were infatuated with her. She was all right."

"She is all right but—"

Mimi interrupted him with a gesture.

"One moment, please," she begged. "Let me ask a question. Why do you think I went away to-day, Jill?"

The English girl smiled cynically.

"You and Glen had some slight tiff, I suppose, and you left the house out of pique. Then he became alarmed and thought you'd run away to Paris."

"It was logical, your thought, Jill." Again Mimi's eyes went to Glen. "I'm afraid we must tell Jill the truth for her own sake."

"We've no right to do so at this tricky stage of affairs," he disagreed. "However, as I'm going to marry this silly kid, I'd better trust her. Here goes, and if you let any human being know, Jill, it may cause a ghastly mess."

Jill was startled by his tone.

"I will tell no one," she promised breathlessly.

"Mimi was drugged and insensible when you saw me carry her upstairs," Glen informed her. "Thinking she was merely tired out and heavily asleep, I dumped her on her bed and left her."

"I'll say the next bit," put in the French girl. "I was on a boat at sea when I opened my eyes. Unfortunately I couldn't keep awake. When I really awoke it was nearly noon and I was locked in a room at Nice."

"By whom?" Jill asked in alarm.

Mimi made a negative gesture.

"*N'importe*. It is better you do not know that just yet. *Alors*, with much difficulty I telephoned to you for help. No, no, *chérie*," she said quickly as Jill's eyes flooded with tears, "you acted as I should have done in your place. Your uncle and Glen searched everywhere for me. By great luck Mr. and Mrs. Reynolds were able to rescue me and take me back to the Villa Lorne."

Suddenly Mimi remembered the spectacle which had greeted the Reynolds, and shook with laughter. "*Figurez-vous*, Jill dear, I, who love to be chic and *soignée*, in a wet dressing-gown and felt slippers! *Queue toilette* in which to receive my friends."

But Jill had no answering smile. Her heart was full of compunction for deserting her friend.

"I'm sorry," she said softly. "It was terribly stupid of me to misjudge you, Mimi."

"Not a sign of grief for having misjudged me," put in Glen "However, we'll let the past, including Franz, be very dead, angel," He turned to the French girl. "Mimi, if you're not afraid to go home in the dark, this is where you obligingly fade out. Or shall I find you a handsome gigolo to dance with while Jill and I wind up our quarrel in the old, old way?"

"And now it's our turn, my sweet," Glen said as Mimi left them. "I've given you a thin time. Forgive me."

Jill nestled into his arms, silent and content, in the darkness of the deserted terrace.

Their peace was disturbed at last by the moon which, streaking slyly from behind a cloud, directed a beam as clear as a spot-light upon them.

Jill drew away from Glen's arms laughingly.

"I always knew he was nothing but a prying old man," she declared.

"Who?"

"The man in the moon. Let's go, Glen. I can't share you even with him."

He caught her by the shoulders.

"No more philanderings with Franz," he ordered sternly.

"No more," promised the girl. "Glen, he is an odd person. I mean Franz Van Godchen. He is devoted to me in a queer desperate fashion. I believe that is the real side of him."

"And what is the other side? If we must discuss that frozen image at such a moment." There was veiled eagerness, however, in the question.

"His submission to his father. Not only about me. That is understandable. Lots of fathers would not wish their sons to marry penniless girls. And I am penniless, you know."

"You don't mean it!" Glen clasped his head and groaned. "Leading me on; that's what you've been doing, while I hoped you would inherit your uncle's billions. However, I'll overlook it and let you drag me to the altar. Tell me more about Franz," he added, as they walked towards the Casino.

"His father dominates him," Jill went on, "and Franz hasn't the courage to resist. He would never have asked me such questions otherwise, I'm sure."

"What questions?"

"Oh, about uncle; who he was and why he came here."

"Did you tell him?" Glen asked sharply.

"Of course not. I became beautifully vague, chiefly because I didn't know the answers myself. Poor Franz. He's really quite a simple soul. What do you think his great interest in life is?"

"Knitting bedsocks," guessed Glen.

"Butterflies and moths. He begged me to go on some expedition after one particular variety."

"Has he got his gadgets with him? Tins and nets and things."

"Yes, I saw him leaning over his balcony very early one morning trying to catch a butterfly with a long-handled net." Jill smiled. "Suddenly out came 'father' roaring like a lion, and in went 'son' with his toys like a lamb. Wasn't it funny?"

"Very," Glen said dryly, and hailed a cab. "In you go."

He was curiously silent on the way back to the Villa Lorne. They stood for a while in the scented darkness of the drive, after the cab had gone.

"Do you know, Glen, that when I first came I thought you were in love with Lady Daventry," Jill ventured.

"You did, eh!" The man chuckled. "Well, there indeed you might be jealous, for I've kissed Eve hundreds of times. I've likewise bitten, scratched and slapped her."

"She is so beautiful and dignified that one can't imagine you'd dare to do that."

"We were both bald, fat-faced babies then, and fought savagely in adjoining cots, I believe. Her parents were drowned when she was a few months old, and my mother brought her up. We're distant cousins."

Jill gave a sigh of relief.

"Oh, I understand now. Have you seen much of her?"

"Before this winter we hadn't met for years. Then she was in a spot of trouble and I came to see what I could do about it. I couldn't do much. She wouldn't let me for fear of hurting someone else. Eve's a dear pig-headed fool and always was."

"I adore her," the girl said fervently.

"What was Mr. Caryll's motive for bringing you here, Jill?"

"I don't know, and I'd rather he told you how we met." She touched his arm gently. "You too have secrets that you can't tell me, haven't you?"

"Yes," he agreed. "At least, it's safer that you are in ignorance of them. You see, my sweet, you're the world's worst actress, and a child could read your sweet face. I'm glad of it. Now do something for me. I've an idea that things may be happening here to-night and I want you out of it. Say you're tired and go to bed."

"Of course," she promised. "Good night, Glen." He kissed her upturned face.

"Good night, beloved. When all this mess is cleared up, you'll be surprised what a nice young man you'll have."

XXXIV, THE GIGOLO

Thursday night.

GIGOLO! Glen's casual phrase struck a forgotten chord in Mimi's memory as she left him and Jill on the Casino Terrace. Guido was a gigolo, and he had been the dead Mrs. Lucas's friend. He was also sympathetically inclined to Mimi and would probably be dancing at the Café de Paris at this moment. It was worth going there on chance.

There was something else, however, of equal importance that she must do first.

Re-entering the Atrium she was able to perform one portion of that task. Franz was gazing around forlornly.

"Where is Miss Caryll?" he asked when the French girl approached him. "She promised to meet me here."

"Jill is detained with friends for an hour, monsieur," Mimi replied politely. "Will you please stay here in case she returns earlier?"

Franz bowed stiffly.

"I will await Miss Caryll's pleasure."

That was nicely fixed up, Mimi reflected.

Near the door stood a Casino official. He gave a start of recognition as Mimi approached him.

"The pearl necklace belonging to Mrs. Lucas was discovered soon after you and the police officers left the Villa Lorne, monsieur," she observed pleasantly.

"Thank you, mademoiselle. It was very disagreeable to me, that search," the official volunteered.

"Who suggested it?" inquired Mimi.

"A man with a huge voice, who refused to give his name, rang up the Casino and also the police station. He spoke in French with a foreign accent and was undoubtedly very angry."

"Thwarted people often are," Mimi told him cryptically, and at once rang up the Villa Lorne and asked for Reynolds.

"We've just arrived," he told her in a moment over the wire. "Anything wrong?"

"*Au contraire,* all is very well." She related what she had just learned, adding, "Franz Van Godchen will be in the Casino for one hour. I told him to wait there for Jill."

"Excellent," Reynolds remarked. "Are you going to stay with him?"

"*Mais non.* Me, I go to see a gigolo." Mimi chuckled. "Now that the wise Inspector Reynolds is doing his stuff, I am free to amuse myself."

"Listen to me, brat," he said sternly. "You've been in enough mischief for one day, and I'm not going to yank you out of fresh troubles at this time of the night. So, be careful."

Inside the smart restaurant where Guido danced with his clients, Mimi looked round for him in vain. Inquiries from the manager produced the information that Guido was very ill.

"La grippe," he diagnosed. "If mademoiselle wishes to dance—"

"Not now," Mimi replied, trying to slip away before two people, who had just entered, observed her.

The manager escorted her to the door, an act of politeness that was not wholly disinterested since he wanted to greet the two new guests.

"Guido lives in Beausoleil; it is quite near," he explained, with one eye on the huge elderly man and the red-haired, impressive-looking woman who accompanied him.

Making a vague reply, Mimi edged towards the door.

"You come to dance at the café, Miss Mimi?" the hearty voice of Van Godchen boomed in her ear.

"And now I go to work at the villa," she said with an attempt at gay retort.

"Because your Guido is not here?" he persisted.

"No. Because it is late," she replied irritably, conscious that Hester Pertzoff's malicious gaze was watching her discomfiture.

Evading further questions, she sped from the café and hailed a cab.

"Beausoleil, quickly. I will give you the address in a moment," she ordered the driver, and searched her handbag for Guido's card. The encounter with Hester and the Hollander had shaken her nerve.

At the door of the gigolo's lodgings she paid off the cab.

"Yes, Monsieur Guido lives here," the aged concierge told her. Adding with a cackle, "If he still lives!"

"He is very ill?" Mimi demanded.

"He is dying: it is an affair of hours only," the old woman replied. "Already the priest has visited him for the last rites. No one can see him." Greedy fingers closed on a note that Mimi pressed into them. "On the second floor, mademoiselle. The door is open. You will see a light which I have put there. One should not die in the dark."

The girl's feet almost flew up the staircase to the dingy room which the immaculate gigolo occupied.

The glimmer of one candle shed fantastic shadows on the ceiling as she hurried to the bed.

"You know this poor boy?" asked a gentle voice. Startled, Mimi swung round and saw a nun sitting in the semi-darkness.

"Yes, Sister. Is he conscious?"

The nun bowed her head and rising, murmured, "The end is very near. If you wish, I will leave you."

The girl bent over the bedside.

"Guido, do you remember me?" she asked.

The man's eyes opened and he looked at her, at first dazedly. Presently a faint smile hovered on his white lips.

"It is Mademoiselle Mimi," he whispered with an effort. "I am glad you have come." His hand groped feebly beneath the pillow. "Madame Lucas gave me this weeks ago. Take it, please. I cannot guard it any more."

Giving her an envelope, he sank back with a tired sigh and closed his eyes.

For a moment Mimi watched him retreat further into a remote land. Then, with a light touch of her fingers on the unconscious boy's forehead, she called the nun and hurried to the staircase.

Half-way down from Guido's room, Mimi paused on the landing, startled to hear Hester Pertzoff's voice, in conversation with the concierge.

"Oh, so mademoiselle is with Guido! I will go up," Hester announced.

"I go with you," came the deep voice of the old Hollander.

"No, stay here and hold that girl if she tries to slip away," Hester ordered him peremptorily.

Frantically Mimi tried the other two doors on the landing. Both were locked, and already Hester's feet were on the stairs. If that envelope which Guido had given into her care contained what Hester was seeking, Van Godchen might take it by force.

There was not a second to lose. The stairs had no carpet behind which she could hide it, but on the walls there were two or three dusty pictures.

Slipping the envelope behind one of them, Mimi darted up the second flight of stairs again.

Her fingers were actually on the handle of Guido's bedroom door when Hester came into view.

"He is barely conscious, Baroness," she said.

Hester swept her aside and went into the room.

With a shrug, Mimi walked down to the hall and gave an effective gasp of surprise when Van Godchen grasped her wrist.

"You are very interested in this gigolo," he observed.

"Guido was a good dancer, and hearing that he was ill, I called to see him," was the girl's defence. "Why are you detaining me?"

"That you shall know when the Baroness returns," Van Godchen told her.

In a few minutes Hester came hurriedly downstairs.

"Ah, good, you have caught her," she exclaimed as she saw the Hollander's captive. "Now then, girl, give me that blue envelope at once," she ordered Mimi. "Don't pretend any nonsense. Guido was able to tell me that he gave it to you and the nun heard him say so."

"I have not got it," Mimi replied.

In a flash she guessed that Hester would search the house if necessary, unless she was told that the envelope was not there. "It has gone," she added.

"You are lying."

Hester dragged the girl into the hall and searched her swiftly.

"I told you that the envelope has gone," Mimi observed calmly. "Do you think that I should be such a fool as to come here alone, knowing that you would follow me?"

"You had just come from Guido's room when I saw you," Hester said furiously.

"I appeared to do so." Mimi smiled. "Have I never heard of throwing an envelope from a window to someone who is waiting below, Baroness? It was nearly as simple as my trick with the water in your flat." She glanced across the road where several people were passing. "Will you release me or shall I scream?"she inquired. "Those people will willingly help me, one of their own nationality. They may not be so amiable to an Austrian and a Hollander."

"Let her go," Hester told the man. "I must reach the villa before this girl's messenger does. Who was it?"

Mimi realized that somehow she must delay them from going to the Villa Lorne.

"Please don't blame your son," she said to Van Godchen, assuming a tone of uneasiness.

"My zon! You brought him, my Franz, here with you!" thundered the old man. "Where is he?"

"You will find him in the Casino Atrium. How could I know you wanted the envelope?" Mimi said falteringly.

Directly they were out of sight, she re-climbed the stairs, and taking the envelope from its hiding-place, set out for the Villa Lorne.

What had Inspector Reynolds discovered there in the meantime, Mimi wondered as she hastened along. And was this blue envelope, which Guido had given to her, the key of freedom for Lady Daventry?

XXXV, Information Received

Thursday night.

AN hour earlier when Inspector Reynolds with Eve and her friends had returned from the Casino, the butler stated that a man was waiting for Mr. Lucas.

"His name is Staines, sir. He arrived direct from London about nine o'clock to-night."

"Where is he?" Lucas asked after a moment's pause.

"In the housekeeper's room, sir. He seems a decent chap, so I've arranged for him to sleep here to-night as it's so late."

"Very thoughtful of you, Oswell. Bring him up to my room, will you?"

Lucas squared his shoulders and drew in a long breath, as might a brave man facing a firing squad at dawn.

"Eve," he said, drawing her aside, "Staines is here. You remember: he was my chauffeur."

She nodded. "I've not forgotten," she replied. "It's too late now that so much water has gone under the bridge. You always suspected that he suppressed evidence at my trial. It was probably for your sake. Staines worshipped you."

"Well, whatever happens to me," Lucas said, "I know what I must do now."

Bill Staines' stolid countenance was obviously working with emotion when he grasped his master's hand.

"I had to come, sir," he said simply.

"Thank you, Staines. I knew you would, one day. I never blamed you for clearing off."

"It wasn't only the money I got for holding my tongue, sir, honest. That, part preyed on my conscience bad enough. I'd have gone if I hadn't had any money, for your sake."

Lucas wrinkled his brow.

"I don't understand; nor about money, you received. Let's put our cards' on the table, Staines. Do you know where the lady is now?"

"In this villa, sir. She is Lady Daventry. I recognized her photo to-night" The chauffeur rubbed his head. "Of course, now I come to think of it, as she's a widow and you're free, it's natural you should be here, seeing as you was in love with her."

"I wasn't free when I came here weeks ago. It was my wife's wish to do so. She hated Lady Daventry, as you know."

The chauffeur's face darkened.

"I didn't know," he asserted, "or I might have made a bit of trouble with my tongue that Mrs. Lucas wouldn't have liked. What's more, I could have proved it. Had it happened in England I wouldn't have minded so much. But I was scared of that foreign island, and not knowing the language. French or German's civilized, so to speak; Greek is a kind of heathen lingo, and who knew what the interpreter was saying in court? You fought hard for poor Miss Eve—"

"Leave it at that," Lucas urged quickly. "Walls have ears in this place. So far as I'm aware, only the Baroness Pertzoff and an old Hollander know Lady Daventry's maiden name."

"That woman here too, sir!" The chauffeur's face hardened. "A dangerous bit of goods."

"Perhaps not altogether bad, Staines. She was doing risky work and got trapped," Lucas said. "I bribed people on that island to get Miss Eve free. I forged my wife's signature, and sold shares worth thousands of pounds belonging to her for half their value to get money quickly for those bribes and the lawyers. My wife never forgave

me. She made me sign a document admitting my guilt
and that I owed it."

"As her husband, you'll get her money now, sir, and
you can burn that confession."

Lucas shook his head.

"By her will, read a few days ago, she has left
everything to the Baroness Pertzoff. That means I must
pay the Baroness. I wish I'd faced the music years ago.
You see the hole I'm in through my silence."

"Couldn't you have earned that money and paid your
wife back, sir?"

"She preferred to keep me in her power; also, once a
man in my profession has retired, it's not so easy to begin
again and make a fortune."

"Lady Daventry must be very grateful for what you
did for her sake."

"She has never known and never shall know who paid
the money. She thought that my wife's hatred was
jealousy." Lucas leaned closer to the man. "Tell me, did
Lady Daventry's fiancé commit suicide, was he murdered,
or don't you know?"

"He was murdered, sir. I know who did it and I can
prove it easy."

"Your word isn't sufficient, Staines."

The man pulled out a pocket-book and gave something
to Lucas.

"There's the proofs, sir. Six of 'em on one film. Hold it
up to the light—*if you're sure you want to know.*"

Lucas took the strip of negative and examined it.
Clear as crystal before his eyes, as it would always be in
his memory, was that corner of a balcony on which the
death of Bromley, Eve's fiancé, had occurred, in that far-
off island years ago.

Only a camera film, yet it pointed an accusing finger
with deadly accuracy at Bromley's murderer.

"This is incredible, Staines. Ghastly!" broke from him.

"You never guessed, guv'ner, and I hadn't the heart to
tell you," the chauffeur said gently. "I was trying my new

camera in the summer house not fifteen yards away that afternoon. The first snap I took was of Mr. Bromley, sitting reading."

"How had you the courage to take the others?" Lucas inquired.

"I don't know, sir; I was so dazed I didn't realize. It seemed like a bit out of a play at the time. Look at number two. There she is standing beside him; Mr. Bromley couldn't see the gun in her hand. Number three is where she's by his right side with the gun near his head."

Lucas peered closely at the third tiny picture. 'Bromley evidently knew nothing of her intention, poor devil. He's even smiling as she stands looking over his shoulder."

"Number four snap is after he's been shot," Staines went on grimly. "You can see her half way across the balcony. She went away through the garden. Number five shows Lady Daventry come on the scene. She must have heard the shot and run in. The sixth picture is where she's picked up the gun."

"That's how she was when they arrested her," Lucas said with a groan. "Why didn't you save her, Staines?"

'And hang My guv'ner's wife?" the man exclaimed. "I couldn't do that to you, sir, even though I didn't like Mrs. Lucas. If Miss Eve, as she was then, had been found guilty, of course I'd have shown these negatives. But you got her off and I bolted to England with the money Mrs. Lucas gave me to hold my tongue."

"My wife knew of this evidence against her!" Lucas tapped the strip of film.

Staines nodded shamefacedly.

"I'd lost a pretty packet in those Greek gambling dens, sir. In desperation I printed off copies of the film and went to your wife with them. I told her I'd destroyed the negatives. She gave me two hundred quid to go away."

"But why, why did my wife kill Bromley? She had nothing against him."

"Mr. Bromley laughed at her when she said that you and Miss Eve was in love—and worse he said she was jealous of a lovely girl. Mrs. Lucas told me so herself. She got Mr. Bromley's gun and killed him, meaning Miss Eve to be found guilty. That would keep you from her. She knew Miss Eve was going to see her fiancé that afternoon."

"It fits in with terrible truth, Staines. Everyone thought Bromley was mixed up with Baroness Pertzoff because he'd been seen with her a lot on the island, and that Miss Eve, when she landed, shot him through jealousy."

"Why was that red-headed piece there at all, sir?"

"She was in the pay of her country, and Bromley was in the pay of his, though officially he ran an agency. Bromley got hold of some Greek fortification plans that she wanted. So she tried to vamp him. It didn't work. Then Miss Eve arrived by boat to marry him. A few days later he was killed."

"Who got the plans in the end?"

"I neither know nor care," Lucas replied. "But sometimes I think that either Miss Eve or my wife had them, otherwise why is Baroness Pertzoff here?"

Staines did not know the answer to that question. Instead he asked:

"Excuse me, sir, when you was all arriving to-night, I took a squint out of the housekeeper's room. Who's that tall clean-shaven gent about fifty years of age? You was talking to him. He had a little blue flower in his coat."

"That must have been Mr. Caryll. He's an American, staying here with his niece," Lucas told him indifferently.

Staines appeared to be puzzled

"Caryll!" he exclaimed "Well, sir, you be careful. He's no American, and his name ain't Caryll."

"Does it matter?" Lucas smiled faintly. "He's a good fellow, and it's not my business if his name is Brown, Jones or Robinson."

"Isn't it, sir?" the man said dubiously. "Any-how, you get him up here a minute, will you? I'd like to be sure for your sake."

For a moment Lucas hesitated. Staines was a shrewd fellow and a loyal servant, but in this case loyalty had probably outrun judgment.

"Very well, Staines. But I can't trap Mr. Caryll. I shall say that you think you recognize him, and that I fancy you're mistaken."

Lucas found John Caryll in the corridor, and explained the situation.

"I'll see your chauffeur in a minute," Caryll promised. He lowered his voice. "I'm on guard here until Inspector Reynolds comes out of Franz Van Godchen's room."

"*Inspector* Reynolds!" echoed Lucas.

"Yes. Quite a pretty bit of work he's doing, too. Don't let Pertzoff or the Van Godchens know who he is."

"Of course. I won't." Lucas was mystified. "Does Lady Daventry know of this search?"

"She does, and a whole lot of her happiness rests on its success. Here's Reynolds now," Caryll added as Franz's door was opened cautiously. Any luck?"

Reynolds nodded.

"The works!" he said curtly.

"Fine," Caryll exclaimed. "Come with me, Inspector, to meet Mr. Lucas's old chauffeur. You'll be interested."

Lucas looked from one man to the other as if making up his mind.

"I want you to know what my chauffeur has just told me, Inspector," he said gravely, and related Staines' story in poignant sentences that showed the humiliation he was suffering.

"The negative proves it to the hilt," he added.

The inspector touched Lucas's shoulder sympathetically.

"You've been through a lot," he said. "Cheer up. There's one thing certain. Baroness Pertzoff will not take proceedings against you to recover your wife's money. I have an ace in my hand which will make that lady pause and think. She, an Austrian, drugged and kidnapped Mimi, who is a French subject. There's another charge, too.

"Also," Reynolds went on, "Mimi is not only a French subject, but an unofficial member of the Paris Sureté, the French equivalent of our Scotland Yard. Mimi is known to both those forces'—greatly respected by them for her valuable help on many occasions."

"I might have guessed it," Lucas observed. A flash of suspicion crossed his countenance. "What is she doing in the Villa Lorne, masquerading as Lady Daventry's secretary?"

"Fulfilling most faithfully the duty required of her," Reynolds replied. "Lady Daventry, worried until she was nearly frantic by the jewel thefts in her villa which in more than one case could have been attributed to her, resolved to protect herself. She wrote to the Paris Sureté asking them to put her in touch with a private detective, preferably a lady, who could act presumably as her secretary and find out who was trying to plant guilt on to her shoulders. Hence Mimi. She has had a busier time than I'd care for. Thanks to her skill, only one or two small links are missing from this tangled chain."

"We'll give you one link right now, Inspector," Caryll remarked. "Come along with me and see Lucas's chauffeur."

Staines rose as his employer entered with the two men. Caryll advanced towards him with extended hand "Do you remember me, Staines?" he asked

"Quite well, sir," the chauffeur replied.

"Tell Mr. Lucas and this gentleman where we met," Caryll ordered.

"On that blasted Greek island, sir, the day after the murder trial ended. You got off the very boat I was going on to. You spotted me on the quay, and seeing I was English, asked me what the verdict was. You didn't know I'd been a witness then—a witness who'd concealed facts."

"You said that you didn't want to talk about it as you were fed up," Caryll put in "What was it that induced you to give me a few details?"

"You gave me ten bob and said you was the murdered man's brother, sir. Mr. John Bromley was your name then." Staines looked doubtful.

"My full name is John Caryll Bromley. For my Californian business I dropped the surname of Bromley long ago. I went to the island to discover who had killed my brother, but failed. The case was over, and mouths had been effectually closed. Years afterwards I learned by a photograph in a magazine that my dead brother's fiancée had become Lady Daventry. I concocted a ruse to enter her household and find out if she were guilty."

Lucas started forward.

"Then you came here as her enemy," he said in an agitated manner.

Caryll bowed in agreement.

"I came as Lady Daventry's enemy, Mr. Lucas. I leave as her friend. We'd better see her immediately with the inspector, and show her these photographs." He grasped Lucas's arm. "Don't you realize what a burden will be lifted from her mind? At last she is entirely vindicated of guilt."

"And at last," said Lucas, "she can be free of these people who, trading on Eve's horror of the past being exposed, clung like leeches to her."

XXXVI, Links in the Chain

Thursday night.

WHEN Mimi reached the villa, she found Mrs. Reynolds waiting for her in the hall.

"Come up to Lady Daventry's room, Mimi. We have a lot of wonderful news to tell you before the Van Godchens and Baroness Pertzoff arrive."

The French girl followed her friend upstairs to the study where the inspector, with Lucas, Glen Armitage, Mr. Caryll and Tony, were gathered round Eve Daventry.

Without a word, Mimi laid the envelope on Eve's knee.

"Guido is dying, madame. He gave me this which he had been keeping for Mrs. Lucas," she explained.

With trembling fingers Eve passed the packet to Reynolds.

"Open it, please," she begged. "I cannot."

Slitting the sealed envelope, the inspector drew out a sheet of transparent blue paper with black tracings showing upon it.

"Mrs. Lucas took this from Mr. Bromley's pocket after she had killed him," Reynolds explained gravely. "I will take it to the Home Office when I return."

"Of what use was it to my wife?" Lucas inquired. "She certainly was not a spy."

"Should Lady Daventry have escaped arrest, it would have served to throw suspicion of guilt for Mr. Bromley's murder on the Baroness Pertzoff, who wanted this tracing very much. This doubly safe-guarded Mrs. Lucas. As it happened, no suspicion fell upon the Baroness, because Lady Daventry came upon the scene of the tragedy first." Reynolds took six small photographs from the envelope. "Have you ever seen these before?" he asked, holding them out to Eve.

She glanced at them with a shiver.

"Mrs. Lucas showed me this one only," she said. It was the print in which Eve was holding the gun and standing by the dead man. "She said it proved my guilt, and that as her husband had squandered her fortune to save me, I must pay her five thousand pounds for it. Hence—lodgers at the Villa Lorne!"

"Eve dear, why didn't you give her some of my father's money?" Tony asked.

"I couldn't, Tony. Your father was hard but just. He had done his part in marrying me and taking me away after that ghastly business.   It would have been repugnant to me to use his money to buy my peace of mind. So, foolishly, I tried to earn it."

"How did you come to be drawn into the Van Godchen and Pertzoff net, Eve?" Glen demanded with a touch of impatience.

The inspector interposed.

"Mr. Armitage, when misfortune attacks an innocent person, it unfortunately makes him or her the easy victim of unscrupulous people. Van Godchen was on that island at the time of Mr. Bromley's murder. Later, when it suited him, he traded on that knowledge and forced Lady Daventry into taking this villa and accepting him and his son as guests. It aided him in his unlawful exploits. Baroness Pertzoff came because the Lucases were here, and she knew that Mrs. Lucas had this blue tracing. To obtain that tracing, the Baroness was more or less in league with the Hollanders, although their purposes were different."

"Which one of that trio put the lights out on the night of the dance?" Caryll inquired.

"The housekeeper told me that bit," Reynolds replied. "Mrs. Warren loved Tony Daventry as if he were her own son, although she acted sternly towards him. In her desire to get him out of this house, where she knew he was in bad company, she accepted a bribe from Van Godchen. He said if she would pull the fuse out of the electric meter in the cellar, he would cancel Tony's debt to him and persuade Lady Daventry to send him back to London."

"I'd been gambling and owed the old shark thousands of francs," Tony admitted shamedly. "He charged me exorbitant interest."

"Mrs. Warren saw Van Godchen shoot at Mr. Caryll from his balcony one morning," Reynolds went on. "Probably it was intended merely to frighten him into leaving the villa."

"Did he mean to wound Hester Pertzoff on the night of the dance?" Eve asked.

The inspector shook his head.

"I think that shot was fired merely to distract attention from the theft of Mrs. Kellner's jewel. By chance the shot passed through Tony's coat sleeve and then through Baroness Pertzoff's shoulder."

Caryll leaned forward.

"Who stole Mrs. Kellner's jewel, Inspector?"

Reynolds glanced with a faint smile at Tony Daventry.

"Would you like to tell us?" he asked.

Tony flushed.

"Maybe I'll feel less of a skunk if I own up," he answered. "Old Van Godchen got me into his clutches completely, partly because I owed him money, partly because he threatened to expose Eve's past if I didn't help him."

"That's one up for you, my lad," Glen murmured, "Go to it."

"Well, Van Godchen made me get a fake duplicate of Mrs. Lucas's necklace."

"I saw it," Glen cut in. "That's why I took Mrs. Lucas's real necklace at the Casino. For Eve's sake I was trying to prevent Tony from taking the pearls. Later, I pushed all Mrs. Lucas's jewels, which I'd taken from her case for safety, into Tony's drawer, hoping to give him a fright. I apologize for that nasty bit of work, Tony."

"I deserved it and more, Glen," the young man admitted.

Glen's brow puckered comically.

"Who took that real necklace from my pocket at the Casino?" he demanded. "And who put it next day in Eve's drawer in this study? Was that done out of malice or kindness, I wonder?

"Out of mistaken kindness," John Caryll said ruefully. "I saw you take Mrs. Lucas's necklace, Glen. It was simple for me to lift it from your pocket. Next morning I placed it in this drawer, knowing that Lady Daventry would return it tactfully."

"Why, oh why didn't you tell me what you had done, monsieur?" Mimi reproached him.

"I didn't know you so well as I do now, young woman," was Caryll's smiling rejoinder. "Had Lady Daventry been there I should of course have told her. For"—he looked kindly at Eve—"I had not been in this house more than a few hours before I knew that you were being cruelly victimized. That knowledge weakened my belief that you had killed your fiancé, my brother. I had come here bent on private vengeance, you see, thinking that you had cheated justice. That explains my ignoble reason for being in this villa as your guest, Lady Daventry. Try to forgive me."

Eve held out her hand to him.

"When one has suffered so much as I have, Mr. Caryll, one forgives easily."

"I'm going to make reparation," Caryll told her by taking Tony out to California. "There's plenty of work for him there in my factories."

Tony's face beamed.

"My hat, you're a good sport, sir," he blurted out. "Oh, but I forgot. Maybe I'll have to go to gaol instead. You've not heard the worst yet, inspector. The dirtiest job I ever did was to drive Mimi, when she was drugged, in Hester

Pertzoff's car to the harbour and dump her on board that boat. Hester made me do it. She said that Mimi was spying on all of us, including Eve."

You see." Mimi spread her hands in appeal to Reynolds. "Mr. Tony could not avoid obeying the Baroness."

Reynolds nodded.

"Let's hear the rest of his story," he urged. "She will be here with the Hollanders presently. I want to straighten out these tangles first. To-night after I received Mimi's telephone call that she had persuaded Franz to wait in the Casino, I searched his room. In it, amongst other suspicious articles, I found a sheet of gold such as gilders use, and a butterfly net of very fine mesh with a long screw-on handle."

"Franz is only the tool of his clever old father," Tony explained. "Old Van Godchen stole Mrs. Kellner's jewel, and fired that shot to create a scene and draw off attention. At that signal, Franz leaned over his bedroom balcony with the net and his father dropped the stone in."

"I noticed wet footprints on his bedroom floor," exclaimed Glen. "That really roused my first suspicion of him. Continue, Tony."

"Franz wrapped the stone in putty, gilded it at once and concealed it in the mirror frame on the stairs. Old Godchen must have pushed the coral bracelet into my pocket to implicate me if trouble arose."

Mimi cocked an amused eye in Glen's direction.

"I told you, monsieur," she reminded him.

"Van Godchen ordered me to get the stone during the night," Tony went on. "It wasn't there, and that's all I know. How long a sentence shall I get, Inspector?"' he asked seriously.

Reynolds caught imploring glances from his wife and Mimi, and cleared his throat.

"Young man, I am on holiday and this is neither my country nor my affair," he said. "So far as I'm concerned you'll get hard labour—in California as soon as Mr. Caryll can arrange it."

"Thank you, sir," Tony said with relief. "I tried to get out of my share in this foul business. On the night that Mrs. Lucas died, Hester Pertzoff dragged me—"

"Into Mrs. Lucas's bedroom," interrupted Glen "I was behind the curtain. Hester was looking for the blue tracing. She said you'd got the real necklace, had emptied the jewel-case, and that Van Godchen would ruin Eve unless you gave the stuff to him."

"You and I, Monsieur Armitage, have done much espionage this week," Mimi remarked. She touched her ear whimsically. "*Ma foi*, how this thing has listened. And now I think it hears an automobile arriving!"

Reynolds scanned Lady Daventry's face and admired its composure. She would keep her head if an earthquake happened, he decided.

Aloud he said to her, "Please try to detain the Hollanders and Baroness Pertzoff in the lounge. They will have no cause to be wary if Mimi remains here.

"You and she will come down presently, Inspector?" Eve asked

Reynolds nodded grimly.

"We certainly shall, after the police have arrived. I'll telephone to them immediately. You know what to do when I come on the scene?"

"Quite well," agreed Eve. "It will be a moment of joyous triumph for me after years of fear and slavery."

XXXVII, Hester's Final Curtain

Thursday night.

TWENTY minutes later, when four stalwart police officials were concealed in the house, Reynolds and Mimi entered the lounge together.

The Hollanders and Baroness Pertzoff stared at the French girl with varying expressions. Franz was the first to speak.

"You wished me to remain in the Atrium to await Miss Jill," he complained. "She did not come, mademoiselle."

"No," Mimi replied. "She has gone to bed. I also allowed your father to think that I had given you the envelope which I had obtained from Guido. It was in my possession all the time."

"Give it to me," ordered the Baroness imperiously. "It is mine."

Reynolds stepped into the conversation. "The document it contained will go to my country," he said smoothly, and gave a faint signal to Eve.

At once she pressed the bell and calmly waited for her summons to be answered.

There was a tense silence in the room as if something ominous were about to happen. Yet it was merely Eve Daventry's moment of victory which the inspector, who secretly loved a sense of drama, had determined should be hers before the grim wheels of the law revolved.

The lounge door was opened and the butler entered.

"Your ladyship rang?" he inquired.

"Yes, Oswell. I have decided to close the Villa Lorne to-morrow and return to England with the staff, and all except three of my guests. It will mean a great deal of work, I'm afraid."

A look of relief came over the butler's usually impassive face.

"We'll manage it easily, my lady," he assured her. "I'll tell the housekeeper at once."

"Thank you, Oswell."

"Thank you, my lady," he replied fervently, and retired with the good news.

"You will not leave this villa," Van Godchen shouted in a hectoring manner. "Recall your servant and say that you have changed your mind."

"Since when has a landlord the right to compel a tenant who has paid the rent in advance to remain in his house?" Eve demanded.

"I have that right," Van Godchen declared. "Otherwise your stepson can be arrested for theft. You will not dare to disobey me."

Eve raised her head proudly.

"With the information that Inspector Reynolds of Scotland Yard has discovered against you, I can dare anything," Hester Pertzoff appeared to suppress a bored yawn. And at that second Mimi approached her and said something in an undertone.

Hester replied to her and rose.

"If we leave to-morrow, I must pack," she announced to the party, and moved languidly across the room. Reynolds barred her way.

"One moment, Baroness," he said. "That little scene you witnessed in the Casino this evening was for Mimi's benefit. By its means she recalled that it was you who gave the scent bottle containing prussic acid to Mrs. Lucas, from the fumes of which she died. And," he added, with a shrewd guess, "it was not the one you took from Lady Daventry."

For a second Hester Pertzoff stared blankly. Then she smiled.

"So that cat is out of the bag, eh! My only regret is that I used a duplicate of Eve Daventry's scent bottle. I had carried it for days, awaiting my chance." She walked towards Robert Lucas. "I killed Bella as much for your sake as my own, Robert. Goodbye," she added in a low tender tone, and stooping, kissed him.

With head still poised high, she moved with supreme grace to the door, her power defeated, her personality unscathed.

Outside in the hall stood two police officers.

"Your services are needed in that room, messieurs," she told them with courteous command, and stood aside for them to enter the lounge.

Dazzled by her magnificent and imperious manner, the men entered.

Reynolds advanced to meet them.

"There are your prisoners. You will find many pieces of stolen jewellery in their luggage," he said, indicating the Van Godchens, who made no movement of protest as handcuffs were placed on their wrists.

"And the third prisoner?" inquired one of the police when the Hollanders were secure. "In your telephone message you said there was also a lady, monsieur."

Reynolds frowned.

"It was the woman who left this room as you entered. Did you not hold her? There are four of you, and I gave you a description of her when you arrived."

Leaving a man to guard the Van Godchens, Reynolds and the other officer hurried out in search of Hester Pertzoff.

"Where is the Baroness, Oswell?" Reynolds inquired when they reached the hall.

"Gone off in her car, sir," was the butler's stolid reply. "It was standing in the drive with the engine running."

"Was it, indeed?" Reynolds glanced thoughtfully at him and then at Mimi.

The French official went outside and called to his colleague who was on guard.

"Why did you let that woman pass? I told you that no one must leave the villa," he asked.

The man pointed to a newly-made scar on his. forehead.

"She bowled me over as she shot down the drive, monsieur," he explained. "Her automobile raced down the road. It was impossible to stop her. *Ma foi*, how she swept round those curves!"

His superior officer grunted. "No matter. She cannot escape far. We will get her at the Ventimiglia frontier, if not before. Take the Hollanders away while I make preparations to find this Austrian woman." He added to Reynolds, "She will surely make for Italy. I will telephone to you.

*   *   *   *   *

The French police had taken away the Van Godchens but still Daventry and her friends remained waiting for news of the fugitive. They talked over the events of the evening, while subconsciously their ears were strained for the sound of the telephone bell.

"It's only about twenty miles to the Italian frontier," Eve said with a sigh "Hester could have reached it easily by this time, if she were going there"

"Yes," agreed Reynolds, "if she were going there." With a deliberate desire to avoid the distressing topic, he asked lightly, "Are you going to stay long in London, Lady Daventry?"

"That depends, Inspector." Eve looked across at Lucas. "For years I've been trying to pay a debt made on my behalf by a dear quixotic man. A man who is so blind that he has never guessed I care for him, and so modest that I'm afraid he'll never ask me to marry him." Her lips curved whimsically. "It's most embarrassing for me."

A light of incredulous happiness dawned in Robert Lucas's face. With one stride he reached her and caught her hands.

"Is it true, Eve?" he asked

"Quite true," she replied steadily.

Lucas flung back his head. "Then indeed the house of hate has changed," he declared. "It's the place where a miracle has happened."

One by one Caryll, Tony, Mr. and Mrs. Reynolds and Glen offered their congratulations.

Mimi was the last.

"Be happy, dear Lady Daventry," she said.

"I shall never forget how much I owe to you," was Eve's reply.

"Well, well," Glen Armitage remarked, "Now that little episode is settled, Eve, I think we'll leave you and Lucas to gaze into each other's eyes."

His face became serious as he joined the rest of the party, now clustered in the hall.

"D'you think the police will get Hester Pertzoff to-night, Inspector?", he asked.

Reynolds' expression was inscrutable to all except his wife and Mimi. "I think that she will not evade justice," he replied slowly.

The sharp sound of the telephone bell him made snatch up the receiver.

In tense silence those who had contributed to the drama in the Villa Lorne listened to his curt mono-syllablos over the wire, waited breathlessly until he replaced the receiver.

"What's happened?" demanded Glen.

"Baroness Pertzoff has not evaded justice," Reynolds told them. "She met the Austrian who owns the *Anncel* outside the Casino when she left to-night. One of the Casino staff overheard the man say that she was too old for her job. Hester drove away alone down the hill past the station, Her car has just been found. The lights were full on, and in the back seat, with a revolver still clasped in her hand, was Hester Pertzoff, the once famous actress. She had shot herself through the heart."

Mimi nodded gravely, and Reynolds saw her move towards the housekeepers room.

In a moment he followed her, and found Oswell and Lucas's chauffeur listening in awed silence to the news.

Reynolds pursed his lips.

"I should like to know," he said, with an attempt at sternness, "who ordered the Baroness Pertzoff's car to be placed in the drive and left there with the engine running."

The French girl eyed him calmly.

"I did. Oswell and Staines obeyed me and are not at all to be blamed. Also I placed Hester Pertzoff's loaded revolver in the pocket of the car."

"And you cheated the law of your country for this Austrian woman's sake?" questioned Reynolds.

Mimi shook her head.

"Not for her," she replied, "though as Hester was brave enough to choose a dignified exit, I can admire her courage. I aided her to escape arrest for Lady Daventry's sake. It would have been fresh torture for her to have awaited another murder trial; to have been a witness and see another woman in the dock where once she herself stood unjustly." She waved her hand expressively. "So you see, my way was better for everyone, was it not?"

"Perhaps," Reynolds agreed. "Nevertheless, I remember that a year or so ago you blamed me for being a sentimentalist over a criminal. You are worse than I was. Suppose Hester Pertzoff had not found the revolver?"

Mimi's eyebrows moved.

"I told her what I had done," she stated. "She thanked me and gave me her promise. I knew she would not break it."

Glen Armitage gave a sigh of relief.

"Personally," he remarked, "I'm thankful that Hester took this way out, or I'd have had an unpleasant explanation to make in public. It was I who snatched the scent bottle from Mrs. Lucas's hand in the Casino. I thought it belonged to Eve. Having washed out its contents of prussic acid, I refilled it with aromatic vinegar which I bought for the purpose, and, as Hester had thrown Eve's bottle away, I asked the housekeeper to put it in the study." He grinned across at the French girl. "I never knew how beloved I was until I sniffed the bottle to see if that young woman suspected anything."

"Beloved!" Mimi raised her head indignantly. "My anxiety, Monsieur Armitage, was only because you would have been slightly more nuisance dead than you had been alive, and I was rather busy at the moment."

THE END

Other Resurrected Press Books in *The Chief Inspector Pointer Mystery* Series

MYSTERIES BY ANNE AUSTIN

Murder at Bridge

When an afternoon bridge party attended by some of Hamilton's leading citizens ends with the hostess being murdered in her boudoir, Special Investigator Dundee of the District Attorney's office is called in. But one of the attendees is guilty? There are plenty of suspects: the victim's former lover, her current suitor, the retired judge who is being blackmailed, the victim's maid who had been horribly disfigured accidentally by the murdered woman, or any of the women who's husbands had flirted with the victim. Or was she murdered by an outsider whose motive had nothing to do with the town of Hamilton. Find the answer in... **Murder at Bridge**

One Drop of Blood

When Dr. Koenig, head of Mayfield Sanitarium is murdered, the District Attorney's Special Investigator, "Bonnie" Dundee must go undercover to find the killer. Were any of the inmates of the asylum insane enough to have committed the crime? Or, was it one of the staff, motivated by jealousy? And what was is the secret in the murdered man's past. Find the answer in... **One Drop of Blood**

AVAILABLE FROM RESURRECTED PRESS!

GEMS OF MYSTERY
LOST JEWELS FROM A MORE ELEGANT AGE

Three wonderful tales of mystery from some of the best known writers of the period before the First World War -

A foggy London night, a Russian princess who steals jewels, a corpse; a mysterious murder, an opera singer, and stolen pearls; two young people who crash a masked ball only to find themselves caught up in a daring theft of jewels; these are the subjects of this collection of entertaining tales of love, jewels, and mystery. This collection includes:

- **In the Fog - by Richard Harding Davis's**

- **The Affair at the Hotel Semiramis - by A.E.W. Mason**

- **Hearts and Masks - Harold MacGrath**

AVAILABLE FROM RESURRECTED PRESS!

THE EDWARDIAN DETECTIVES
LITERARY SLEUTHS OF THE EDWARDIAN ERA

The exploits of the great Victorian Detectives, Poe's C. Auguste Dupin, Gaboriau's Lecoq, and most famously, Arthur Conan Doyle's Sherlock Holmes, are well known. But what of those fictional detectives that came after, those of the Edwardian Age? The period between the death of Queen Victoria and the First World War had been called the Golden Age of the detective short story, but how familiar is the modern reader with the sleuths of this era? And such an extraordinary group they were, including in their numbers an unassuming English priest, a blind man, a master of disguises, a lecturer in medical jurisprudence, a noble woman working for Scotland Yard, and a savant so brilliant he was known as "The Thinking Machine."

To introduce readers to these detectives, Resurrected Press has assembled a collection of stories featuring these and other remarkable sleuths in The Edwardian Detectives.

- The Case of Laker, Absconded by Arthur Morrison
- The Fenchurch Street Mystery by Baroness Orczy
- The Crime of the French Café by Nick Carter
- The Man with Nailed Shoes by R Austin Freeman
- The Blue Cross by G. K. Chesterton
- The Case of the Pocket Diary Found in the Snow by Augusta Groner
- The Ninescore Mystery by Baroness Orczy
- The Riddle of the Ninth Finger by Thomas W. Hanshew
- The Knight's Cross Signal Problem by Ernest Bramah

- The Problem of Cell 13 by Jacques Futrelle
- The Conundrum of the Golf Links by Percy James Brebner
- The Silkworms of Florence by Clifford Ashdown
- The Gateway of the Monster by William Hope Hodgson
- The Affair at the Semiramis Hotel by A. E. W. Mason
- The Affair of the Avalanche Bicycle & Tyre Co., LTD by Arthur Morrison

RESURRECTED PRESS CLASSIC
MYSTERY CATALOGUE

Journeys into Mystery
Travel and Mystery in a More Elegant Time

The Edwardian Detectives
Literary Sleuths of the Edwardian Era

Gems of Mystery
Lost Jewels from a More Elegant Age

E. C. Bentley
Trent's Last Case: The Woman in Black

Ernest Bramah
Max Carrados Resurrected:
The Detective Stories of Max Carrados

Agatha Christie
The Secret Adversary
The Mysterious Affair at Styles

Octavus Roy Cohen
Midnight

Freeman Wills Croft
The Ponson Case
The Pit Prop Syndicate

J. S. Fletcher
The Herapath Property
The Rayner-Slade Amalgamation
The Chestermarke Instinct
The Paradise Mystery
Dead Men's Money

The Middle of Things
Ravensdene Court
Scarhaven Keep
The Orange-Yellow Diamond
The Middle Temple Murder
The Tallyrand Maxim
The Borough Treasurer
In the Mayor's Parlour
The Saftey Pin

R. Austin Freeman
The Mystery of 31 New Inn from the Dr. Thorndyke Series
John Thorndyke's Cases from the Dr. Thorndyke Series
The Red Thumb Mark from The Dr. Thorndyke Series
The Eye of Osiris from The Dr. Thorndyke Series
A Silent Witness from the Dr. John Thorndyke Series
The Cat's Eye from the Dr. John Thorndyke Series
Helen Vardon's Confession: A Dr. John Thorndyke Story
As a Thief in the Night: A Dr. John Thorndyke Story
Mr. Pottermack's Oversight: A Dr. John Thorndyke Story
Dr. Thorndyke Intervenes: A Dr. John Thorndyke Story
The Singing Bone: The Adventures of Dr. Thorndyke
The Stoneware Monkey: A Dr. John Thorndyke Story
The Great Portrait Mystery, and Other Stories: A Collection of Dr. John Thorndyke and Other Stories
The Penrose Mystery: A Dr. John Thorndyke Story
The Uttermost Farthing: A Savant's Vendetta

Arthur Griffiths
The Passenger From Calais
The Rome Express

Fergus Hume
The Mystery of a Hansom Cab
The Green Mummy
The Silent House
The Secret Passage

Edgar Jepson
The Loudwater Mystery

A. E. W. Mason
At the Villa Rose

A. A. Milne
The Red House Mystery
Baroness Emma Orczy
The Old Man in the Corner

Edgar Allan Poe
The Detective Stories of Edgar Allan Poe

Arthur J. Rees
The Hampstead Mystery
The Shrieking Pit
The Hand In The Dark
The Moon Rock
The Mystery of the Downs

Mary Roberts Rinehart
Sight Unseen and The Confession

Dorothy L. Sayers
Whose Body?

Sir William Magnay
The Hunt Ball Mystery

Mabel and Paul Thorne
The Sheridan Road Mystery

Raoul Whitfield
Death in a Bowl

And much more!
Visit ResurrectedPress.com
for our complete catalogue

About Resurrected Press

A division of Intrepid Ink, LLC, Resurrected Press is dedicated to bringing high quality, vintage books back into publication. See our entire catalogue and find out more at www.ResurrectedPress.com.

About Intrepid Ink, LLC

Intrepid Ink, LLC provides full publishing services to authors of fiction and non-fiction books, eBooks and websites. From editing to formatting, from publishing to marketing, Intrepid Ink gets your creative works into the hands of the people who want to read them. Find out more at www.IntrepidInk.com.

www.ingramcontent.com/pod-product-compliance
Lightning Source LLC
Chambersburg PA
CBHW070835250626
47159CB00003B/790